Blind Vengeance

Blind Vengeance

Barry Hoffman

Printed in the United States of America

Cover by Harry O. Morris
Design by Elizabeth E. Monteleone
ISBN 978-1-948929-42-4

For information address Crossroad Press at 141 Brayden Dr.,
Hertford, NC 27944
www.crossroadpress.com

To my children Dara, David and Cheryl
and my granddaughter Tyler

Prologue

They passed by her in the Acme Supermarket, and Shara's instincts to keep a low profile suddenly deserted her. They seemed so cute on first glance. Two teens, possibly twins, walking down the aisle hand-in-hand. Both slender, fair-skinned with blond hair so bright it almost lit up the dim market. But Shara saw the boy holding the girl's hand a bit too tight. The girl's bangs almost obscured her eyes. *Almost* . . . but not quite. And those pale blue eyes, which refused to make eye contact with Shara, showed a world of hurt.

Shara knew those eyes. They had been *her* eyes when she'd been with her half-brother. The eyes of a youth sexually or physically abused.

Shara felt the urge to flee, but ignored it . . . this once. She vigorously maintained her anonymity. She didn't butt into other's business. Everyone had problems. If it wasn't job or family related, it wasn't her concern. Shara was no Good Samaritan. Get involved and you invited scrutiny, and Shara did nothing to draw attention to herself.

". . . the cereal Alexis likes."

"What?" Shara asked, looking at Lamar Briggs. They were both bounty hunters. Technically Shara was Briggs's boss, but they had become equals. And with Briggs being a former homicide detective, Shara deferred to him whenever they had to involve the police. Shara knew her capabilities. She didn't have to strut her stuff. She much preferred the background, where she was barely noticed. Briggs would get credit for nabbing a skip, though Shara was equally responsible for the capture. It irked Briggs that Shara was all but ignored. It pleased Shara to no end that to them she was all but nonexistent. She derived her pleasure from the hunt, not the glory that came with the capture.

They were back in Philly, in Southwest Philly, where Briggs resided. He had some shopping to do on his way home and had dragged Shara with him.

"They don't have the cereal Alexis likes," Briggs repeated, seemingly lost in his own personal hell of hundreds of cereals to choose from *except* the one he desired.

Shara took her eyes off the two blond teens for a moment. She scanned the shelf and handed Briggs a box of Fruit Loops. "This will do," she said.

"Just a few more items," Briggs said, looking at a list his wife had prepared for him.

"I'll catch up with you outside," Shara said, seeing the pair heading toward the checkout line.

Outside, Shara saw the two enter a silver Toyota Corolla. The *backseat* of the auto. Shara watched for a few moments until she was certain her gut reaction had been correct. Shara saw the girl struggling in the backseat. She needed no more confirmation.

Making her way to the car, Shara flashed to images of her half-brother, Bobby, sneaking into the bathroom while she showered when she was eleven. Saw Bobby taking pictures of her as she tried to cover herself with her hands. Bobby laughed and shot a few more photos then slithered out. Worse . . . far worse was to follow.

At the car window, Shara saw the girl's blouse unbuttoned. The boy was massaging her small, milk white breasts. The girl's eyes appeared dead, as if she knew the battle was lost and had escaped within herself. At some point she may have fought off his advances, Shara thought, but it had proven fruitless. She no longer struggled, but let her brother have his way with her.

Shara opened the back door. "Get your hands off her," she said.

The boy looked momentarily startled. Then his eyes filled with rage. "Fuck off, lady," he said, his voice a deep baritone, at odds with his appearance. "Ain't no business of yours what me and my . . . my girlfriend are doing."

"Your sister's your girlfriend?" Shara asked.

"Look, lady—" the boy started, not quite as indignant as he had been. Shara knew she'd been correct.

"Are you his sister?" Shara asked the girl.

The girl nodded. Her eyes were filled with terror and focused on her brother, as if to gauge his mood.

"I'm not going to tell you again, lady—"

Shara ignored him. "Do you want to have sex with your brother?" Shara asked.

The girl said nothing, her eyes still on her brother, but tears ran down her cheeks. With her upper teeth, she bit her lower lip.

"One more question?" Shara *had* to ask. "Does your mother know?" Shara's mother had known Bobby had snuck into the bathroom to photograph Shara. Thought it was a hoot. Her mother had detested Shara. Resented Shara. Shara had no idea why, and though her mother was still alive, she knew she would never find the answer to that question . . . or any others for that matter. As far as Shara's mother was concerned, Shara was dead. Literally, having committed suicide at the age of eleven.

The girl closed her eyes and more tears fell. Shara had her answer.

"Get out—" Shara started and only then saw the boy pull the gun from under the seat. Shara's hand went for her own gun, but she knew she was too late. *That's what you get for not minding your own business*, a voice in her head chided. She heard a single shot and saw the boy jerk back, blood spurting from his shoulder. The gun fell from his hand.

Shara turned and saw Briggs behind her, his bag of groceries scattered at his feet. "Get his gun," Briggs said.

Only when Shara had the youth's gun did Briggs holster his weapon. He took out a cell phone and made several calls.

Shara led the girl out of the car while Briggs tended to her brother.

"Is he dead?" the girl asked. Shara thought she heard a trace of hope in her voice. Dead, she would be free of him forever.

"No, but he won't hurt you anymore," Shara said, reading the girl's mind. "I promise."

Shara saw panic replace the momentary relief. "You've only made it worse—"

Shara put a finger to the girl's lips. "We only have a few minutes until the police arrive. I'm not going to abandon you. What's your name?"

"J'aime," the girl said. "J'aime Maynard."

"Has he raped you?" Shara asked.

The girl nodded.

"How old are you?"

"Sixteen."

"When did he start?" Shara asked.

"When I was twelve."

"And your mother knows?" Shara asked.

The girl nodded again.

"What about your father?" Shara asked.

"He left when we were seven," the girl said, her voice just above a whisper.

"Do you have any relatives you could stay with? Someone you could trust?" Shara added.

"My aunt," the girl responded after a brief pause.

"Does she know?" Shara asked.

The girl shook her head. "I was too embarrassed. Too scared. Brett . . . my brother, threatened to kill me if I told anyone."

It was just how Shara felt even after she had been placed with a foster family. Somehow Bobby would get to her. Shara would never be safe. "He'll never come near you again," Shara said. "You have my word."

For the first time, the girl made eye contact with Shara. "Why do you care?"

"I've been there," Shara said. "Just tell the truth when the police come. Don't look at your brother. Imagine he doesn't exist." Shara handed the girl a card with her cell number on it. "Day or night," Shara said.

A police car and ambulance arrived almost simultaneously. As Briggs was speaking with one of the two uniformed cops, a third car pulled up. It was an unmarked police car. Nina Rios emerged. She had been Briggs's partner before he had been forced to resign from the police force. She conferred with the uniform who had been talking to Briggs. The cop nodded. Rios had established Briggs's credentials with the officers. Shara could see the young officer visibly relax.

Shara approached with J'aime. Nina Rios introduced Shara to the officer.

"The boy is her brother," Shara said. "He's been sexually abusing her for four years."

The officer looked from Briggs to Rios then back to Briggs again, as if he wanted to be told what to do. Shara guessed he was fresh out of the Academy. He was definitely out of his element. "Let's call her parents," he finally said, his voice uncertain.

"The mother knows of the abuse and did *nothing*," Shara told him. "There is no father."

"Still, I gotta—"

"You gotta do nothing," Shara said. "Except protect this child. You bring the mother in, J'aime will recant. She's afraid of both her mother and brother. There's an aunt you can call," Shara added.

"Look, I don't know," the officer said. "I really gotta call her mother."

"Do so, and the next time you see this girl, she'll be in the morgue," Shara said, raising her voice. "You want that on your conscience?"

The cop again looked from Briggs to Rios. Nina Rios finally interceded.

"I'll take responsibility for her, Officer Hopkins," Rios said. "We'll sort this out at the Round House." She patiently told the young officer what should be done. She wasn't condescending, Shara noted. She was just sharing her experience with a green officer. "That fly with you?" Nina asked when she had finished. He nodded, thanked her, then hustled off to his partner, who was with the brother. The boy was being lifted into the ambulance.

Nina turned to Shara. "We can't keep the mother from J'aime. Not for long, anyway. Knowing you, I assume you have an alternative."

Shara nodded. She and Nina Rios would never consider the other a friend. What they shared in common was Briggs. Rios had initially been jealous when she'd lost her partner to Shara. She erroneously assumed Shara had become Briggs's confidant—a role Nina had filled until Briggs had been forced to resign—but nothing could be further from the truth. Shara had finally convinced Rios that Briggs still valued her. Briggs spoke to Nina of his frustrations working with Shara, of Shara's secretive nature and unwillingness to share. Nina finally got it—that while she and Briggs no longer worked together, they were still joined at the hip. In this analogy, Shara was no more than an appendix. An uneasy truce followed. Shara knew that Rios respected her abilities and would have Briggs's back in any altercation. "Take a statement from J'aime," Shara said. "But I wouldn't rush her, if you get my drift. She's badly shaken up. Maybe something to eat . . ." Shara said, not needing to finish.

Rios nodded.

"I'll call my attorney. He'll take care of the rest," Shara said.

Again Rios nodded.

"Can you make sure the case is turned over to someone who won't allow J'aime to get fucked over again?" Shara asked. Shara knew that as a homicide detective, Rios wouldn't retain jurisdiction of the case.

"I know just the person," Nina said with a smile.

The second officer, no older than the first, now came over to Rios, and the two spoke for a few moments. Briggs then came over to Shara.

"They got your gun, I see," Shara said, nodding toward a senior officer who had appeared on the scene.

"Standard procedure," Briggs said, sounding irritated.

"You gotta give a statement?" Shara asked.

"We both do, but not now," Briggs said. "I told them what happened. They have the little prick's gun. Nina vouched for me, and the girl corroborated what went down. Forensics is on its way, and these two will be canvassing for any possible witnesses, but I don't anticipate any problems."

"Thanks, Briggs," Shara said. "You saved my ass."

"Not like you to miss the kid's weapon," Briggs said, locking eyes with Shara.

"Caught me by surprise," Shara said.

"I don't buy it," Briggs said.

Shara shrugged.

"It's also not like you to play the Good Samaritan," Briggs said. "This seemed personal. What gives?"

"She's just a kid," Shara said.

"You gotta do better than that," Briggs said. "I know you, Shara. You don't get involved. I'm glad you did, don't get me wrong, but you owe me an explanation . . . if we're going to continue to work together. Shit," he said, then paused a moment. "That didn't come out right. What I mean is, just like Nina and me, there's gotta be mutual trust. You were sloppy, careless . . . call it whatever you want. I need to know it's not going to happen again. I might not be there to save your ass, and I have no desire to attend your funeral."

Shara couldn't tell Briggs the truth. But she understood where he was coming from. J'aime's brother had gotten the drop on her because she had been flashing back to her own past instead of focusing on the threat in front of her. Shara had spent a good portion of her life lying, so what she now said came naturally. "Renee's been working at The Haven, the shelter for battered spouses and their abused children. Alexis helps out once in a while," she added.

Briggs nodded.

"I've done some work there myself," Shara went on. "I guess when I saw J'aime's eyes . . . well, I've seen that look too often at The Haven. I knew in the grocery store she was sexually abused. I let my emotions get the better of me. I let my guard down, not even considering he might be packing. I won't make that mistake again. Satisfied?"

Briggs said nothing.

"Honestly, Briggs, there's nothing more to tell," Shara said. "Cut me some slack. I fucked up. I learned my lesson. Consider me chastised."

Briggs shrugged. "One day you'll confide in me," he said sadly.

"I'm not bullshitting you, Briggs," Shara said.

"I believe you," Briggs said. "But that's not the whole story. Tell me I'm wrong?"

Shara remained silent.

"Bugs the hell out of you that I'm getting to know you . . . just a bit," Briggs said with a smile.

"Smartass," Shara said, then gave him a hug. She held on tight, not wanting to let go. Now that she finally had a life and others who depended on her, being disassembled in the morgue had little allure.

Chapter One

Briggs, I'm the Vigilante, Shara said to herself, then shook her head. Too abrupt.

Briggs, I killed Bobby Chattaway. He was my half-brother. He molested me when I was eleven. No, Shara thought, that didn't explain the first five sexual predators she had killed. Briggs would pick up on that immediately.

Briggs, I'm not who you think I am— she started, then stopped, disgusted. *That* sounded lamest of all.

Shara stared into the mirror that was on the wall of her room. Ever since she'd had a place of her own, she surrounded herself with mirrors. Mirrors on all walls. Mirrors on the ceiling and on the floor. She'd needed the mirrors *before* she'd killed her half-brother. She'd feared his eyes—*his hungry eyes*. With mirrors encircling her, Bobby couldn't sneak up undetected. Even with his death, the mirrors were Shara's womb, far more comforting than any alarm system.

For twenty minutes she'd been rehearsing words she thought she'd never utter to the former-homicide detective who had unsuccessfully attempted to track her down. She could unbutton her blouse and show Briggs the tattoos that adorned her breasts. Six pair of eyes. One for each of those she'd killed. *That* would get his attention. She shook her head again. No she couldn't. Briggs wouldn't hear her words. He'd be aghast at Shara baring her breasts before him. They'd gotten close. Possibly far closer than Shara had wanted. But not *that* close.

Still, it was time to tell her partner. Shara had hired Briggs after he'd been forced to resign from the Philadelphia police force. He'd been arrested for murdering a rapist. Shara had exonerated him. She'd hired him solely to keep him from moving from Philly. He was a hero to many cops who believed he really *had* killed the bastard who had destroyed the lives of three children. He could have easily gotten a job with another police department. But Shara couldn't allow him to leave . . . not with Alexis, his daughter.

Shara didn't give a shit about Briggs at the time. It was all about Alexis. If Alexis hadn't been raped and beaten, Briggs wouldn't have gone on his rampage. Not only couldn't he protect his own daughter, he also hadn't captured her rapist. Lysette Ormandy, dubbed The Nightwatcher by the media, had killed the albino who had raped Alexis. Briggs had felt even more impotent.

Alexis had been little more than a vegetable, except in a forest that ever-so-slowly cured her. Only Alexis, Lysette, and Shara knew of its existence. Shara had offered Briggs a job so the healing could continue. Briggs worked *for* Shara. They had never been partners in the sense some cops become a team. Shara divulged nothing of her personal life to Briggs. She couldn't. Doing so would mean baring her secret, if not her tits.

The two of them had worked together for close to two years. Briggs had slowly burrowed under Shara's defenses. Alexis was cured. Briggs was no longer the brooding presence Shara had first encountered. He had his daughter back, cured, whole. He was a happy camper.

Shara could never confide in Briggs as she did with Alexis. But after he saved her life when J'aime's brother pulled a gun on her, Shara thought she owed Briggs the truth. They had become partners, she thought grudgingly. And lately, on more than one occasion, she wanted to blurt out the truth. Get it over with. Hope he wouldn't go off the deep end. Her encounter with J'aime three days before had convinced her the time had finally come. She hadn't appeared herself, wading into the affairs of a stranger. Her explanation to Briggs sounded lame even to her.

Fuck it, she thought. No amount of rehearsing would prepare her. She would wing it.

Her cell phone rang. Briggs was a block away. When he pulled up, Shara was on the stoop of her Center City townhouse waiting. She had told him there was a case she wanted to talk to him about.

"Go down to Washington, then left on 21st," she told him when she got in his car. She would take him to the scene of the crime, so to speak. To Loretta Barrow's South Philly row house. Her birth mother who thought Shara dead.

Briggs was uncommonly quiet as he drove. Odd, Shara thought. He always had something to say. She caught him glancing at her briefly. Furtive looks. She did the same, neither making eye contact with the other. Something's on *his* mind, Shara thought. Now that she was prepared to unburden herself, she didn't want him preoccupied. At 21st, Briggs pulled over and parked in a vacant spot.

"I've been offered my job back," Briggs said, sounding as if he'd been preparing before a mirror just as Shara had, with equal success. "On the force. Homicide detective," he added.

"Get out," Shara said, looking at Briggs carefully for the first time since she'd gotten into the car. Though it was pleasantly cool outside on this November afternoon, there were beads of sweat on his shaved head. His dark-skinned face was somber. He was trying to grow a beard, but he was dismayed there was as much gray as black. What could he expect? Shara had told him. He was in his mid-forties, no longer a young stud. "When did all this come down?" Shara asked.

"Yesterday," Briggs said.

When he said nothing more, Shara was irritated. "We going to play twenty questions? Yesterday what?"

Briggs sighed. "The new chief of police asked me to drop by. I had no idea why. Morales was there." Morales, Shara knew, was Briggs's old Sergeant. "What with the scandals that have hit the department, he's cleaning house," Briggs went on. "Detectives with a lot of seniority are being forced out. He talked about my indiscretion—"

"*Indiscretion!*" Shara said. "Shit, you near beat that rapist to death. You didn't shoot him, but indiscretion my ass. Gimme a break."

Briggs laughed, and his body language showed he was more relaxed. The worst was out, Shara thought. He was no longer sitting as if he had a stick up his ass.

"That was *his* word," Briggs said. "Odd phrasing, but I held my tongue. Anyway, both my record and what Morales had told him about me gave him a pretty accurate picture what I was going through at the time. What most impressed him was, though I had a temper, I was clean. He's bringing some retired cops back, some only temporarily, until he gets his house in order."

"And he wants you . . . a bounty hunter?" Shara asked.

"He asked me about that," Briggs said with a tight smile. "It was more like an interrogation than an interview, if you want to know the truth. Bottom line, he wanted to know if I was a bounty hunter or a cop in need of a job. Know what I mean?"

Shara knew all too well what Briggs was referring to. It had been a bone of contention between the two. Briggs was never comfortable as a bounty hunter. The shortcuts Shara savored were troublesome to Briggs. Entering a house without a search warrant, illegal wiretaps, lying, conniving, and ignoring the rights of the accused grated on Briggs like fingernails on a chalkboard. He was a cop at heart. Had been for twenty years. Always would be, even if he never carried a shield again.

"You taking the job?" Shara asked, though she knew the answer.

"Not if you tell me not to," Briggs said.

"Bullshit, Briggs," Shara said. "You know it's what you crave. Don't feel you're under some obligation to me. Granted, you're an asset. You've opened doors for me because you're male and considered a rogue cop. But I got along without you, and I've proven my worth with you. Those doors aren't going to suddenly shut because you're leaving. Take the job, Briggs. You'll end up embittered and resentful if you don't. Ignore this opportunity, and guaranteed, you'll regret the decision. Your bitterness will fester. You'll want to leave. Hell, I'll want to push you out the door, but that offer from the new chief of police will then be history. Spare me the drama and go back to doing what you do best."

Briggs looked at Shara. Before he could say anything, Shara answered for him. "I'm sure, Briggs."

Briggs visibly relaxed. Briggs did owe Shara a debt. Several, actually. But she hadn't known Briggs would find it so difficult to dissolve their . . . well, partnership. "I can tell him I need a couple of weeks—"

"We've got nothing pressing," Shara cut him off. "It's not like I won't see you. I'm as tight with Alexis as ever. If I want to run something by you, I won't hesitate."

"What about the case you wanted to talk to me about?" Briggs asked.

It was all Shara could do from bursting out laughing. Once a cop, always a cop. She felt she'd been slapped in the face with a cold dose of reality. How could she have thought she could tell Briggs her secret? It would have destroyed whatever relationship they had. What a fool she'd been. "Just another cold case I thought we might check out. It's nothing that won't wait."

Briggs went silent for a moment. "I appreciate all you've done for me and Alexis," he said finally. "We've had our moments, haven't we," he said with a laugh.

"That we have," Shara answered.

"Tell me I'm not letting you down," Briggs said. "I couldn't—"

"Take the job, Briggs," Shara said, suddenly irritated. "I'm a big girl. We never had a marriage. Know what I mean?"

He nodded.

"Look, we found our stride these last few months, but you know I'm a loner by nature. So no regrets," Shara said.

Later at home, Shara was a ball of nervous energy. She felt claustrophobic. She changed and went for a jog. She had come so close to making the biggest mistake of her life. So close to destroying all she had built after she rid herself of Bobby and his hungry eyes. She'd been blinded. Thank goodness he'd been offered his old job back. There was only one way he would have responded to her revelation. Badly.

Chapter Two

When Shara returned from her jog, there were two messages on her cell from J'aime. Seemed to Shara everyone had a cell phone and it was forever plastered to their ear. Walk the streets and every other person was texting or having a conversation on their cell. And for some reason, most people had no desire for privacy. With the hustle and bustle of the city, most seemed to be yelling when speaking. It grated on Shara's nerves. Even fellow joggers couldn't seem to part with their precious communication device when they went out for a run. Shara intentionally left her cell at home when she jogged. She treasured her privacy. She wasn't about to talk business in public. And even an emergency could wait. After all, she had done just fine most of her life without a cell phone.

J'aime's messages reinforced Shara's desire to jog without the latest in technology. She really didn't want to talk with J'aime, but she had given the girl her word. *She would be there for her.*

J'aime had proven to be a puzzle. Initially it had all gone down as Shara had envisioned. Douglas Frazier, an attorney she often worked with, cut through the bureaucratic red tape with ease. With a copy of J'aime's statement outlining her brother's abuse and her mother's knowledge such abuse had taken place, Frazier had called in a favor with a contact at the Department of Human Services. Frazier traded in favors. To his credit, far more were owed to him than the other way around. "You can bank them for just so long," he had once told Shara. "It's not like you can take them with you when you're dead or will them to your family. I use them judiciously, but I don't hoard them like a squirrel with acorns."

When J'aime's mother had finally been called, she was greeted at the Round House by a caseworker from DHS. J'aime was being removed from her mother's care while allegations of negligence were being probed. A day later, Frazier had arranged temporary placement for J'aime with her aunt. He had also obtained a restraining order to keep both J'aime's mother and brother at bay while the investigation progressed.

When Shara had thanked Frazier, he seemed troubled. "J'aime hasn't been totally forthcoming," he told Shara. "It could be there's enough to get J'aime out from under her mother, but a judge could go either way."

"And the brother?" Shara asked.

"For the moment, he's not an immediate threat," Frazier said. "He'll be hospitalized for probably a week. And he's looking at a host of charges lodged against him: attempted murder, weapons offenses, and statutory rape. I'm trying to convince an ADA to have him tried as an adult. With no priors, if he's treated as a juvenile, he might just get a slap on the wrist."

"And continue to be a threat to J'aime," Shara said.

Frazier nodded. "Talk to the girl, Shara. I spoke to her briefly, and I know there's a lot more here than meets the eye. She won't confide in me. You seemed to have touched a nerve, though. Maybe she'll open up to you."

Shara had reluctantly agreed to try to get the girl to open up to her. She chastised herself for getting involved. The world was full of sick perverts like Brett Maynard and his mother. Shara had no burning desire to rid the world of the scum that populated most street corners. She was no social worker and, after killing her half-brother, was no longer the avenging angel ridding society of sexual predators. Still, she had given her word to J'aime, and she wouldn't abandon the girl.

Shara called J'aime and agreed to meet her at Liberty Place, a Center City mall at 16th and Chestnut Streets. They bought some pizza and sat at a table on the second floor of the mall that overlooked the first. Shara knew Frazier was right. Just looking at the youth, Shara was certain something was disturbing her. She gnawed on her lower lip, just as she had when Shara had first met her. A telltale sign she was nervous or worried. She was dressed carelessly in a grey sweat suit that seemed two sizes too big for her. While just three days had passed, J'aime seemed to have lost weight. She had been scrawny to begin with. She picked at her food while Shara ate. The girl's breath smelled of mints. Shara wondered if she smoked—not that it made any difference to Shara—and was attempting to mask the smell. Shara had no illusions that J'aime was simply a victim. She and her brother had bought nothing at the supermarket where Shara first saw her. Thinking back on it, Shara was certain they had come to shoplift. And Brett Maynard didn't carry a gun in his car for self-protection. J'aime would have to make her own decisions. If she ended up in prison or on the street hooking, so be it. Shara's only desire was to separate the girl from her abusive brother and mother. She had promised J'aime no more.

If Shara needed a lesson on keeping her distance from strangers, she had only to recall the treachery of Denise DeShields. The sister of Deidre Caffrey, someone she considered a friend— though Shara manipulated her time and time again—Shara hadn't known of Denise's existence until Deidre had been murdered. After helping wean Deidre's sister from a heroin addiction and getting her a job at the newspaper Deidre had worked at, Denise had repaid

Shara by blackmailing her. Denise was not the lost young woman she appeared to be. She was as manipulative as they come, and Shara's kindness had come back to haunt her. Shara had promised herself she wouldn't be duped again. So she wasn't about to let J'aime into her life.

Shara watched as J'aime stared into space seemingly oblivious to the swarms of humanity in the mall. Shara, ever an observer, could sit for hours looking at those who passed. Shara became absorbed by two students arguing, a male and a female, wearing University of Pennsylvania sweat shirts. Were they having a heated debate about a classroom discussion or had she caught him gazing at or sleeping with another coed? When they were out of sight, Shara turned her attention to the reaction of others in the mall as a group of six black teens wearing baggy jeans hung low so their underwear was exposed walked among them, loudly talking trash. While harmless, they nevertheless appeared threatening. They were given a wide berth as they sauntered about checking out window displays.

"So, how are things with your aunt?" Shara finally asked J'aime. She felt irritated, then chastised herself. Play nice, she told herself. She had gotten herself into this mess. There was no reason to take it out on J'aime.

J'aime shrugged. "She's okay," she said.

"Would you want to stay with her for good?" Shara asked.

Again, the girl shrugged. "Better than the alternative, I guess."

Shara was becoming annoyed. J'aime had called *her* after all.

"Look, J'aime, I said I'd be there for you if you needed me," Shara said. "And I will. But you leave two messages for me and now have nothing to say to me. I got a life, J'aime. Tell me what's bothering you or I'm outta here."

"My . . . my mother's been calling," J'aime said, then

fell silent.

"You speak to her?" Shara asked.

J'aime shook her head. "My aunt won't let her speak to me. I don't want to. I know what she'll say."

"To recant what you said about your brother," Shara said.

J'aime nodded.

"There's nothing that can be done about her calling, but you don't have to speak to her," Shara said. "And there is a restraining order to keep her from you."

J'aime shrugged.

"Let me lay it out for you, J'aime," Shara said, tiring of the girl's reaction. "You've talked to a lot of people the last few days. All of them think there's something you're holding back. You've got to trust someone. Your brother is going to deny raping you, and your mother will stand by his side. All I saw was your blouse unbuttoned and you struggling, so I won't be of any great help as a witness—"

"Why?" J'aime interrupted. "You saw him attacking me."

"Problem is, a defense attorney will tear my testimony to shreds," Shara said. "'Was she screaming for help?' he'll ask. I'd have to say no. 'Was she hitting him, trying to fend him off?' I'm not going to lie, J'aime, so don't even ask. Maybe I interceded too soon, but I didn't see you fighting him off. 'Were his pants down? Was he penetrating his sister?' Again, I'd have to say no. So, no, J'aime, the prosecutor will have me testify, but the only thing definitive I can say is, 'He raised a gun to shoot me.'"

J'aime was again picking at her food, her eyes avoiding Shara.

Shara sighed. "This isn't the time to be coy. You know what awaits you if DHS places you with your mother. You got something to tell me, this is the time. Otherwise there's nothing more I can do to help."

J'aime got up. "I shouldn't have called. My mother doesn't give a good god damn about me. I've known that since . . . well, since forever. But she *is* my mother. Talk to my aunt. I'm told you're a bounty hunter. That's kinda like a detective, right?"

Shara was tempted to correct her, but decided against it. The girl was trying to tell Shara something without actually saying the words. Keep her talking, Shara decided. "I find things out," Shara said.

"*She's my mother*. Understand?" J'aime said. "But if you happen to, you know, use your . . . skills and . . . find something out, well, then it wouldn't be me telling you, right?"

"I'll speak to your aunt," Shara said. "But you've got to start trusting—"

"She's home now," J'aime interrupted. "I can hang here for half-an-hour while you talk to her."

Shara nodded. Damn, she thought, this is what comes from being meddlesome.

Chapter Three

J'aime's aunt lived in a high-rise two blocks west on 18th Street. J'aime's aunt, Tricia McCauley was an older version of J'aime. She had the same trim build and blond hair. It was cut shorter than J'aime's and styled, but there was no mistaking the resemblance between the two.

"I want to thank you for helping J'aime," Jaime's aunt told Shara after she had ushered Shara into her spacious living room. Shara had declined the offer of a beverage.

"Did you know J'aime's brother was abusing her?" Shara asked.

"Heavens no," Tricia answered. "I love my niece. Had I known, I would have called the authorities myself. I hadn't seen much of her, though, in the past few years."

"You know she says her mother knew of the abuse," Shara said.

"My sister . . . doted, I guess the word is, on Brett," Tricia said. "He's her only son."

"And J'aime is her only daughter," Shara said.

"Her only *living* daughter," Tricia said. She got up, went to a mantel, and returned with three photos. "It's truly tragic. Before J'aime and Brett were born, my sister had three other daughters. Each died of crib death . . . SIDS they call it now."

"You're sure it was SIDS?" Shara asked.

"My sister loved her children, Miss Farris," Tricia said tartly. "What are you inferring?"

"Look, Mrs. McCauley, J'aime won't tell me anything, but she said I should talk to you. Obviously she felt there was something you'd tell me that would arouse my suspicions. This could be it."

"Are you suggesting my sister killed her three girls?" Tricia asked.

"I'm just trying to make sense out of J'aime's cryptic comments," Shara said. "She thinks I'm some sort of detective. She's given me a morsel—*talk to my aunt*—and I'm supposed to find out something that J'aime feels guilty putting into words herself." Shara paused. "Three children dying of SIDS . . . isn't that too much of a coincidence?"

"What you're surmising is incomprehensible," Tricia said. "My sister always wanted sons, I'll grant you that. We have no brothers. She was disappointed that she couldn't give birth to a son, but it's a long stretch saying she . . . she killed her daughters."

"J'aime told me her father left when J'aime was seven. Do you know why?" Shara asked.

"Once she had given birth to the twins . . . once she had Brett, she seemed fulfilled. She had the son she always craved. She and Stan . . . that was her husband, they seemed to drift apart after the twins were born. Doris spoiled Brett something awful. I think Stan resented the attention."

"How did she treat J'aime?" Shara asked.

"My sister's life was filled with girls. Me . . . her other daughters. I never saw her raise a hand to J'aime, but to be truthful, she never showered her with the affection she offered Brett."

"And her husband left because . . . ?" Shara asked again.

"He had an affair," Tricia said. "I can't blame Stan, if you want my opinion. My sister just seemed to lose interest in him after Brett was born. So he strayed. He even told her. He would have broken it off, but . . . I know this sounds terrible, but she actually encouraged him to continue the affair. That was the last straw. He didn't leave right then and there. It must have been six months later. He came by, told me he was leaving, and asked me to keep an eye on J'aime. I haven't seen him since. I do know he sends my sister money for the children, even though she never asked for a dime."

"He asked you to keep an eye on J'aime, but *not* on Brett?" Shara asked.

"Brett had his mother," Tricia said. "I think he felt J'aime needed attention."

Shara thanked J'aime's aunt and left. Exiting the building, she saw J'aime at the corner. Shara waved, but the girl turned away, as if she hadn't seen Shara. What have I gotten myself into? Shara wondered again.

Chapter Four

When Shara returned home, Renee was in the kitchen cooking spaghetti and meatballs. Shara was Renee's legal guardian. She had taken the sixteen-year-old girl in a year and a half before. Shara stood at the kitchen entrance and smiled. Renee could eat spaghetti and meatballs every day and not tire of it.

"Hey," Shara said. "Wonder what's for dinner?"

Renee smiled. She had an infectious smile that never ceased to amaze Shara. Renee was tall, slim, and athletic. Though bi-racial, she could have passed for white. Her long, straight, silken black hair was tied in a ponytail with a scrunchy. Shara kept nothing from the youth and now told her of Briggs rejoining the police force and what she'd planned to tell him before he sprung his news. She'd tell Renee about her strange meeting with J'aime and then her aunt later.

Renee came over and felt Shara's head, as though Shara had a fever. "You were going to tell Briggs you're a murderer, and because you kept him out of prison and helped nurse Alexis back to health, he was going to shrug at your news and say, 'Thanks for sharing.' You got to be kidding."

Despite herself, Shara began to laugh. "Pretty stupid, right?"

Now Renee was laughing. "You could have introduced him to your birth mother."

"I was planning to . . . sorta," Shara said, her laughter building, and she told Renee she was going to confide in Briggs near her birth mother's home.

"Then tell him Deidre knew the truth all along." More laughter. "Alexis knew the truth . . ."

"And you knew the truth," Shara added, between bouts of laughter.

"Just about everyone but good old Detective Lamar Briggs knows of your sordid past," Renee said.

Shara shrugged, then laughed again.

"You sometimes have shit for brains, Shara," Renee said.

"Now you've done it," Shara said, going into the living room and returning with a Nerf bat. "Show some respect for your elders," Shara said, chasing Renee.

Renee ran into the living room and began pelting Shara with Nerf balls that littered the floor. Some people chilled with stress balls. Since she had been living on her own, Shara had watched a lot of television and interacted with the hosts of various talk shows. When they angered her, well, she lost control and threw whatever was at hand at the TV. She had broken several picture tubes before she bought Nerf balls and used those to pummel her foe on the tube. Now she and Renee used the Nerf balls against one another whenever there was tension in the air. "Since when did you become self-destructive?" Renee asked, absorbing a whack from Shara's bat.

"Since I began trusting people like you and Alexis," Shara said, then stopped. "I'm such a fool, Renee," she said.

"For letting Briggs get close to you?" Renee asked.

Shara shrugged.

"There's nothing wrong with that. You're human. But Briggs is . . . well, Briggs."

"I lost sight of that," Shara said. "Alexis warned me.

Long ago. There are just some things I have to withhold from him. I got burned once. For a second time, I almost forgot he's a cop, whether he has his shield or not."

"Better you learned *before* you put him in an . . . awkward position," Renee said.

"Awkward my ass," Shara said. "An impossible position."

Renee pelted Shara with another Nerf ball and the battle raged for another ten minutes. Both finally lay on the carpet exhausted.

"Thanks," Shara said.

"For what?"

"I was feeling depressed for my sorry ass. Foolish, too. If I were alone, I would have sulked and pouted."

"And obsessed," Renee said.

"That, too," Shara said with a smile. "You helped me put it into perspective."

"Just don't think of doing anything foolish like that without consulting me first," Renee said.

"Yes, Boss," Shara said. "I've learned my lesson."

"I'm going to finish dinner," Renee said. "You . . . you take a shower. I didn't want to say it before, but you smell kinda funky."

Shara got up and slapped Renee on her butt with the Nerf bat before scurrying to the shower.

Chapter Five

When Shara walked into Club Aphrodisia, an upscale strip club on Chester Pike, just outside of Philly proper but still within city limits, she was looking for Lysette, the club's manager. As usual, the first to spot her was Luther, affectionately known to Shara as Sweets. A former pro-wrestler, he had been a bouncer at the club and was now head of security. Physically, he could have passed for Briggs's brother. A dark-skinned black, shaved head like Briggs, just as powerfully built. He exercised and lifted weights obsessively. Nobody at the club fucked with Sweets. Yet to Shara, he was a Teddy Bear with his quick and engaging smile. His keen sense of humor and laid back approach is what differentiated him from the brooding Briggs. Shara had to admit Briggs had lightened up, especially with his daughter's improved health, but to Shara, no matter how good things were, Briggs was somber.

"You looking good, Little One," Sweets told her, after smothering Shara in a bear hug. Shara had managed the club when Lysette, a vigilante known as The Nightwatcher, had been hospitalized. Shara and Sweets had hit it off immediately. He was one of the few who saw through Shara's tough exterior. Always respectful in public—she was Ms. Farris and later Shara—in private he referred to her as Little One, a term of endearment. It was also accurate, as he dwarfed her by over a foot. "Life been treating you good," he said. It was an observation, not a question. He could gauge Shara's mood as only Renee and Alexis could. Before Shara could answer, he did have a question. "Any work for me?" he asked, a twinkle in his eyes.

"As a matter of fact, yes," Shara said and saw the look of surprise on Sweets's face. Before she had hooked up with Briggs, Shara had employed Sweets if her prey was particularly nasty. Bail bondsmen wanted bounties returned, but in one piece and not the worse for wear. Returning a skip bruised and abused in the litigious atmosphere of the new millennium might find the bondsman facing a civil suit. Shara could fend for herself, and with a gun in her hand, she was seldom challenged. Still, a drunken hulk of a bail jumper might underestimate Shara. Though muscular and proficient both in martial arts and street fighting, she was short and didn't appear physically intimidating. And truth be told, some could do her serious harm if she wasn't prepared to inflict damage of her own. The sight of Sweets sobered up even the meanest drunk in a hurry. Driving back to Philly with her cargo, Sweets often charmed their quarry with tales of his exploits while on the pro-wrestling circuit. With Briggs as her partner, Shara had used Sweets sparingly. Still, whenever she visited the club, he always asked if she needed his assistance. It had become a running joke between the two.

"You wouldn't be shittin' me, would you, Little One?" he asked.

Shara told Sweets about Briggs rejoining the police force.

"You let him into your life," Sweets said when she had finished. "You must be hurtin'."

Shara was reminded how perceptive Sweets was. Most looked at him and saw his muscle. He was far more complex and a good judge of human nature. Little escaped his notice. Shara hadn't had enough time to consider how she felt about Briggs rejoining the police force. She knew it was best for him. Still, she would miss his presence, she had to admit. Even if she offered nothing to him about her personal life, bouncing ideas off him had proven productive. And with Alexis now in school, Shara saw far less of her than before she had been healed. Briggs always had stories about his daughter that he shared with Shara. She didn't know if she would be hurting without Briggs, but she had to admit she would miss the man.

"Living means accepting pain," Shara said. It was something she had accepted only two years earlier when she first let others into her life. "This is more a flesh wound. You know cops. Briggs was never cut out to be a bounty hunter. Without him, I could use you on occasion."

Sweets put a huge hand to his ear spread out in the sign of answering a phone. "You call, and I'll be there," he said.

Shara saw Lysette across the room mingling with customers. It was a far more confident, relaxed Lysette than Shara was accustomed to.

Sweets must have been following her gaze and read her mind. "Lysette gone and got herself a personality transplant," he said with a playful laugh.

"You're bad," Shara said, swatting him playfully on the shoulder.

"Just being honest," he said. "She don't be keeping to herself holed up in her office no more. She's growing comfortable within her skin."

"Ya think?" Shara asked, still concerned for her friend.

"That smile of hers is genuine," Sweets said. "That laugh . . . well, I hadn't heard it since back when she was a dancer. Now it comes natural and often."

Looking her way, Shara caught Lysette's eye. Lysette smiled broadly and beckoned for Shara to come over. That, too, Shara thought, was a far different greeting than she received when Lysette decided she no longer wanted Shara in her life. That had been over a year and a half ago. They'd only recently resumed their friendship.

The two embraced after Shara made her way over. Shara saw the smile hadn't left her friend's face.

"Thanks for being a shoulder to cry on," Shara said. She had called Lysette four days before and told her Briggs was rejoining the police force.

"I'm glad you called," Lysette said. "I mean you've got Renee and Alexis . . ." she said and tailed off.

"Both ten years younger than me. That's a whole lifetime at their age," Shara finished for Lysette. "I missed you when we . . . weren't speaking. I missed having someone my own age who could identify with how I felt." She paused. "Is everything all right? When you called me back—"

"Everything's fine," Lysette said. "Look, I gotta mingle for another five or ten minutes. Go to my office and make yourself comfortable. I won't be long. Promise."

When Shara entered Lysette's office, she saw a woman her age lying on a couch reading a magazine.

"I'm sorry," Shara said. "Lysette told me . . . . Look, I'll wait outside—"

"Nonsense," the woman cut her off. "This *is* Lysette's office after all." She stood up. "Cheyenne. Woods. Cheyenne Woods," she said with a laugh.

"Are you a dancer?" Shara asked, feeling confused. Dancers she knew had stage names, but few used both a first and last name. It was all part of the fantasy. Your name was your persona. And if customers didn't know your real name, they couldn't hassle you outside the club.

"No I'm a . . . friend of Lysette's," Cheyenne said. "Actually more than that. We're lovers. Lysette called you to meet me. I think she wanted your approval."

Shara looked more closely at the woman now knowing she and Lysette were intimate. Cheyenne was Lysette's height, 5' 10", more than a head taller than Shara. She had Shara's tawny complexion but, like Shara, appeared to be Caucasian. Yet, while Shara's complexion was natural, Cheyenne seemed tanned from the sun. Maybe she worked outdoors, Shara thought. The woman was attractive and knew it. Her bearing exuded confidence. The total package was . . . exotic, Shara thought, searching for an apt description, and the various parts were equally alluring. Her long, curly brown hair flowed far past her shoulders, which accentuated her ample breasts. Skin-tight jeans drew Shara's eyes to long, muscled legs that reminded Shara of a dancer's. The only flaw was a birthmark of veins that reminded Shara of a spider's legs on the right side of her forehead. It was almost exactly where Alexis had scarring from her beating. Oddly, the blemish was just as seductive as her overall beauty.

Shara wondered if beneath the attractive facade was a mind to match. Too often gorgeous women lacked depth. Like athletes, they had been coddled and coveted all of their lives. Beauty too often covered shallowness. Lasting relationships rarely succeeded when the surface attraction was no longer a novelty. Cheyenne's emerald green eyes, though, sparkled with intelligence and wit.

"Lysette wanted us to meet?" Shara asked, more confused than ever. "She doesn't need my approval—"

"Cheyenne needs a job," Lysette said from behind Shara, startling her. "She's a bounty hunter—"

"You set me up," Shara said, but she wasn't angry with her friend, just perplexed.

"Cheyenne's a bounty hunter," Lysette repeated. "She recently moved to the area and . . . well, with you and Briggs . . . " she tailed off.

"Not set up," Shara said. "*Ambushed.*" She should have been angry but knew Lysette's intentions were good. Shara just couldn't summon any indignation.

"Why don't you two talk," Lysette said. She looked at Cheyenne. "Shara's not going to give you a job as a favor to me. Hell, I wouldn't want her to hire you for my sake. I do think you'd be good for one another," she said, now looking at Shara. "Is an interview too much to ask?"

"I've been bushwhacked," Shara said, but she was smiling. "We'll talk. No promises," she said, locking eyes with Lysette.

"I'll be mingling," Lysette said, not able to hide her own smile. She left, closing the door behind her.

"Are you and Lysette serious?" Shara asked.

"Is this part of the interview?" Cheyenne asked in return, not hiding her irritation. "My relationship with Lysette—"

"Is all I give a damn about right now," Shara interrupted. "She's fragile. She was recently in a relationship that went sour—"

"Denise," Cheyenne said, now cutting Shara off. The two of them stood face to face, neither ready to back down. "Lysette told me all about her."

"*All* about her?" Shara asked, wondering just *how* much Lysette had told her. Denise had befriended then bedded Lysette to get information to use against Shara. When she had what she wanted, she'd discarded Lysette. Lysette had let down her guard with her first lover, telling things about Shara that she *knew* were meant to remain secret. Shara feared Lysette had done so again. Just how much had Lysette told this stranger? Shara wondered.

"Just that Denise had been the first woman Lysette had slept with . . . been in love with," Cheyenne said, as if reading Shara's mind. "Their affair . . . if that's what you want to call it, was like a brush fire. Hot, torrid, passionate, but short-lived. Lysette thought they'd parted friends, but Denise had other ideas. Is there more I should know?"

The hell not, Shara thought. Denise had tried to blackmail Shara with what Lysette had told her. Denise hadn't succeeded. But that was not for Cheyenne to know. "I don't want Lysette hurt again," Shara said. "She's still . . . *becoming*. That's the word she uses. It's up to her to fill in the blanks for you, if she wishes. Let's just say she's not quite sure who she is. She doesn't even know if she's a lesbian," Shara added.

"You're assuming I am?" Cheyenne asked.

Shara shrugged.

"I'm bi- myself. Lysette and I are lovers, but we're not *in* love. We're both looking for companionship. The sex ain't bad. Ain't bad at all. Neither one of us are looking for a long-term commitment, though."

"Just don't fuck with her mind like Denise did," Shara said, more harshly than she intended. She was feeling overly protective of her friend.

"Lysette's lucky to have a friend like you," Cheyenne said. "I assume our *interview* is over," she added.

"It's just begun," Shara said. "Look, I don't need a partner like Lysette seems to think. But Lysette does need my protection whether she's willing to admit it or not. I'm just looking out for her." She paused. "Lysette said you were a bounty hunter. Tell me about yourself."

"Not a hell of a lot to tell," Cheyenne said, massaging the spidery birthmark on the side of her head. "I was a cop in Colorado. The town's a dot on the map. I spent my time giving out speeding tickets, writing up fender benders for insurance claims, intervening in the odd domestic dispute. That was my life. Mundane. I had accumulated a good deal of vacation time when my mom passed away suddenly. She left me some money. Not a whole lot, but I decided to travel across the country. I walked in on a liquor store robbery in St. Louis. Cold-cocked the bastard with a bottle of wine. He had a bounty on his head, and I had a new vocation."

"Because the money was good?" Shara asked.

"The money isn't *that* good," Cheyenne said. "I like the freedom. My own hours. Being my own boss. My own rules. No asshole supervisor to have to kiss up to. No need to go to bed with some fucking supervisor to get a promotion. No need to get out of bed at all on days I don't want to. When I tire of a town or city, I move on. What's there not to like?"

"Why work for me, then?" Shara asked.

"I pack my bags when I want, but there are drawbacks," Cheyenne said. "I have no connections here. Bad enough for any bounty hunter, but worse for a woman. Tell me you didn't have to fight tooth-and-nail to earn the respect you deserved."

Shara nodded.

"It's those first few months I can do without," Cheyenne continued. "Work for you and I don't have to prove myself all over again. Give me thirty or forty percent of each skip. Whatever you think is fair. I don't have a hell of a lot of expenses."

"And when you've earned the respect of bail bondsmen, you go off on your own," Shara said.

Cheyenne nodded. "I won't lie to you. I *do* value my freedom."

"And you might blow town at any time," Shara said.

"You got it," Cheyenne said. "But not in the middle of a case we're working on," she added. "I don't renege on my responsibilities."

"You know there's a lot of grunge work—" Shara began.

"I'm no novice," Cheyenne interrupted. "I know what's involved. You're the boss. It's up to me to prove my worth. That's all I ask. If it doesn't work out, we'll both know."

Shara smiled. "You work for me, and I get to keep my eye on you. Make sure you do right by Lysette. Got a problem with that?"

Cheyenne shook her head.

"You staying with Lysette?" Shara asked.

"Got a place of my own," Cheyenne said, giving Shara the address.

"I'll pick you up tomorrow at eleven. Introduce you to some people you'll be working with and give you some files. I've got no office. I work from my home. However, my home's off limits." Shara gave Cheyenne a card with nothing on it but a phone number.

Cheyenne took a piece of paper from Lysette's desk, wrote something on it, and handed it to Shara. "My cell number."

"This is purely professional," Shara said. "I'm not looking for a partner, confidant, buddy, or friend. I don't want to hear about your love life or you bitching if you and Lysette quarrel. I take you on, we help each other out and Lysette's happy. Those are my terms. Non-negotiable."

"I wouldn't have it any other way," Cheyenne said.

"Let's break the good news to Lysette," Shara said.

Chapter Six

Norman—don't call me Norm—Flowers sat down and placed the *Philadelphia Inquirer* to the right of his breakfast. A glass of fresh-squeezed orange juice sat on first base of his plastic Philadelphia Phillies placemat. A glass of two-percent milk nestled on second base. No coffee for Norman with its artificial stimulants. On the pitcher's mound was a plate with a single piece of unbuttered toast. Butter contained too much cholesterol. At fifty-one Norman was no kid and clogged arteries and a heart attack were inevitable if he didn't avoid temptation. And margarine just wasn't the real thing, and Norman eschewed anything fake. No NutraSweet, no Sweet 'N Low, and no margarine. Twice a week he'd indulge himself with a dash of jam or fresh honey on his toast. But Norman never overindulged. Jam or honey, not on Tuesday. The crust had been cut off, just as his mother had done for him as a child. Next to the toast was a thin slice of pound cake, which he'd baked himself from scratch. A bowl of freshly cut grapefruit occupied third base. No canned fruit, with its artificial preservatives, was acceptable.

Norman tucked a cotton napkin into the collar of his shirt and methodically attacked his breakfast. With a knife and fork, he cut off and ate a piece of toast, then going counter clockwise washed it down with some juice. A sliver of pound cake followed by milk. And last some grapefruit. He repeated the process, without deviation, until not a crumb remained. Waste not, want not. Only then did he unfold the morning paper.

The headline story dealt with the ongoing scandals within the Philadelphia Police Department. Norman smiled. He took perverse pleasure as almost daily the ineptitude of the city police was paraded before the public. Chaos would reign, Norman thought joyously. Convictions would be overturned. Careers ruined. Civil suits would be filed that would cost the city millions. He almost felt exonerated.

The story continued on page twenty-two, and there Norman's festive mood turned foul. Near the bottom of the page a second story discussed the recent hires by the embattled newly hired police commissioner. With senior officers being transferred, demoted, retiring, or being outright booted off the force, the department resembled a rudderless ship. To plot a new course, a number of recently retired officers had been recruited to fill the void. One name jumped out at Norman. Lamar Briggs. *Lamar-Fucking-Briggs*. Not only was he returning, but he had been reinstated as a detective to the coveted homicide division. Norman recalled the vindication he'd felt just shy of two years before when Briggs had been forced to retire from his beloved homicide unit. Lamar Briggs had committed a crime. He'd admitted to beating an alleged rapist to within an inch of his life. Even though he'd been absolved of the rapist's murder, Briggs had been forced to resign from the department. That had been one of the sweetest days in Norman Flowers' life. Poetic justice. If Lamar Briggs couldn't be a cop, his life lacked meaning, Norman knew. Norman had celebrated non-stop for a week. He'd been avenged even if it had taken fifteen years.

But now Lamar-Fucking-Briggs was returning to the prestigious homicide unit as if nothing had transpired.

Norman stood up shaking. There was no justice in the world, he was reminded yet once again. He ripped the napkin from his collar. He picked up the empty glass that had held his orange juice and flung it against the wall. Then the milk glass and plate. He tipped over the flimsy kitchen table, kicking it as if it were Briggs himself. His rampage continued unabated for half an hour until every glass, every plate, and every glass bowl had been obliterated. He stood at the kitchen sink for ten minutes feeling lightheaded and nauseous. He vomited his breakfast into the sink, then lay down amid the broken glass, curled into a fetal position. He wept, uncontrollably, without the slightest trace of embarrassment.

Chapter Seven

Shara shook her head as Cheyenne walked up the steps to her home on Baltimore Avenue just east of Cobbs Creek Parkway. She'd actually rented the entire two-story house. Seemed a bit excessive for someone who spent little time at home, Shara thought. Cheyenne and Lysette were still seeing one another, but after a few weeks Shara could sense the flames of passion giving way to smoldering embers that wouldn't be rekindled. As she vowed, Shara didn't discuss her observation with Cheyenne. Their relationship was purely professional. Would remain so if Cheyenne valued her job. Shara *had* discussed the subject with Lysette at the club. She wanted to make sure her friend was not about to be unceremoniously dumped.

"You two have an argument?" Shara had asked Lysette the day before.

"You're worried about me," Lysette answered, without answering Shara's question.

"After Denise—"

"This is nothing like Denise," Lysette cut in, sounding testy. She paused a moment, then smiled. "Sorry. With my history, your concern's not out of line." There was another pause, and then Lysette shrugged. "Whatever we had has just about run its course. But Cheyenne isn't Denise. I don't know how much longer we'll be lovers, but we *will* remain friends." Lysette paused again, then laughed. "Funny thing is, lately I've been thinking I'd like to find a man. Not *the* man," she said when she saw the expression on Shara's face. "I've enjoyed being with Cheyenne, but lately I've seen some men at the club . . . hell, men on the street, that I've fantasized going to bed with. So don't go blaming Cheyenne when we split. It's mutual. Maybe when I'm through with men, I'll start with animals," she added, and they had both broken up.

Shara was going to say something but held her tongue. Lysette's *becoming* wasn't entirely healthy. Shara knew three distinct personalities lay within Lysette that hadn't yet come to grips with one another. Lysette was pragmatic, even-tempered, introverted, and conscientious. She didn't take risks. Cassandra had been Lysette's stage persona as a dancer but was actually a part of Lysette that had been repressed for years. Cassandra was outgoing, liked to live on the edge, was an exhibitionist, and was temperamental. It was the Cassandra in Lysette who had probably prompted her to seek female sexual companionship. Finally, there was Angel, the most dangerous of them all. Angel was Lysette's lost youth, a teenager inhabiting the body of a twenty-something woman. Cassandra and Angel were defense mechanisms Lysette had created when Lysette's family had been brutally killed in front of her when she was eleven. Lysette herself had been left for dead. The Lysette persona had been in control most of her life. First Cassandra had emerged, when Lysette was eighteen, and then several years later, Angel appeared. Hence the *becoming*. Lysette needed a shrink, but it wasn't Shara's place to suggest it. She just hoped Lysette wouldn't now go jumping from the beds of one man to another as she had with Denise and Cheyenne. Shara thought Lysette needed stability in her life, something Shara now had for the first time and prized.

Shara had dropped Cheyenne off at her apartment a number of times since they began working together. She'd been naturally curious how Cheyenne surrounded herself, but Cheyenne had never invited Shara inside. A part of Shara was pleased. Cheyenne was keeping up her end of the bargain. No female bonding. No chit-chat or gossip. Shara had feared Cheyenne would want a shoulder to cry on. Too many women aired their dirty laundry to co-workers. To her credit, Cheyenne seemed professional to the core.

Shara had to admit she was impressed with Cheyenne. Any fears Shara might have had proved unfounded. Cheyenne did the grunge work assigned her without complaint, and she was thorough. In the time she had been working with Shara, she had ferreted out two bail jumpers. Shara had intentionally gone after the first herself to test Cheyenne. To her credit, Cheyenne hadn't sulked. Shara knew how badly Cheyenne had wanted to accompany her. Shara had noted a musky odor permeating Cheyenne when she'd told Shara where the skip could be found. When Shara was on the scent of her prey, she would sweat like a pig. And as Renee has commented more than once, on such occasions, she would smell ripe. Yes, Cheyenne had wanted to go badly, but had handled the disappointment without pouting.

When Cheyenne located a second fugitive, Shara let her tag along. Everything had gone smoothly. Cheyenne was a long way from replacing Briggs, Shara thought, but was pulling her own weight. It might work out after all.

After letting Cheyenne off, Shara drove to Club Aphrodisia. She had been a stripper herself while still a teen. She hadn't worked at an upscale club, though. With a fake ID, the body of an adult, and the owner greasing the palms of local cops, Shara had never been hassled at what was little more than a bar with a long table and a pole for the dancers. Club Aphrodisia, on the other hand, was almost like home. Besides talking to Sweets and Lysette, Shara enjoyed the atmosphere. Each dancer had her own signature calling card, so to speak, and Shara liked watching them reel in the day's catch. The customers intrigued her as well. For some, the club was a home away from home. They didn't keep their wives or girlfriends in the dark and weren't the least bit embarrassed. For others, visiting the club was a guilty pleasure. These men looked furtively about, as if a co-worker, friend, or relative would walk in and their secret would become public knowledge.

Renee was spending the night at Briggs's house with Alexis. The two had become close. It was good for both of them to have someone their own age to confide in.

Thinking of Renee and Alexis brought Shara full circle to J'aime, the *other* teen in her life at the moment. With the news Shara earlier brought, she thought J'aime could move on . . . and out of her life.

After she met with her aunt, J'aime had called Shara daily. Shara intentionally refused to respond until she had something to report. J'aime had to learn she didn't have Shara on a leash. Shara had to set boundaries. The calls became less persistent, but never stopped altogether.

Shara had met with J'aime once again at Liberty Place. J'aime was dressed as she'd been at their first appointment, in her gray sweat suit. She continued to nibble on her bottom lip when Shara questioned her. She still picked at her food. And she was no more forthcoming than she had been previously.

"What you wanted to tell me, but felt you couldn't, is that your mother killed your three older sisters," Shara said. "Twenty years ago there was far less scrutiny when an infant allegedly died from crib death. Only your sisters were murdered. Is that what you wanted me to find out using my *investigative powers?*" Shara asked.

J'aime nodded.

"You *could* have told me," Shara said. "Forget about it for now," she added, as she saw J'aime chewing more vigorously on her lip. "I've convinced a homicide detective to reexamine the deaths. They're going to exhume Valerie's body." Valerie had been the last to die. "Anything else I should know?"

J'aime shrugged, but said nothing.

"I don't know why you continually call me, then when we meet you button up," Shara said, then paused. "I'll call *you* when I find out the results of the autopsy." This time Shara got up to leave. When J'aime didn't stop her, she walked off.

Now she had the results of the autopsy. They sat at what had become their *regular* table at Liberty Place. J'aime was dressed as she'd been the two prior times. Shara wanted to ask her if she had other clothes. Her aunt was reasonably well off, Shara knew from inquiries she had made. She was certain J'aime didn't dress this way for school. This girl was certainly a puzzle. As usual, she picked at her pizza as if she were grossly overweight. If anything, she had lost another few pounds. Her face also had an unhealthy sheen, and her blond hair was unkempt.

"Your mother has been arrested," Shara said and paused. J'aime didn't react at all. Shara shook her head and went on. "For manslaughter . . . in the death of your sister Valerie."

For the first time, J'aime looked up. She had stopped gnawing at her lower lip. Was that a smile playing at her lips? Shara wondered.

"How do they know?" J'aime asked.

"The autopsy. Like I told you before, autopsies on children who are thought to be the victims of SIDS are far more exhaustive now than when Valerie died. You've seen enough TV. Forensic science has come a long way. Today's pathologists can do wonders with bodies far older than Valerie's." Shara paused. "Valerie was suffocated."

"And my other sisters?" J'aime asked. She took a bite

of her pizza. What an odd girl, Shara thought. Told that her mother was a murderer and her appetite returns.

"Their bodies will be exhumed. If the results are the same, your mother will face additional charges."

"How long will she be in jail?" J'aime asked.

"I honestly can't tell you," Shara said. "Your mother will undoubtedly mount some cockamamie defense to gain the sympathy of a jury. Postpartum depression. She was depressed, overwhelmed. A lot of crap, but it's better than no defense at all. The prosecution will counter by calling your father. And there's the question as to why you and your brother didn't suffer the same fate—"

"She finally had a son," J'aime said, cutting Shara off. This was the most animated Shara had seen J'aime. "That's what she wanted all along."

"And you?"

"Maybe she feared being caught," J'aime said. She was really digging into her pizza now. "I mean she now had the son she craved, so why tempt fate. Know what I mean?"

"It's as good an explanation as any," Shara said. "In any event, I'm inclined to think your mother will be offered a plea to avoid the circus of a trial. If she's smart, she'll take whatever deal is negotiated between the ADA and her attorney."

"How long will she get?" J'aime asked. She had stopped eating.

"If I was the District Attorney, I wouldn't budge for anything less than fifteen years," Shara said. "Three infants killed, and there's the added charge of child endangerment regarding your situation."

J'aime took another bite of her pizza. "Can you do anything for Brett?" she asked, not making eye contact with Shara.

"You mean making sure he gets tried as an adult?"

"No, I mean dropping or . . . lessening, I guess, the charges against him," J'aime said.

"You want him out?" Shara asked, bewildered. "He raped you."

"He had sex with me," J'aime said. "He wasn't rough with me. He didn't beat me. He even said he loved me. He comforted me when my mother made me feel like an unwanted shit. You know, like he built up my self-esteem. No one else did."

"But the sex was against your will, wasn't it?" Shara said.

J'aime looked at Shara. She was munching on her lower lip again. She finally nodded. "Look, I'm glad my mother is getting what she deserves. But maybe Brett was a victim, too."

"In what way?" Shara asked.

"It's like my aunt told me. My mother spoiled him rotten. He thought he was entitled to anything he wanted. My mother never taught him the difference between right and wrong. Yet, he was good to me. The police may call it rape, but he was really gentle with me. I think he thought he was making love to me. What I'm saying is, he's not this abusive asshole the assistant district attorney assigned to the case wants me to portray him as. Can't he get counseling or something?"

"He pulled a gun on me, J'aime," Shara said, her anger mounting. "If it hadn't been for my partner, he might have killed me. Your brother lives by his own rules."

"But he *can* be helped," J'aime said. "I've been doing some reading. I also spoke to a counselor at school. She not *just* a school counselor. She works with troubled teens, has her own practice. She says Brett needs counseling, not prison."

"I did what you asked of me, J'aime," Shara said, not wanting to prolong this discussion. "Neither your brother nor mother are a threat to you anymore. Your aunt will take good care of you. I have no desire to see your brother walking the streets six months or a year from now. Neither should you. He'll probably be incarcerated until he's either eighteen or twenty-one. That's not a lifetime. His fate is out of my hands. If that pisses you off, so be it."

J'aime sighed. "I'm sorry. I appreciate all you've done. I guess I was feeling a little guilty." She took a last bite, finishing off her pizza. "Can I still call you? Can we meet and have lunch and just chat?"

No way, Shara wanted to blurt out. J'aime reminded Shara even more now of Denise DeShields whom Shara had helped out. Both were totally self-absorbed. It had turned out bad with Denise. Shara already had Alexis and Renee. She was not about to become a big sister to this stranger who still made her feel uncomfortable. She'd try to let her down gently. "I like you, J'aime. I really do. But to be totally honest, my plate is full. I've got my job. Sometimes I'm out of town for weeks at a time. It's not like I can be counted on, is what I'm getting at. And I've got family of my own that screams out for attention when I am home. You need friends your own age. And you've got your aunt. And, there's the school counselor you mentioned."

J'aime shrugged. "So this is it," she said. "Nice knowing you. Don't let the door hit you on the ass on your way out."

"That's not what I said," Shara said. "What I said may hurt, but you'll get over it. The worst thing I could do would be to string you along. You'd become dependent on me, and I might not be there for you when you need me. You don't always get what you want in life, J'aime. You seem to be on good terms with your counselor at school. Tell her what I've told you. Get her take on it. And find some kids your own age you can confide in."

Leaving J'aime, Shara had a feeling she hadn't heard the last from her. For some reason, the thought depressed her.

Shara left the club at around 2:30 a.m. She now turned onto Chestnut Street, with its staggered lights and lack of traffic, to head home. She'd get to Fifth and Lombard in fifteen minutes tops. She popped in a *Best of Harold Melvin and the Blue Notes* CD. She was partial to R&B music, especially Old Skool rhythm and blues of the sixties and seventies. Teddy Pendergrass was at the top of his form on the plaintive "If I Could Love You Now." Shara was humming along—she couldn't sing worth a lick and knew it—when her cell phone rang. It was Briggs.

"Shara, can you come over?" he said. His voiced sounded strained.

"Now?" Shara asked.

"Now."

"What's wrong?" Shara asked. Instinctively, she knew something was terribly amiss. "Is Renee all right?" It could just have easily been Alexis, but Shara knew otherwise.

"Not over the phone," Briggs said and hung up. He knew Shara would bully him for answers he wasn't about to give over the phone. If he didn't hang up, he knew Shara would persist. Fine, Shara thought and speeded up.

It took twenty minutes for Shara to get to Penrose Park, the area in Southwest Philly where Briggs lived. Shara ignored red lights and a steady downpour. *Something was terribly wrong. Renee was in danger.* Shara had heard it in Briggs's voice.

Shara parked in the driveway next to a car she had never seen, a dark, nondescript sedan. A detective's car. Shara knew it didn't belong to Briggs. Down toward the end of the block, Shara noticed a second car. It was just as ordinary as the sedan but looked to be at least five or six years old. She thought she could make out the figure of someone in the driver's seat. She noted the license plate but went straight to Briggs's front door. This wasn't the time to satisfy her curiosity.

While in Philly proper, Penrose Park skirted nearby suburbs. In the seventies, when newly built, the two-story single family dwellings had been integrated, something uncommon for Philadelphia. As more blacks moved in, white flight followed. Middle-class Blacks and Hispanics now almost exclusively inhabited the area. A shame, Shara had often thought, that even middle-class blacks and whites couldn't co-exist together.

Briggs opened the door before Shara could knock. His face was slack and drawn, his brown eyes lifeless. "You're soaking wet," Briggs said. "Let me get you a sweater."

Shara grabbed Briggs's arm as he was about to turn. "The hell with a sweater. Where's Renee?" Shara asked. "Don't sugarcoat it."

Briggs sighed. "She's been kidnapped."

Shara shut off her emotions. She wanted answers. Nothing must cloud her judgment. Later she could vent. "From a mall?" Shara asked when Briggs went silent.

"Right here," Briggs said. "I'm so sorry. So sorry."

Shara thought Briggs might be in shock. Getting answers from him was like pulling teeth. "Tell me what happened, Briggs," Shara said. "I don't give a fuck how sorry you are. Just don't keep me in the dark."

"Come into the living room," Briggs said with a little more life.

Entering, Shara saw Alexis, Briggs's wife Vivian, and a cop she recognized but couldn't put a name to.

"Paul LeBrea, from the Special Investigation Unit of Southwest Detectives," Briggs said, as if reading Shara's mind. "He's dealt with a number of kidnappings."

"You called the police without consulting me first," Shara said. "You shouldn't—"

"We don't have the resources or the expertise," Briggs said without emotion. "And frankly, I didn't want to get into an argument with you. I knew how you'd respond. It's a done deal."

"Fine," Shara said tersely. "We won't argue. The decision's been made. Now start at the beginning, Briggs."

LeBrea stood up. He was thin, medium height, in his mid-thirties, with a close-cropped

Beard and straight black hair. "Briggs already filled me in," he said. "And a forensics unit has already been here. Discretely," he added as Shara began to speak. "We mainly dusted for prints and took some impressions from the carpet. We don't need a circus with Brash outside lurking. I can fill you in on the results. It's not much."

Shara nodded. Shara noted LeBrea stroked the beard around his chin when he spoke. He had just the hint of a South Philly accent and spoke calmly. His hazel eyes were alive, in contrast to Briggs, and he seemed very much in charge.

"At approximately one forty-five this morning, a single male broke the back door window in the kitchen and entered—"

"There was no alarm?" Shara asked. She knew Briggs had a state-of-the-art alarm system.

"It hadn't been turned on," LeBrea said. "Come with me. I'll walk you through it."

Shara followed LeBrea into the kitchen. There was broken glass on the floor and muddy footprints.

"I'm going to lay out the facts for now, Miss Farris—"

"Shara," Shara said.

"Okay, *Shara*. While waiting for you to arrive, Detective Briggs and I have speculated. I don't want to cloud your judgment with our thoughts. I know what you do for a living. I want . . . *I need* your observations. Then we'll compare notes."

LeBrea took Shara to the stairs leading up to the bedrooms on the second floor. "This was no burglary gone awry. From his tracks, our perp went directly upstairs."

Shara nodded.

LeBrea stopped outside what Shara knew was the master bedroom, where Briggs and his wife slept. LeBrea pointed at the footprints. It was as if someone had been pacing, trying to make up his mind, Shara thought. Tracks over tracks over tracks.

"He stopped here," Shara said. "He didn't enter. Why?"

"A CD player was on in Alexis's room. Rap music, not something that would normally appeal to adults in their forties—Briggs and his wife," LeBrea said, without answering Shara's question. "You'll get a clearer picture in a moment. Our perp must have figured Alexis slept in the room where he heard the music."

LeBrea led Shara to Alexis's room. "When our man entered, Alexis was in the bathroom. He saw Renee and assumed it was Alexis. The music was loud enough so Alexis didn't hear anything amiss going on in the bedroom. Also because of the music, the abductor was almost certainly unaware there was anyone in the bathroom. After going to the bathroom, Alexis took a shower. She estimates she was in the bathroom for twenty minutes."

Shara looked at a mirror atop a vanity table, and many of her questions were answered. In lipstick was scrawled the words "Payback . . . It's A Bitch."

"The fucker has a grudge against Briggs," Shara said. "He entered, considered killing Briggs," Shara continued, pacing about the room. "That's why there are all the footprints outside the master bedroom. He hadn't planned this out. He was deciding what do to on the fly. He heard the music and decided to snatch Alexis. That would devastate Briggs far more than killing him outright."

"Speculation," LeBrea said.

"Tell me I'm wrong," Shara said.

"No, his message says it all," LeBrea said.

"He must have taken Renee at gunpoint," Shara said. "She wouldn't have put up a fight if she thought Alexis, Briggs, or his wife might be in peril."

LeBrea nodded. "He left the way he came. When Alexis came out after her shower, she assumed Renee was in the kitchen. She came down, saw the broken glass—"

"I get the picture," Shara said. "The kidnapper thinks he has Alexis," Shara said, almost to herself. "That complicates things, doesn't it, Detective," Shara said.

LeBrea nodded. "Call me Paul. Or LeBrea," he said.

"Renee's abductor is not interested in any ransom. He wants to hurt Briggs. So he'll kill Renee thinking he's killed Briggs's daughter."

"That's one scenario," LeBrea said.

"The only one," Shara said. "It's just a matter of how much time we have to find him, isn't it?"

LeBrea nodded again.

"He won't kill her right away," Shara said, thinking out loud. "He hadn't planned on snatching her. But once he made his decision, it felt right. Briggs is impotent. Briggs is suffering. Payback for something Briggs did to him." Shara paused and looked at the detective. "How am I doing?"

"Briggs and I came to the same conclusion."

"So how long do we have, in your expert opinion, before he kills Renee?" Shara asked. "Don't bullshit me, LeBrea," Shara added. "I know there are a thousand variables. Give me your gut reaction."

"Forty-eight to seventy-two hours," LeBrea said. "It's difficult to approximate because this doesn't fall into a pattern where there's sufficient information to make an informed guess. Nationwide, there are no more than a hundred children abducted by strangers a year. Most abductions deal with domestic disputes. The circumstances here are so unique, we don't have other cases for comparison. This was no premeditated, carefully planned crime. The only footprints outside are those leading to the kitchen door and exiting. He didn't stand out in the rain for half an hour waiting for the light to go off or deciding what to do. For whatever reason, he decided to get revenge on Briggs tonight. Only once in the house did he consider kidnapping Briggs's daughter rather than harming Briggs himself. That can work for or against us. He could panic and decide to dispose of the body . . . of Renee . . . right away. Or, having committed to a new course, he might need time to mull over what to do. It could go either way. Another variable is Renee. If she blurts out she's not Briggs's daughter, whoever snatched her could decide to kill her right away."

"Renee won't let that happen," Shara said. "She's good at thinking on her feet. Once she's aware he thinks she's Alexis, she'll play along with him. She knows to do otherwise would immediately jeopardize her."

"You don't think she'll panic?" LeBrea asked.

Shara shook her head. "She knows the danger she's in. I believe in Renee. You have to, as well. She'll play for time. Consider it my gut instinct." She paused a moment, in thought. "Something triggered him," she finally said. "We figure out what and we narrow down the list of suspects. Did forensics come up with anything else?"

LeBrea shook his head.

"Have you canvassed the neighborhood?" Shara asked.

"Briggs says there were no lights on in any of the surrounding homes. We wake people at two in the morning, and someone will alert the media. Briggs is not only a cop, but a well-known figure, what with his beating the crap out of a rapist and all. We'll check with the neighbors at daybreak. We'll come up with a plausible reason without mentioning the abduction."

"There was a car down the block," Shara said, suddenly remembering. "One of yours?"

"No. A reporter from the *Daily News*. Sam Brash," LeBrea said.

"Does he know anything?" Shara asked.

"He must have been monitoring traffic with a scanner. He's sitting tight, so no, I think he's in the dark. At some point he's going to figure out there's a story. Before he does, I want to have a chat with him," LeBrea said.

Shara nodded. "Let me get Briggs out of his stupor. I want to hear your plans."

"One more thing," LeBrea said, not looking happy. "Briggs pulled some strings to get me assigned the case. He knew there were complications that would hinder our investigation. My sarge agreed on one condition," LeBrea said, and paused.

"Don't keep me in suspense," Shara said.

"He's going to alert the FBI," LeBrea said.

"Fuck," Shara said. "Why don't we just take an ad out in the papers. The more people we involve— "

"I know," LeBrea cut her off. "They're not going to arrive in a convoy," LeBrea said with a tight smile. "My sarge knows the situation. We've already got a tap on the phone in case we're mistaken and there is a call for a ransom."

"Or if the bastard wants to fuck with Briggs's head," Shara said.

LeBrea looked at Shara.

"It's a long shot," Shara elaborated. "If we're right and this guy is making it up as he goes along, he may decide to torment Briggs. He may not care if he's caught. Hell, now that he's done the deed, he may assume he will be captured. What does he have to lose? He's been fucked over by Briggs. What a rush if he can actually talk to his tormentor and hear the pain and resignation in his voice. If he calls, we have to figure how to lengthen that time frame of yours."

"Convince him keeping Renee alive will push Briggs to the brink," LeBrea said, nodding.

"Briggs cracked before when he couldn't bring Alexis's rapist to ground. This guy's got nothing to lose. I'm convinced he'll contact Briggs." Shara paused. "Your sarge, can he work with the FBI so we're not hamstrung?" Shara asked.

"That a cop's daughter has been kidnapped, or so the abductor thinks, works for us," LeBrea said. "It's family. They can't brush us aside."

"Let me talk to Briggs. He's putty in my hands," Shara said with a weak smile.

"I don't doubt it for a moment," LeBrea said with a smile of his own.

Chapter Eight

As Norman Flowers shaved, his eyes caught the news article he'd taped next to the mirror in the bathroom. Norman shaved daily, though there was hardly a need. He had once tried to grow a beard without success. His facial hair sprouted at the speed of a tortoise. After three weeks, he didn't have a beard. He didn't even have a five o'clock shadow. Still, he felt dirty if he didn't shave daily, and he loathed filth.

His apartment, while seedy, was immaculate. He had spent almost an entire day cleaning up the broken plates and glasses he'd tossed in his fury at reading of Lamar Briggs's reinstatement.

Norman couldn't put Lamar-Fucking-Briggs out of his mind. He didn't want to. Seeing the article daily as he shaved stoked his anger. It had taken him years, but he had finally accepted losing his job, his home, and even his family because of Lamar-Fucking-Briggs. He was now a sales associate—a glorified title for a cashier—at a Barnes & Noble bookstore. With no family and few expenses, he wasn't leading much of a life, but he could easily make ends meet. Not making the money he once did really didn't bother Norman. With no family, money would just gather dust in a savings account. He had long ago accepted his lot. But this . . . *this* was just too much. If there was a god, he had a perverse sense of humor, Norman thought, and was probably having a good belly laugh now at Norman's expense.

Until that morning when life had kicked him in the balls yet again, things had been going relatively well for Norman. Everything was relative in Norman's world. He would never retrieve his dignity or reputation. Wealth would forever elude him. He hadn't had a serious relationship since his wife had left him fourteen years earlier.

But the last two months had been better than most. Rose had unexpectedly returned. He hadn't seen his youngest daughter since his wife had left him. When his wife had moved to Michigan and soon after divorced him, Norman had been too full of self-pity and despair to fight for even shared custody or visitation. After losing his job and being rebuffed by every other public relations firm in the city, he had begun to drink heavily. He had even dabbled with drugs, uppers to keep the depression he felt at bay. Thoughts of his family were stored deep in the recesses of his frazzled mind.

The first few months after his wife left, she had called once a week out of genuine concern. She wasn't adverse to visitation. She told Norman their children *should* see their father. Norman hadn't given a damn at the time. Soon the calls stopped, then the divorce papers arrived. Jan had called when she remarried not soon after. It had been awkward. Norman still hadn't hit rock bottom. He hadn't asked about his children. He hadn't called or sent a card or present for their birthdays. He'd then sent nothing for Christmas. Hell, he'd spent Christmas in a drunken stupor.

His children must hate him, he thought the following June after he'd sunk as low as he could and had finally began to claw his way out of the sewer that was his life. He convinced himself he was no longer a part of their life. They'd forgotten him. They had a new father. He had nothing to offer.

Then in September, just a few weeks earlier, there had been a knock on his door. At first he was mortified by the girl who asked if he was Norman Flowers. Her face resembled a pincushion with numerous piercings on her right eyebrow and left ear. Her lip was pierced, and when she spoke, he saw so was her tongue. A nose ring completed the grotesque tableau. What kind of parent would allow a girl who appeared to be seventeen or eighteen to mutilate herself? The girl had numerous tattoos, and on her arms there seemed to be burns. They formed patterns, and Norman was certain they were self-inflicted, not the result of being caught in a conflagration.

Norman wanted nothing to do with this girl. She must be soliciting money or a signature for a petition for some cause, he thought. Still, Norman was nothing if not polite. He would hear her out, then gently see her on her way.

"It's Melissa, Daddy," the girl said, tentatively. "Your daughter," she added, when Norman didn't respond.

"My daughter's name is Rose," Norman said.

"Rose Melissa," the girl said. "I go by Melissa."

"My Rose," Norman said, his eyes widening in disbelief. "My baby, Rose. Come in. Sit down," he said and rushed into his bedroom. He returned with a photograph, looked at it, then at the teen sitting with her hands in her lap. His eyes went back and forth. Photo. Girl. Photo. Girl. *Yes*, the eyes were the same. His Rose had returned.

Their first meetings had been awkward. She told him she'd wanted to reconnect with him. She had intentionally applied to Temple University to be close to him.

For his part, initially, Norman was often at a loss for words. What questions were off limits? What did she know about him? What lies had Jan concocted? Soon, though, they grew comfortable with one another. Norman asked Rose about the burns. He referred to her as Rose, never Melissa. She was Rose, and Norman would never accept her name change.

"They're brandings, not burns," Melissa said.

Norman had laughed. "You brand cows to prove ownership. So who do you belong to?"

"I belong to me," she'd said and laughed in return.

Privately, Norman was appalled at his daughter's appearance. He alternately blamed Jan and himself. How could his ex-wife allow it? But he knew he was as much to blame. He hadn't been there for Rose or April, his oldest daughter. What right did he have to condemn Jan when he'd abdicated responsibility for fourteen years?

Soon he began to accept Rose for the young woman she was. He would never get used to the piercings. And she dressed far too provocatively for his taste. She had small breasts, but he could see her nipples through her skin-tight tops. One was pierced. She wore her jeans low, and her top exposed her midriff so he could see yet another ring in her navel.

"How do you get through airport security?" he'd joked one day. "You must set off alarms."

"I *do*, Daddy," she'd said and laughed. "They use those wands. But it's their problem, not mine."

He saw her twice weekly. Once a week he cooked dinner for her. The other day he saw her, he would take her to a restaurant. New to Philly, every restaurant was a novel experience. There hadn't been much variety in her diet in Michigan, she told him. She was eager, though, to try new foods and seemed to enjoy everything she sampled. Chinese, Italian, Thai. She loved exotic meals but was just as happy with a Philly cheesesteak from Genos or a pizza from a hole-in-the-wall greasy-spoon pizza parlor. Norman took her to elegant restaurants, as well. Rose ignored the stares. Norman marveled at her self-confidence. She wasn't the least bit intimidated or embarrassed by the reproach of others.

Things had been going so well . . . until Lamar-Fucking-Briggs re-entered Norman's life. He couldn't get the man off his mind. Since the article appeared, he'd tried to relax when he was with his daughter. He tried to free his mind of thoughts of his nemesis. But Briggs wouldn't be denied. Norman became curt, abrasive, then detached. Rose would be talking about campus life or a professor she had and Norman hardly heard a word. Worse, as he became more obsessed with Briggs and his rage mounted, Norman began to give his daughter the bum's rush. At home, he'd cook a frozen dinner for her visits rather than slave over a gourmet meal as he had before. When they finished, he'd make an excuse about work that had to be done and usher Rose to the door, almost pushing her out. He would then sit and stare blankly at a TV show he paid no attention to, thinking about Lamar-Fucking-Briggs eating dinner with his family, discussing his day at his dream job.

And just four days before, he had called Rose around noon and told her he couldn't take her to the Irish Pub on Walnut Street where he told her they had thick, juicy hamburgers to die for.

Norman knew he was on the verge of losing his Rose yet again. Someone would pay. Lamar-Fucking-Briggs would pay. Pay dearly.

Chapter Nine

Renee enjoyed hanging with Alexis, though both were aware they continued to vie for Shara's undivided affection. It was actually Shara, more than anything, that bound the two together. While Renee enjoyed Alexis's company and considered her more than just a friend, they didn't share that much in common. Renee was athletic and competitive—compulsively so. She jogged whenever she could with Shara. Not much of a team player, she had been on her school's cross country and track teams. Alexis had been interested in athletics before Renee knew her. Since her attack, though, Alexis had been little more than a vegetable physically until she had been healed by the forest some six months earlier. While almost completely healed, Alexis still walked with a limp, so athletics was pretty much out of the question. No way Alexis could keep up with Renee if they jogged, for instance. The two did share one athletic endeavor—boxing. While Alexis was handicapped by her leg, she had been taught to compensate and use her disability to her advantage. Alexis, big-boned like her father, was a far more powerful puncher than Renee. Agility, a long-arm reach, and quick hands that could deliver numerous jabs to the body allowed Alexis to fight Renee to a draw.

Renee was glib while Alexis was withdrawn. Again, this was the result of the rape and beating Alexis had suffered. For a good year after her attack, Alexis had been unable to speak. When in the forest with Shara, Alexis had been her old self, but once outside the forest, she could communicate only via sign language. Even though she was now healed, she spoke without emotion in a dull monotone. There was only so much the forest could do in healing her. She had her limp, and while within her emotions churned, the words she spoke were flat and remote. You would only know she was angry, upset, frustrated, or happy by reading her eyes, something Shara was an expert at, something Renee was learning as her fondness for Alexis grew.

Truth be told, if it weren't for their mutual interest in Shara, Renee doubted they would have become close.

Several times a month Renee slept over at Alexis's house. Renee had brought a sleeping bag along with her, but it was still in the corner of Alexis's room. With no school the next day, and neither tired, there was no need to open the bag yet. The two were on Alexis's bed playing chess. They had each won four games, and this last one was for all the marbles. Renee saw, though, she had misplayed her last move and if Alexis realized her mistake, the game would soon be over. Renee knew the only way to possibly stay in the game was to distract Alexis.

Thinking how to distract Alexis, Renee was unaware she was staring at her friend.

"What are you looking at?" Alexis asked.

Renee was aware Alexis was self-conscious about her body. *That* could be her distraction. "You've . . . grown," Renee said, shrugging.

"My body had a lot of catching up to do after I was healed," Alexis said. "I'll never be as tall as you, but I no longer have the body of an eleven-year old."

Alexis had explained to Renee any number of times that her body had been in what she called a state of hibernation from the time she was attacked at eleven until she was healed just after she had turned sixteen. When she was raped, she had been tall for her age, but she hadn't grown more than an inch in the intervening years. She hadn't had her period. She had no breasts to speak of. She was still a kid. After she was healed, it was as if her body clock was racing to catch up to her chronological age. In less than five months, her body had aged five years.

"I wasn't referring to your height," Renee said, looking at Alexis's full breasts—far larger than Renee's.

"There, too," Alexis said and signed a smile. "I've gone through three different bra sizes in the past month alone."

"Getting noticed by boys now," Renee said, with a smile of her own.

"Getting stared at, yes, but I'm still considered a freak," Alexis said. "It's not the limp," she clarified. "It's my lack of emotion when I speak that scares most away. What do you make of someone who never laughs or raises her voice when she's angry? I can feel boys looking at my tits. They wouldn't mind getting a handful," she said, and again signed a laugh. "But they don't want to get to know me . . . get too close to me to even have a chance to cop a feel."

The two fell silent for several moments.

"Shara worries me," Alexis finally said, breaking the tension. "Without Deidre I'm sometimes afraid that dark side of hers will surface again."

"We're her conscience now," Renee said, repeating what Shara had told her several times before. "Shara doesn't deny her dark side exists. What she did to Denise proves it. She promised me she wouldn't kill Denise, but giving her to the forest is as bad . . . maybe worse. But I don't think it was Deidre who kept her in check. It was you. And now it's both of us. It's not like she's grown a conscience. She doesn't want to disappoint us."

"But that didn't stop her from . . . well, destroying Denise," Alexis said.

"Shara considers what she did to Denise self-preservation. Self-defense," Renee said.

"So she'll kill again if she feels it necessary," Alexis said.

"That's going a bit too far," Renee countered. "Look, I think your initial premise is wrong. You think Deidre somehow held Shara in check. With Deidre dead, Shara can do as she pleases." Renee shook her head. "Deidre hadn't been a part of Shara's life for a good six months before she was murdered. Shara can control her demons. But even if Deidre were alive, if Shara feels threatened or if you or I are endangered, there's nothing that's going to stop Shara from doing whatever she feels is necessary to protect us or herself. That's not a bad thing, Alexis."

Alexis shrugged. "Still, we should both keep an eye on her."

Now it was time for Renee to shrug. She no longer wanted to argue the point.

Alexis looked at the chess board and signed a smile. She moved and Renee saw she hadn't distracted Alexis at all. "Good try," she said, "but it's just a matter of time now."

After the game, Renee yawned.

"I'm going to the bathroom and then taking a shower," Alexis said. "Maybe you can beat me tomorrow," she said, scooting off the bed before Renee could slap her on her butt.

Chapter Ten

Norman hung up the phone, wiped a tear from his eye, then went out for a drive. As before, he had driven aimlessly for half an hour or more yet invariably ended up in Southwest Philly at Penrose Park where Lamar Briggs resided. He'd driven by Briggs's house three times previously. The first time, a week earlier, it was out of curiosity. Norman had lost his home because of this detective. Norman wanted to see what Briggs called home. Briggs's lodgings were nothing to write home about. It couldn't compare to the Lower Merion house Norman had lived in fifteen years before. It if hadn't been for Briggs, he was certain he would have had a far more luxurious home by now. He had been a highly valued member of his public relations firm with a knack for knowing what would please a client.

Still, the Briggs property had the feel of home, not just someplace to hang your hat, like Norman's apartment. It further fueled Norman's resentment and rage.

After the first visit, he'd been drawn there a second then a third time. He didn't know why. He had never consciously expected to end up at Briggs's home after his first visit.

Tonight it was raining steadily when he left his apartment. This was the first time he had driven to Briggs's home in the evening. His daughter's words echoed in his mind. The day after he had canceled dinner with Rose, he had felt terribly guilty. Here he'd been given a second chance with his daughter and he was pissing it away. He'd called to apologize. He'd suggested dinner, but Rose had declined.

"My classes are catching up with me. I really have to study," she told him.

He called the following day. Now it was his daughter who seemed distant and aloof.

"I'm sorry, I can't, Daddy. That job I got. Someone's sick. I agreed to fill in."

He'd called again tonight. He couldn't lose her again. He'd spent the afternoon cooking as soon as he'd returned from his job. "I've made something special for you, Rose. Can't you come over for dinner? You can leave right after."

"You're making this really difficult for me, Daddy," she replied.

"What's wrong, Rose?" he asked. He heard her sigh, then pause. Finally she spoke words he dreaded.

"I'm transferring to Michigan State at the end of the semester," she said, then fell silent.

"I thought you liked it here," Norman said. "The restaurants, classes, life in the big city, friends you've made—"

"I came here because I wanted to be close to you," Rose cut in, talking in a rush. "Lately you've been so distant . . . so consumed by bitterness. That's the way a counselor on campus I've been seeing put it. *Consumed by bitterness*. This detective you talk about all the time . . . Briggs, your hatred for him is more important than your love for me. I guess that's why mom left you in the first place. I don't blame you, but it was a mistake for me to come here."

"I can change," Norman pleaded. "I *will* change."

"I'm lonely, Daddy," she replied. "A lot of my friends went to Michigan State. I had this fantasy when I decided to go to Temple. I enjoyed our time together. I truly did. But you've also opened my eyes. I've got a life of my own to live, and I feel like a stranger here. With you drifting away . . . well, I have to do what's best for me."

Norman started to protest, but he knew it was useless. He could make all the promises he wished, but each morning when he shaved, his mind would be on Lamar-Fucking-Briggs. And now he'd lost his Rose for a second time because of the bastard.

His anger toward Briggs mounted as he drove. Soon he found himself just a block from Briggs's home. The storm had abated and it was just drizzling when he parked his car a block from Briggs's home. He opened the glove compartment and took out a gun he kept there. He tucked it in the waistband of his trousers. There was a pair of gloves on the back seat. He put them on and made his way to the back of Briggs's house, the rain mixing with tears that flowed down his cheek.

Why was he here? What was he going to do? He had no plan. But tonight Lamar-Fucking-Briggs would pay. Norman had lost Rose again because of Briggs. There was just so much a man could take.

Norman approached the house from the rear. He paused near some bushes. If Briggs had a dog, it would begin to howl at the smell of a stranger. The only sounds he heard were raindrops and crickets. At the backdoor, Norman used his elbow to break a window pane on the kitchen door. He was poised to run if an alarm rang out. But again there was silence. Norman shook his head. A cop, Briggs must have felt himself invincible. No dog. No alarm. A lock that could be easily accessed. Such an arrogant bastard, Norman thought.

Norman walked through the kitchen, then went upstairs. While curious, he couldn't chance looking around to get a sense of the life Briggs led. He might knock something over and alert the detective. And Norman knew Briggs had a gun and wouldn't hesitate to use it.

There were two bedrooms on the second floor. The door of the one furthest down the hall was slightly ajar. Briggs heard the sound of music. Nigger music, he thought, as he listened for a moment. Music kids listened to, not adults. Norman didn't consider himself a racist, but the lyrics of rap music sickened him. Nigger music, unlike jazz or sixties Motown songs he had enjoyed as a child. Hell, he thought, the rappers often referred to blacks as niggers during their vile diatribes.

He stood by the room with the closed door. He could envision Briggs and his wife inside sleeping. Some parents, he thought, letting their daughter stay up on a school night so late. He'd looked at his watch in the car. It must be close to one-thirty in the morning now. His hand was on the butt of his gun. His father had taken him hunting when he was young. He could use a rifle. He could use a gun. But could he walk into Briggs's bedroom and shoot the detective? He paced back and forth for what seemed an eternity but was actually less than a minute. Killing Briggs was the easy way out. *Easy for Briggs.* He wanted Lamar-Fucking-Briggs to suffer. No, killing him wasn't the solution.

A decision made, Norman went to the other bedroom. Peering in, he saw Briggs's daughter lying on her stomach, her head propped upon on her hands looking at the radio and softly mouthing the vulgar words to the music that played. She was fully clothed. Didn't she have school in the morning? he wondered. He crept inside so he was behind the girl . . . Alexis was her name, he recalled from an article he had read several years back. He remembered she had been raped and beaten. He had almost felt sorry for Briggs then. *Almost.* Norman put his hand over the girl's mouth and the gun to her head.

"Scream or struggle and I'll kill you, *then* your parents," he whispered. "Understand?"

The girl nodded.

"We walk out together without a sound, Alexis. Try anything and you . . . your mother . . . and then your father dies. Understand?"

Again the youth nodded.

Ten minutes after he had arrived at Briggs's home, Norman was in his car. He had locked Alexis in his trunk after tying her hands and feet with string and gagging her with a towel he used to wipe dew off the inside of his windshield.

Once he'd formulated his plan outside of Briggs's bedroom, he seemed to have an answer for every question that popped into his mind. He had a cabin he had never sold about ninety minutes outside of the city. He would take Alexis there. He still visited it once a year to get out of the tumult of the city. It was isolated, which made it ideal. On the outside, it had fallen into a state of disrepair. Norman thought it ironic that because he didn't have the money for upkeep, it now suited his purposes to perfection. Especially at this time of year, it would seem like an abandoned property. He had kept the inside clean. Norman couldn't abide filth. It was also well-stocked with non-perishable food. He would stop at a convenience store, once out of the city limits, to buy milk, bread, and a few other essentials.

He whistled as he drove. Soon, maybe even now, Briggs would begin to experience the torment that had been Norman's life for the past fifteen years.

Chapter Eleven

Shara peered out the front window to look outside before going over to Briggs. The reporter was still keeping vigil. She saw it had stopped raining.

"Let's talk, Briggs," Shara said, seeing he still had the look of a beaten fighter.

Briggs rose and walked toward the front door.

"There's a reporter camped across the street," Shara said. "I don't want him seeing the two of us together. Raising questions. Drawing conclusions. Let's go out back."

Briggs shrugged and followed Shara. They stood next to a swing set that hadn't been used in at least eight years, Shara thought. Its green metal posts were littered with rust.

"I've been meaning to get rid of this," Briggs said. "Inertia," he added as a means of explanation why it remained in the backyard.

"Briggs, I don't blame you," Shara said, ignoring his banter.

"But I blame myself," Briggs said. "I'm an arrogant asshole thinking being a cop would insulate me from crime. I should have learned with the attack on Alexis. I'd made a habit of not setting the alarm. It shouldn't have been Renee . . . " he said, unable to finish.

"You'd feel better if it *had* been Alexis?" Shara asked.

Briggs shrugged.

"I love Alexis and Renee equally, you know that," Shara said. "You'd feel less guilty if it were Alexis. That I can understand. But this is no longer about you. It's about getting Renee back safely."

"If anything happens to Renee, I don't know how I'll live with myself," Briggs said.

"But you could live with your own daughter being harmed?" Shara said.

"That's not what I said," Briggs answered, his voice rising.

Good, Shara thought. She had to get through to him if Renee was to have a chance. "To put it bluntly, Briggs, Renee can cope with this better than Alexis."

Briggs looked at Shara.

"Alexis has already been traumatized once," Shara said, knowing she had his attention. "She's been sheltered most of the past five years while she's been recovering. You've given Alexis a safe haven, sanctuary, whatever you want to call it. And her values are your values. Renee has been around me, and I'm no pillar of the community. I'm a bounty hunter who takes shortcuts. I've schooled Renee in survival. She'll read her kidnapper. She'll play him." Shara grabbed Briggs by his shirt so he had to look at her. "Time's our enemy, Briggs. Only you can narrow down the list of suspects. Give it your best shot. That way I can live with the consequences if we come up short."

Briggs nodded. "No more wallowing in self-pity is what you're saying."

"I'm saying no one comes into *your* house and messes with *your* loved ones. No one fucks with Lamar Briggs."

"Anyone tell you you'd make a hell of a motivational speaker," Briggs said. "You sure know what buttons to push." He paused. "Okay, let's catch this mother."

Chapter Twelve

Shara, Briggs, and LeBrea went into Briggs's study, which served as his home office. Alexis reluctantly stayed to comfort her mother. LeBrea commandeered a chalkboard Briggs often used.

"We brainstorm," LeBrea said, taking charge. "Regurgitate anything that comes to mind no matter how insignificant. What do we know about Mr. X?" LeBrea asked writing the name at the top of the board.

"He's got a grudge against me," Briggs said.

"Long-simmering," Shara added. "This has been building over time."

"But he's not fixated on you," LeBrea said.

"How so?" Briggs asked.

LeBrea jotted words on the chalkboard as he spoke. "He didn't know Renee wasn't your daughter. They look nothing alike."

"He's an amateur," Shara said.

"Elaborate," LeBrea prodded.

"The manner he broke in. Briggs had an alarm system. How would he know it wasn't activated? He hadn't spent weeks or days observing your habits or he would have known Alexis had a guest over," Shara said, looking at Briggs.

"He's impulsive," Briggs said. "For whatever reason, *tonight* he decided to avenge himself."

"But he had no firm plan other than revenge," Shara added. "He considered striking directly at you," she said, again looking at Briggs. "The pacing outside your door indicates his indecision. He hadn't planned to kidnap who he thought was your daughter until the opportunity presented itself."

They continued for another twenty minutes.

"Why tonight?" LeBrea asked.

"Something recently triggered his rage," Shara said, her admiration for LeBrea mounting. He *was* good. He knew the questions to ask. He wasn't interpreting. Now was not the time. He also knew when to move on. *What triggered him?* He wrote on the board and followed with another question.

"Who is he?"

"Someone I put away," Briggs said. "Possibly spent a good deal of time in prison, his anger mounting."

"Now his life's in shambles," Shara said, playing off what Briggs had said. "He gets out of prison but has nothing to return to. Maybe his wife has left him. Remarried. Relocated. His kids may not know he even exists. He has a dead-end job. A loner."

"So his anger builds," Briggs said. "Not at his wife. Not at society. Against the man who put him away. Against *me*."

"What do we do?" LeBrea asked.

"Check out anyone I put away who fits the profile," Briggs said.

"And if that doesn't pan out?" LeBrea asked.

Shara stifled a smile. Smart, she thought. Keep the momentum going. Come up with alternate suspects if those on list A take them nowhere.

"A spouse, relative, or child of this guy who also feels victimized," Briggs said.

And on they went for another ten minutes. Finally LeBrea held up his hand. "Unfortunately, time is our enemy in more ways than one. The FBI will be here soon. I also want to speak to our intrepid reporter before the Feds arrive. So let's prioritize. Where do we start?"

Shara saw LeBrea was now intent on keeping them on track. Any new extraneous ideas or details were to be jotted on the board, but not discussed.

"Who do we have at our disposal?" LeBrea asked. "Our task force, so to speak. My sarge can spare two other detectives. If the shit hits the fan and the media gets wind of what occurred, we'll have a hell of a lot more manpower—"

"But Renee will be dead," Shara said.

"I've got two detectives in mind whom I trust completely," LeBrea said. "Briggs, who can you provide?"

"I've already spoken to my sarge, Morales. He'll help personally. And my partner, Nina Rios. She knows my fucked-up filing system and is familiar with a number of the cases we'll be looking into," Briggs said.

Shara sensed Briggs's excitement building. He had absorbed a number of body blows but had got his second wind.

"Shara?" LeBrea asked.

"Cheyenne Woods works for me," Shara said. "There's also another bounty hunter I'd trust with my life. Depending on our needs, there's others I can enlist. Each have their own area of expertise and all are totally loyal. For now, though, just the two."

"Well, we've got our Task Force," LeBrea said.

"Independent of the FBI," Shara said.

"We'll have to see about that," LeBrea said. "I won't make promises I can't keep. I've got to keep my sarge in the loop. He won't keep me on a tight leash, but these are not the best of times for the department, if you catch my drift."

"CYA," Shara said. "Cover Your Ass."

"*That* my sarge will do," LeBrea said. "Can't blame him, if you want the truth. Let's worry about the Feds when the need arises." He looked at his watch. "We've got four problems as I see it. One," he said, holding up one finger, "is time. Forty-eight to seventy-two hours. Two," this time he raised two fingers, "the media. Forgetting our friend outside for a moment, everyone must be on the same page. Briggs has been receiving harassing phone calls. We're investigating. We all know what happens if the media reports Renee and not Alexis was kidnapped."

"The FBI," Shara said, raising three fingers.

"Yes, the FBI," LeBrea said. "Until we know who we're dealing with, let's not speculate."

"My list of enemies," Briggs said, raising four fingers.

"Extensive, from what you've told us," LeBrea said. "Other than canvassing the neighborhood, tomorrow we concentrate all our efforts on Briggs's files. We eliminate as many as possible. Anyone who raises a red flag we look into immediately," he said, raising one finger. "Time. We don't have the time to pick and choose, at least not until we've exhausted the files."

There was a knock on the door. Alexis entered.

"The guy in the car across the street just drove off," she said, looking at LeBrea. She then looked at her father. "Detective LeBrea asked me to keep an eye out," Alexis said, tonelessly.

"Good girl," Briggs said.

"Is she still in shock?" LeBrea said when Alexis had left. "Her voice—"

"It's the result of the beating she sustained," Briggs said. "She talks without emotion, but check out her eyes. Plenty there."

"I'm sorry," LeBrea said, his face reddening.

"No need," Briggs said, waving a dismissive hand. "Other than her voice and a slight limp, she's cured," he said, looking at Shara. "She's made a remarkable recovery. Truthfully, I couldn't ask for more." He paused. "What do we do about Brash?"

Shara spoke up before LeBrea could answer. "I know the attorney for the *Daily News*. Anything he writes has to pass through her. What could he have gleaned sitting out there all night?" she asked, looking at LeBrea.

LeBrea's cell phone rang before he could answer. He listened, then hung up. "The Feds will be here between six and seven in the morning. One car. They're flying someone up from D.C. to help us out. We retain jurisdiction. We've all got things to do before the Feds arrive." He looked at Shara. "There's nothing Brash could have learned. Let's see if he comes back." LeBrea walked out of the study. Briggs began to follow, but Shara held onto his arm.

"He's good, Briggs," she said. "You were right to bring him in. I almost forgot we were talking about Renee, I was so wrapped up in the case itself."

"He's going places, Shara," Briggs said. "Police Commissioner someday. Maybe politics. There's a charisma about him. He inspires others, just like he did with you and me.

"A shame," Shara said.

Briggs looked at her oddly.

"This is his element," Shara said. "He's like you in that way. Working a case is what he likes best. But you're right. He's destined for . . . greater things, I guess you'd call it. The shame is, he'll never have the satisfaction he has now as he moves up the ladder." Shara shrugged. "I'll be gone for about an hour. I want to speak to my people in person. Call me if you learn anything."

In her car, Shara made several calls on her cell. She spoke briefly with Rudy, a fellow bounty hunter who had taught Shara the ins and outs of the profession. She said she would meet him in half an hour. Cheyenne wasn't in. Maybe she was with Lysette, Shara thought. She left a message telling Cheyenne to call her.

Her last call was to Lynn Moody. Shara had met Moody after Deidre Caffrey, a reporter and friend of Shara's, had been murdered. Moody had been Deidre's personal attorney. She was the one who broke the news to Shara that Deidre had a younger sister Shara knew nothing about.

Shara apologized for waking Moody up when she answered her phone.

"Not the first time," she said, and Shara could hear her stifle a yawn. "I've been awakened from a sound sleep more times than I can count. Comes with the territory. I take it this is important," she went on.

"I can't give you details, especially over the phone, but Sam Brash might be filing a story that could put someone's life at risk," Shara said. "I know I sound cryptic but—"

"Say no more," Moody said. "I'll call you back in five minutes."

Shara closed her eyes for a moment. She realized she hadn't slept in close to twenty-four hours. She didn't need much sleep. Never had . . . . The phone ringing startled her. Damn, she thought, she must have dozed off. It was Moody.

"I spoke with Carter Hastings," Moody said. Shara knew he was the city editor of the *Daily News* and that Brash would be reporting to him. "Brash thinks he's onto a story, but he hasn't written anything yet."

"Did you tell Hastings what I told you?" Shara asked.

"About someone's life being as risk?" Moody asked in return.

"Yes."

"I did," Moody said. "Look, Shara, before we run anything, I'll call you. I can't make any promises, but I won't approve a story that might lead to someone's death."

"I appreciate it, Lynn," Shara said. "I promise to fill you in . . . over dinner, when this is over."

Shara drove over to Rudy's, then to Cheyenne's. She wanted neither at Briggs's house at the moment. She caught

Cheyenne just after 6 a.m. She came out on her porch when she answered her door, a cup of coffee in her hand. She didn't offer Shara any, which Shara found odd. Cheyenne was dressed and didn't look like she had just woken up.

"I got your message when I came in," Cheyenne told Shara without elaborating. "Thought you'd be showing up, so I didn't bother to go to sleep."

Shara explained the situation. She told Cheyenne she would either e-mail or messenger files over.

"Anything I can do to help," Cheyenne said. "I know I haven't met Renee, what with your rules separating our personal from our professional life, but the few times you've mentioned her . . . well, it's obvious you love her as if she were your own child. Anyway, it's my awkward way of saying I won't let you down."

Shara drove back to Briggs's. The cavalry should have arrived, Shara thought glumly. After she fenced with the Feds, Shara promised herself a short nap. Without some rest, she might overlook something important.

Chapter Thirteen

Renee gave up struggling to escape her bonds ten minutes after she'd been tied up and put in the trunk of her abductor's car. It was useless, and she felt her legs cramping with her efforts. She knew she'd been kidnapped. Knew, too, that the man thought she was Alexis, Briggs's daughter. Initially she'd been terrified with visions of being raped, killed, then dumped where her body might never be found. She knew her thinking was a bit warped at being relieved she was being kidnapped instead. She wouldn't even consider the horrors that might await her or that she might have welcomed a quick death.

Renee had been spending the night with Alexis. Schools were closed the next day for a teacher's in-service day. She and Alexis had talked long into the night. Neither had many close friends. Both had secrets they couldn't divulge except to one another.

Shara was their common link. Both had vied for Shara's attention and had resented the other before having actually met. Shara had known Alexis longer than she knew Renee. With Alexis's psychic powers, she knew all of Shara's secrets. After her father had killed her mother, Renee had lived with Shara for four months before Shara had shared her past with Renee. Shara had done so to gain Renee's trust. Renee had had a secret of her own she felt she couldn't share with anyone. She had been mistaken.

When Renee and Alexis had finally met, they had taken

an instant liking to one another. Both Renee and Alexis understood Shara loved them equally. Shara would go to any lengths to protect them. Their petty jealousy had been totally unfounded. Both still fought for Shara's undivided loyalty, then later felt foolish when Shara chided them. It only further cemented their friendship.

Alexis had been in the bathroom when the kidnapper had entered. The sound of the radio made it impossible for Alexis to hear what was transpiring in the bedroom. It also prevented her abductor from knowing there was someone else in the room.

Now lying in the trunk, Renee had to puzzle out what to do. The kidnapper had said he'd kill *her* parents if she called out. And he'd called her Alexis. His intent, then, was to kidnap Alexis. He'd never seen a picture of Alexis, Renee reasoned, or he would instantly have known she wasn't Briggs's daughter. Alexis was dark-skinned like her father. Renee was bi-racial but she could have passed for white had she desired.

Okay, she decided, she had to pretend to be Alexis. Whether her abductor wanted money from Briggs or revenge, once he knew she wasn't Alexis, Renee was of no use to him. He wouldn't simply let her go. If he found out the truth, Renee knew she would be killed and disposed of quickly. She had to stay alive. The moment Shara found out she'd been taken, she would begin her search.

Like Alexis, Renee had absolute faith in Shara. Briggs was a homicide detective. He wouldn't be able to locate her. But Shara, a bounty hunter, stalked her prey. Shara enjoyed the stalking far more than the capture. No, Renee corrected herself, Shara didn't simply *enjoy* the stalking. The need to hunt humans had become ingrained in Shara when she had killed five sexual predators before dealing with her half-brother. She later found, like serial killers, the kill was necessary for self preservation, with the exception of her half-brother. She no longer killed but had become a bounty hunter so she could satisfy her need to hunt humans. Renee was confident Shara would find her.

Renee had to give Shara the time she needed to locate her. She had to learn what made this man tick. She had to play for time. Shara was good at manipulating others, and Renee was nothing if not observant. Renee had to probe for her abductor's weaknesses then exploit them. She had to stay alive no matter the cost. Given enough time, Shara would find the bastard. Shara played by her own rules. Bending, even breaking, the law was the key to her success as a bounty hunter. And she was relentless. Shara would go to any extreme to find Renee. In the confined, suffocating darkness of the car's trunk, these thoughts comforted Renee and drove the demons of what might lay ahead deep within where she didn't have to confront them.

What would Shara tell her to do now? Sleep. Yes, she was exhausted. She'd have to be at her best to outwit her captor. She couldn't if she was tired. Renee slept, confident Shara would come to her rescue.

Chapter Fourteen

Arriving at Briggs's house, Shara saw Sam Brash had returned, parked just where he had been during the night. She cursed under her breath. A second dark colored sedan was in the driveway. Those cars without personality screamed police.

Shara parked her gold five-year old Nissan directly across the street from Brash. If asked, she couldn't tell anyone what was under the hood. Turn the key. Put the car in gear. Go. She really didn't care. All that counted was the car was fast and reliable. She'd bought it used a year before and had it in the shop only for a change of tires, oil, brakes, and a tune-up. Shara seldom took the car to a carwash. There was a rust spot or two by one door, a ding here, another there. Outwardly, it had the look of neglect Shara desired. Its engine, she pampered. It had personality but wasn't too flashy as to draw unwanted attention. It certainly didn't scream cop like the cars in the Briggs's driveway.

Alexis answered her knock. Alexis looked as exhausted as Shara felt. She probably hadn't gotten any sleep either, Shara thought. She must feel guilty, just like her father. *It should have been me,* she could imagine Alexis telling her. Note to self, talk to Alexis, Shara told herself. Alexis signed to Shara to watch her temper.

Before Alexis had recovered from her rape and beating, she had been unable to speak. She'd learned to sign, as had Shara. Not only could she then communicate, but her hands also expressed her emotions. She could speak now, so why was she signing? And the message?

Shara saw Briggs seated on the couch, his arms wrapped around his body, full of tension. Shara hoped she wouldn't have to rally him again. He was a professional. He was allowed his moment of guilt, but it was time to move on. Briggs's eyes darted across the room, and following his glance, Shara saw the reason for his strange behavior and Alexis's warning. Shara was staring at Claire Cleary, who had a smug look on her face.

"Fuck," Shara said under her breath.

"Miss Farris, so good to see you again," Cleary said, approaching her with her hand out. If there hadn't been a room full of people, Shara could imagine Cleary saying, "*I'm Back!*" and cackling like a witch.

Shara ignored the woman and gestured to LeBrea. "We gotta talk." Without another word, she went into Briggs's study. LeBrea followed a minute later.

"What's going on?" LeBrea asked.

"Briggs didn't tell you?" Shara asked.

"Briggs looked as stunned as you when Special Agent Cleary arrived, but we haven't had a chance to talk in private. He's been tight-lipped and tense—"

"Cleary, Briggs, and I have a history," Shara said, without letting LeBrea finish. "She's incompetent and threatened by a woman who won't kiss her ass." Before LeBrea could speak, Shara went on. "Check with any contact you have at the FBI. Behind her back, she's called C.C. Cleary, as in Carbon Copy Cleary. Others would make pivotal decisions and *then* tell Cleary. She overcompensated. She tried to fit in. Just look at how she dresses. She *could* be a man if you didn't look closely."

"And you know she's incompetent for a fact?" LeBrea said.

Shara nodded. "A year and a half ago, Briggs and I were hired by a woman wanting to know why her pervert of a son was murdered. It seemed like a cold case. The only private bounties we handled were cases no longer under active investigation. The money's good and so is the challenge. Only this wasn't a cold case, and we didn't know it in good part because of Cleary. The trail led us from Atlanta to Philly, where Cleary was heading the investigation by the Feds. It was the sort of case that could make or break a career. Cleary wanted this one bad. She desperately craved a promotion to show she had the balls of males she felt superior to. She's got a chip on her shoulder the size of a boulder."

"And women getting passed over because of their gender has never happened before," LeBrea said sarcastically.

"There were legitimate reasons Cleary had been passed over. Hell, she was bureau chief up here, and she didn't merit that," Shara said irritably. "Long story short, Briggs warned her that the killer wasn't going to strike in the city. She ignored him for no good reason. Cleary had all the answers, so why listen to Briggs? The killer struck just south of Allentown, and Cleary ended up with egg on her face. She was pulled off the case and demoted. I'm sure she blames me."

"Not Briggs?" LeBrea asked, sounding confused.

"Briggs was . . . civil to her, even deferential. I wasn't. We kind of played good cop/bad cop, and it won't take you long to know I don't play good cop well. She jerked us around, withheld crucial information that would have saved us a lot of time. I got into her face. So while she may not think too kindly of Briggs, I'm evil incarnate as far as she's concerned."

That was all Shara was going to tell LeBrea. She left out how she had later sabotaged Cleary, hacking into her e-mail, and was in fact directly responsible for Cleary's demise. She left out a hell of a lot, but LeBrea was no fool and shouldn't need all the dots connected to accept her explanation.

"She must be working her way up the ladder again," Shara continued. "I wouldn't put it past her to have volunteered for this assignment when she saw Briggs and I were involved," Shara said.

"Payback?" LeBrea asked. "Should we add her to the list of suspects?"

Shara laughed. "She's not competent enough to pull it off. Look, Paul," Shara said turning serious. It was the first time she had called him by his first name. "Aside from her failings as an agent, she does harbor a grudge against both Briggs and me. I wouldn't put it past her to leak something to the media. Maybe even use our friend Brash. She has her own agenda. Renee comes a distant second to finding the kidnapper. Do you get my meaning?"

"If Renee is killed, Cleary can still claim it was inevitable," LeBrea said, stroking his beard. "If she captures Renee's abductor, it's still a feather in her cap."

"You got it. We gotta work around her," Shara said.

LeBrea nodded. "You chill. Let me play the bad cop if necessary. Okay?"

Shara laughed. "Alexis told me the same thing when she let me in. Have you briefed Cleary yet?"

"No. She just arrived," LeBrea said. "I'll tell her our theory without going into detail. I've got to tell her Briggs will be checking for someone with a grudge against him. I'll downplay your role. Keep in mind *we've* got jurisdiction. This involves one of our own. Push comes to shove, my sarge will do what's necessary. Can you behave yourself?" LeBrea asked with a smile.

"I'll be a good girl," Shara said.

"This I gotta see," LeBrea mumbled under his breath loud enough so Shara could hear. She laughed.

Back in the living room, Shara sat next to Briggs, who looked at her warily. Shara gave him a nudge in the side and signed she would be on her best behavior. Briggs immediately relaxed. It was all Shara could do to keep from bursting out laughing.

Cleary remained standing, looking almost comical in her charcoal gray pants suit, complete with a tie. Her hair was pulled back in a bun. She wore little makeup. Just one of the guys, Shara thought.

LeBrea stood as well, Shara thought to focus Cleary's attention on him. He succinctly outlined the facts, the theory that the motive was a grudge against Briggs, and the need for discretion.

"Your theory's sound," Cleary said when LeBrea finished. "I do think we can make use of the media, however. Since there has been no ransom demand, I agree our window of opportunity is small. We could use the public's help."

LeBrea flashed Shara a look.

I'll be a good girl and keep my mouth shut, Shara answered with a look of her own.

"It's too risky, Agent Cleary," LeBrea said.

"Claire, please," she said. "Let's not be formal."

"If we go to the media, Claire," LeBrea said, "we have to release a picture. The photo has to be of Renee. It just won't wash. The media covered the attack on Alexis five years ago. They won't be fooled that Renee is Briggs's daughter. We open a Pandora's Box. If the media reports it's not Briggs's daughter, our perp has no further reason to keep Renee alive."

Cleary took out a cigarillo from her purse and slowly lit it, as if playing for time, Shara thought. She'd smoke a fucking cigar if it would earn her the respect of the guys. Shara reminded herself to remain silent.

"Forty-eight hours," Cleary said finally. "From when the kidnapping occurred. If we haven't located or heard from the kidnapper by then, we have to assume the worst. Then we utilize the media to the fullest extent possible."

"Seventy-two hours," LeBrea said. "From now."

Cleary looked at LeBrea, began to speak, but stopped. She took a drag on the cigarillo, then nodded.

They sparred for another fifteen minutes over minutia. LeBrea gave a little but prevailed on all important matters. He argued vehemently on details of insignificance before giving in. He was handling Cleary, Shara saw, and Cleary didn't even know she was being played. Shara wanted to hug the man right then and there.

"If you could come up with a profile of our perp, Claire, that would be of great assistance," LeBrea said. "You've got far more experience than we do." Without waiting for an answer, he turned to Briggs. "Why don't you and Shara attack those files Rios sent over."

LeBrea accompanied Shara and Briggs into the study.

"You're my hero," Shara said to LeBrea. "She doesn't even know she's being manipulated."

"Behave yourself, Shara," LeBrea said with a laugh.

"You're not going to let her hold you to that seventy-two-hour deadline, are you?" Shara asked.

"Of course not," LeBrea said. "It's just that there's no sense arguing about it now."

"What about Brash?" Shara asked. "You didn't mention him to Cleary."

"I wouldn't. Like you said, it might give her ideas," LeBrea said. "Anyway, he's departed again. Your contact at the paper will call you if he files a story?" he asked.

Shara nodded.

"He'll return. When he does, we'll have our chat," LeBrea said. "I'll talk to him in his car to keep Cleary out of the picture. I'll be wired so the two of you can hear. We'll play it by ear. I've got a feeling he's got sources within the department. We may have to tell him Alexis has been kidnapped and offer an exclusive for his silence. You good with that?" LeBrea asked, looking at Briggs.

"I'm in the public eye," Briggs said and shrugged. "Nothing about Renee or Shara, though."

LeBrea nodded. "You look like you're going to nod off, Shara," he said. "Why not get some sleep. I'll wake you up when Brash returns."

Shara didn't protest. LeBrea seemed to be reading her mind.

Chapter Fifteen

Fifteen minutes before he reached the cabin, Norman's mood abruptly changed. He was no longer whistling. His hands clenched the steering wheel.

What had he done? he wondered. He'd wanted to hurt Briggs big time. Separating Briggs from his daughter was poetic justice. After all, Norman has lost his family because of Briggs. And he'd lost Rose a second time because of the bastard.

Yet he was filled with guilt and remorse. Alexis had done nothing to merit Norman's wrath. She'd already been brutalized once before. Yes, he wanted Briggs to suffer, but slowly the ramifications of what he had done began to sink in. For Briggs to *truly* suffer, Norman would have to kill Alexis. Doing so, however, would make him worse than Briggs. Norman had always considered himself morally superior to the detective, even with his life in shambles. For all his insolence, Briggs had been wrong. Norman *had* been innocent. Killing Alexis would validate Briggs's conviction Norman was capable of murder.

Maybe, he thought, he should let Alexis go now, unharmed, in the middle of nowhere. Briggs *would* suffer knowing how vulnerable he was. Knowing how close he'd come to losing his precious daughter might cripple him. And since Briggs had no idea Norman was responsible for the abduction, he would continue to suffer not knowing if his tormentor would strike again. No, not *if*, but when.

Briggs would agonize that the next time the target might be his wife. And this unknown assailant might strike at a mall or anyplace his wife or daughter ventured alone. Briggs would be paralyzed with fear. He wouldn't want his wife or daughter to go anywhere without him. It would put a tremendous strain on his marriage and relationship with his teenage daughter. They might leave him, just as Norman's family had. *It was perfect.* Norman had worn gloves so he'd left no fingerprints. His decision made, he slowed down.

Alexis saw your face. The thought was like a slap in the face. What a fool he'd been. Why hadn't he worn a ski mask? He *couldn't* let Alexis go. His scheme, like his life, was flushed down the toilet. He sped up again, making sure, though, to keep to the speed limit. No, he now knew if he let Alexis go, Briggs would finally get what he'd been denied fifteen years earlier—Norman Flowers in prison.

Norman had no other options. He had to go through with his original plan, spontaneous as it had been. And he now fully comprehended for the first time that he *would* have to kill Alexis. It was no longer an abstract notion. He would have to take the life of another. There was no acceptable alternative. He wouldn't torment her, though. He wouldn't harm her. He'd put her down quickly, humanely, like a horse with a broken leg.

Yet he wondered if he really would. He didn't want to hurt Alexis. But could he control the rage within him? That part of him that *did* want to harm Alexis. *That* Norman was just below the surface. *That* Norman had berated his wife until she was forced to leave him. *That* Norman had treated Rose shamefully so she, too, could no longer tolerate his presence. *That* Norman loathed Briggs and Alexis, an extension of her father. Yes, Alexis was Briggs's daughter. That he couldn't forget. Like father like daughter.

The apple didn't fall far from the tree. He laughed aloud. He was armed with absurd clichés to justify what a part of him deemed necessary. If he could control his fury, Alexis would die a swift, relatively painless death. If he couldn't . . . well, the alternative sickened yet excited him. "Control yourself," he said aloud. He hoped he could for Alexis's sake and for his own peace of mind. Norman knew he would have to live with the knowledge of what would occur if he gave into his darker side. If he lost control, *could* he live with himself after?

Suddenly Norman saw the road that led to his cabin, and thankfully he could ignore his conflicting emotions. There were practical tasks that demanded his full attention. Norman parked behind the cabin so the car would be out of sight. He went inside and found a burlap bag. He returned to the car, opened the trunk, and pointed a flashlight directly into Alexis's eyes. As she turned away, he put the bag over her head. He untied the rope that bound her legs and half dragged her to the cabin. He'd wanted her to walk on her own, but she kept stumbling. Her legs must be numb from being cooped up and tied in the car trunk, he decided.

Norman brought her to the cellar and sat her in a corner, then secured her legs again with rope. He knew what had to be done. He worked feverishly for half an hour, then stepped back. He looked with satisfaction at a job well done.

He untied Alexis and brought her to the wooden cabinet. He had fastened chains to the four corners and tied pieces of leather to each.

"Take off your jeans," he told her.

Alexis stood without reacting.

Norman put a knife to her throat. "Do as I say or die."

Her hands shaking, Alexis removed her jeans.

Norman then yanked off the burlap bag. "Get in," he said.

Alexis complied, blinking and trying to shield her eyes with her hands even though the lights in the cellar were dim.

"Hold your hands over your head," Norman commanded. When she did, he secured them with the strips of leather. If she were a clock, one hand was at the eleven and the other at the one. He did the same with her legs, one at five o'clock, the other at seven o'clock.

For the first time, Norman was able to scrutinize his captive. He was bewildered. Alexis didn't look anything like Briggs. She was tall, like her father, but scrawny, where Briggs was heavyset. And her skin . . . .

"How come you're so light-skinned when your father is dark?" Norman asked. Norman saw Alexis try to speak, but she was unable. "Oh, the gag," he said, and removed it.

"Have you seen my mother?" the girl asked hoarsely.

Norman slapped her. He hadn't intended to do so. He didn't want to harm her, but he wouldn't take insolence. "Don't answer a question with a question."

"She's light-skinned. I get my looks from my mother," Alexis said.

"What do you get from your father?" Norman asked.

Alexis said nothing and Norman moved his hand to slap her again. She was infuriating him with her pigheaded behavior. He had to show her who was boss.

"My strength," she blurted out before he struck.

Norman looked confused.

"My strength of *character*, fool," she said, as if reading his mind.

He smacked her, his anger mounting. "You're not being respectful. You remind me of your father even if you don't look like him," he said, then hit her once more because . . . because he could do anything he damn well pleased. Suddenly, a calm settled over him. For the first time in fifteen years, *he* was in control. *He* had the power. *He* could do as he wished. *Would* do as he wished. He hit her a third time. It felt good.

Chapter Sixteen

Confusion had engulfed Renee from the moment her abductor opened the trunk of his car after what seemed like an endless ride. She felt nauseous from the car fumes. Her back ached. Her head pounded. Her legs had cramped up several times. And now that they'd reached their destination, she knew things could get far worse. He had first blinded her with his flashlight, then put a bag over her head. A good sign, she thought. He didn't want to be recognized. Maybe he *didn't* plan to kill her. But she'd already seen his face at Briggs's house. It made no sense.

He'd dragged her into some sort of dwelling, marched her down a set of stairs, and shoved her into a corner, then trussed her up like cattle waiting to be branded. She was aware of his presence though he was no longer near her. He was tinkering with something. But what? When he'd told her to remove her jeans, she'd panicked. He meant to rape her. Not just once, but again and again, her mind screamed at her.

And then he'd removed the sack and she was staring at him. Any thought that he might let her live instantly vanished. She was in a wooden cabinet, she could now see. He tied her spread-eagled. Maybe that was why he had her remove her jeans. She wore form-fitting jeans. He couldn't tie her as he wished with her jeans on. She *hoped* that was the reason.

When he questioned her about her skin color, she

suddenly became alert. She knew the answers to his questions would determine if he doubted she was really Briggs's daughter. She had gambled that he had never seen Briggs's wife Vivian. She knew he hadn't seen a photo of Alexis. And when he asked what she got from her father, she paused. Her personality? No, the real Alexis wasn't a clone of her father. Alexis did have his strength of will, though. When her captor looked confused at her answer and looked at her arms, she knew what was going through his mind. *Physical strength.* She clarified her answer. She'd called him a fool without thinking. He *had* been a fool not to comprehend. And then she had the answer she had been seeking. *You remind me of your father,* he'd said. *Yes*, she'd have to act like Briggs. Be belligerent even if it meant getting hit. Not giving this man his due. Disrespecting him. *Yes*. By being Briggs, he would want to prolong her agony. He could take out whatever grievance he held against Briggs on her. He might feel he'd have to break her, just as he wished he could make Briggs crumble. It would buy her time. And with time, Shara would find her.

He was talking to her again. *Focus*, she thought. With one swipe of a knife, she saw he now held, he had cut off the buttons to her blouse. What now? she wondered, trying not to panic.

"You don't wear a bra. Why?" he asked.

Why did he care? she wondered. She looked at him a moment. He looked a bit older than Briggs. She noticed his clothes first. Though his pants were wet from the rain, she could see the crease in his slacks. His white dress shirt was spotless and his top button was fastened. He wasn't dressed like a kidnapper. *Forgetaboutit*, her mind scolded. Focus. Focus. *Focus!* She felt the sting of another slap and tasted blood.

"Answer when I speak to you. Why no bra?"

"It's no business of yours what I wear . . . or don't

wear," she said. Yes, that's how Briggs would react. Another smack. For this one she was prepared.

"*Why* no bra?"

She remained silent and was rewarded with another swipe of his hand. Then he shrugged and smiled. A sick smile that made Renee shudder. "You don't want me to hurt you . . . at least no more than I have to. I'm curious. Now, why—"

"I've got no tits to speak of," Renee said. "I'm sure you've already checked." She was going to add *you perv*, but thought better of it. Don't antagonize him too much. His slaps were getting harder. He could break her jaw or even her neck if he got too angry. "I have no need for a bra."

"Modesty," he said. "Briggs's daughter would wear a bra even if she didn't need one."

"I was raped and beaten," she spat back at him. "My father might *want* me to wear a bra, but he still feels guilty he couldn't protect me. Sure, he mentioned a bra. It wasn't easy for him. There are certain things fathers have trouble talking to their teenage daughters about. Like *sex*. A father never thinks of their daughter having sex, even when they're married. So, yes, he mentioned it *once*. I don't need a bra, so I ignored him. It's insignificant, so he . . . he indulges me."

The man smiled again, but this time it was genuine. "Just like your father. You manipulate him just like he tried to maneuver me. Do you do drugs?"

"No."

"Never experimented?" he asked.

"Never," Renee said.

"Drink?"

"No."

"Have you had sex other than when you were raped?"

"That wasn't sex," Renee said. "Rape isn't sex."

He smacked her. "Answer my question."

"No . . . I mean, I'm still a virgin," she elaborated when she saw he misinterpreted her first response.

"Would your father *indulge* you if you experimented with drugs, alcohol, or sex?" he asked her.

"You seem to know my father. What do you think?" Renee asked.

Yet another slap. And the hardest so far. She felt blood drip down her chin. She wanted to wipe it off, but tied as she was, she was helpless. The sight of blood seemed to make the man pause a moment. His eyes looked different. They didn't have a glazed look anymore. He took a clean handkerchief from his pocket and dabbed at the blood on her chin.

"Answer my question, please," he said more softly. "Would your father—"

"No, he wouldn't allow it," Renee said. "He lets the small stuff slide. It's like . . . how do you say it . . . picking your battles. He's adamant when it comes to drugs, alcohol, and sex."

"You idolize your father," the man said. "A great cop. Your hero."

Renee nodded.

"Yet he was arrested and kicked off the police force. Not so perfect, is he?"

"It wasn't his fault," Renee said. "It was mine."

"He was given a second chance," the man said, ignoring her. "I never got a second chance. Your father destroyed my life. Where is *my* second chance?"

He didn't wait for an answer. He gagged her with the towel from the car. He shut the wooden cabinet's door, and Renee was left in the dark . . . literally. She was suddenly angry at herself. Stupid. Stupid. *Stupid*, she said to herself. I'm supposed to find out what makes him tick. I've learned *nothing*.

She replayed the conversation. She *had* learned something. Briggs had done something to this man. He said Briggs manipulated him. Into a confession maybe? And he was pissed that Briggs got a second chance when he hadn't. Next time she would make him talk about himself, even if it took getting smacked in the face several times to convince him.

Renee felt the urge to pee. How long had it been since she had gone to the bathroom? Don't dwell on it. It will only make things worse, she told herself.

An hour later, she couldn't hold it in anymore. As urine dripped down her thigh, she sobbed. She felt totally helpless. Her bladder empty, Renee finally dozed.

Chapter Seventeen

Shara went to Briggs's bedroom at his insistence and was asleep no more than a few seconds after her head hit the pillow. She woke up coughing, her throat parched and her skin dry, forty-five minutes later.

A fever dream, she knew. More like a nightmare. Shara had experienced them before. Though never welcome, they were no longer unexpected. The dream was vivid as always. She lived what she called these fever dreams. They had started when she and Alexis had to encounter and defeat their demons in a mysterious forest in Cape May, at the South Jersey shore. Conquer their tormentors and Alexis would be cured. Shara had left the forest with an unwanted parting gift: the fever dreams.

In the past, she experienced the dreams in fragments through the body of someone else having the same dream. She had felt Alexis's terror when she dreamed of the youth's rape and beating. She felt the sexual desire of Denise DeShields, Deidre Caffrey's younger sister, as Denise made love to another woman . . . before killing her with an overdose of heroin. Like a movie where the reels had been placed improperly, the dream unfolded out of order in short snippets over a period of a week or more. Only after viewing the many fragments did the dream proceed from beginning to end. And no two fever dreams were the same. Alexis's dream had terrified Shara. Denise's had been incredibly erotic and stimulating.

The dream fragment she had just experienced was the worst by far. First there was the fragment itself. Shara inhabited a body looking at a manacled Renee. Renee was tied spread-eagled in a cabinet. Her jeans had been removed. Her blouse was unbuttoned. All of her other dreams had been like silent movies, and this was no exception. Renee was sobbing, but Shara heard nothing. The dream ended with Shara having difficulty breathing. Analyzing the dream, Shara knew the reason she felt so drained. With the other dreams she'd had, she had felt the emotions of the one whose body she inhabited. She'd felt Alexis's mounting terror. With Denise, there had been both the sensual pleasure of lovemaking and the profound sadness when Denise killed her lover. In this dream, she had felt *nothing*. The body she inhabited was merely a husk. No emotions. No memories. There was just an abysmal emptiness. It was as if Shara had experienced the dream through a living cadaver, and that made no sense at all.

Shara got out of bed and tried to stand. Her knees buckled. She felt lightheaded and nauseated. She knew this was only temporary. With each fever dream, there had been lingering physical effects, like an earthquake's aftershocks. She sat on the edge of the bed, and slowly her head cleared. She stumbled to the bathroom and gulped down a cup of water, then a second and a third. She removed her clothes and decided she needed a shower. She felt as dry as a withered leaf. She turned on the cold water and let it cascade over her. It might have been her imagination, but she thought she saw steam rise from her body as the water pelted her.

When Shara had a fever dream, she would discuss it with Renee. Once she understood how the fever dreams evolved, Renee never poked or prodded. She knew Shara was bewildered and anxious until she was provided enough fragments to start putting the puzzle together. Renee gave Shara space until she was ready to share. When Shara divulged the dream to Renee, the youth would pummel her with questions. Many—*most*—Shara couldn't answer right away, but Renee had a knack for getting to the heart of the matter. When Shara strayed afield, Renee's questions would guide her back to the path that ultimately led her to the meaning of the dream.

That Renee wasn't here now to help her untangle this most important of her fever dreams tore Shara apart. One fragment certainly wasn't enough to guide Shara. Yet Shara couldn't patiently wait for the dream to unfold as she had before. There simply wasn't enough time. "What are the important questions, Renee?" Shara said aloud, the water from the shower mixing with her tears.

When Shara came out of the bathroom naked, Alexis was sitting on her parents' bed. Shara wasn't self-conscious. Clothes were a necessity. But after a shower, Shara let the air dry her body. If Alexis felt uncomfortable, Shara would dress. Alexis, though, didn't seem at all concerned with Shara's appearance. She seemed oblivious to her surroundings, which worried Shara.

"I heard the shower and knew you were awake," Alexis said.

"You haven't slept yet, have you?" Shara asked.

Alexis shrugged.

"I have no psychic powers like you, but you're an open book. And you're acting like a child, which is no help to anyone," Shara said.

"What do you mean?"

"Blaming yourself," Shara said.

"It's that obvious?" Alexis asked. Before Shara could answer, she went on. "It should have been me," she said without emotion in her voice, but her eyes blazed with frustration.

"Bullshit," Shara said. "You both should have been safe in this house. Next you'll tell me you'd give anything to trade places with Renee. Don't go there, Alexis. This is as bad or worse as what the albino did to you." Shara sat down on the bed next to Alexis. "You went through hell. I don't know if you would have survived a second trauma."

"But Renee can?" Alexis asked.

"Renee *will*. She knows I'll find her," Shara said.

"A needle in a haystack," Alexis said. "In your world of adults, I'm just a piece of furniture. Detective LeBrea, even my father, they talk around me as if I'm not there. Somebody wants to hurt my father by hurting me. Only he thinks Renee is Briggs's daughter. He's going to make Renee suffer, and you have no clue how to find him. Tell me I'm wrong."

"You can give up if you want, Alexis," Shara said. "It's not part of your makeup, but if you want to wallow in self-pity, like your father was, I have no time to babysit you. I need someone's help, and without Renee, there's nobody but you. Much as you fear for Renee right now, it's all about *you,* and that's selfish." Shara wiped a tear from her eye.

"I've never seen you cry," Alexis said.

"I'm good at hiding my feelings, Alexis," Shara said. "What's ironic is that you can probe my mind. Hell, you *have*. But I wonder if you ever knew how I felt."

Alexis wiped a second tear from Shara's cheek. "Tell me. Make me understand," she said.

"Ever since I killed my half-brother, I've been in control. My life has been about controlling myself and others. But I'm not in command of events here, and it reminds me of when Bobby had me in a cage and made me do unspeakable things to myself while he took pictures. I put up a brave front, but I'm scared shitless for Renee. But I'm not giving up on her."

"What can't you tell the others?" Alexis asked, signing a smile. "You've made your point. If anything happens to Renee, and I could have helped but didn't—"

"I've had a fever dream," Shara interrupted. Alexis knew of her dreams. Shara's first had involved Alexis. "A tiny fragment, but I saw Renee."

"She's alive?" Alexis asked

"In the dream," Shara said. "But as with your dream, I can misinterpret." She told Alexis about the dream.

"You're seeing Renee through the eyes of someone else," Alexis said.

Shara nodded.

"Do you know where she is?" Alexis asked.

Shara shook her head.

"But you do," Alexis said, emphasizing the last word by signing it. "Not the exact location, but there are clues staring you in the face. Are you in the city? What do you smell?"

"It was damp and musty," Shara said, closing her eyes. "There's a window. It's covered with a sheet. The shapes behind it . . . trees, I think. There's a slight crack in the window. Yes, trees. Lots of trees. A cottage or cabin surrounded by woods," Shara said, her excitement building. "It was only a fragment. With more of the dream, maybe there's more I can learn about where he's keeping her," she finished.

"You said you weren't seeing Renee through the eyes of the kidnapper," Alexis said. "If not Renee and not the kidnapper, then who?"

Shara smiled at Alexis's question. It was a question Renee would have asked. Intuitively, Shara knew the answer was the key to finding Renee. Who the hell was it? Was *she*? "A woman," Shara said. "Don't ask me how I know. But there's something terribly wrong with her. It's like she's there but doesn't exist."

"You've lost me," Alexis said.

"Okay, when I dreamed of you, your emotions were crystal clear. They screamed at me. When I dreamed of

Denise, I experienced every sensation she did. But this woman . . . ." Shara paused, got up, and began pacing the room. "This woman I can only liken to a scarecrow. I'm seeing through her eyes, but there's nothing behind them. This woman has some significant connection to Renee. If I can figure out just what it is, I'll be that much closer to finding Renee."

There was a knock on the door. Shara ignored it.

"More fragments may provide the answer," Shara said.

Another knock on the door. "Shara, it's LeBrea. Can I come in?"

"Hold on a sec," Shara said. She slipped into a t-shirt and pullover sweater, then underwear and jeans, and then went to the door.

"Get any rest?" LeBrea asked when he saw Alexis there.

"I live on catnaps," Shara said. "*Seriously*," she said when she saw the look in the detective's eyes. "It's been that way most of my life."

LeBrea shrugged. "Brash is back outside. Time for our chat with him. Briggs is in his study. You'll be able to hear my conversation with him from there."

"Knock yourself out," Shara said as LeBrea led her downstairs.

Chapter Eighteen

Coming downstairs, Shara noticed Cleary wasn't in the living room. "Where's my pal?" she asked.

LeBrea smiled. "Waiting's not her game. She went to Center City to report to her superiors. She left Rappaport. Seems like a decent guy. I mentioned the C. C. Cleary nickname, and he laughed. Said he'd heard the scuttlebutt surrounding the name and it was all true."

Shara grabbed LeBrea's arm, stifling a yawn. She hadn't lied to LeBrea. She *did* exist on catnaps, but what with the fever dream, she didn't feel refreshed as she normally did after a short period of sleep. "Your men been canvassing?" she asked.

LeBrea nodded, then frowned. "No leads yet. Nobody saw anything last night. There hasn't been anyone asking about Briggs the past few weeks. Nobody noticed anything out of the ordinary." LeBrea headed toward the front door to confront Brash.

"Good luck," Shara said and went to Briggs's study.

Briggs was sitting at his desk, a computer screen in front of him and several piles of folders spread on the desk. He pointed to an intercom as Shara entered. "You get any sleep?" Briggs asked.

"You know me," Shara said. "I don't need much sleep. But yeah, I took a nap then showered. How's the search going?"

"Nina and Morales are going over my old cases," he

said. He showed Shara a notepad. "These are still in prison." He pointed to one list. "The ones crossed out are dead." On a second sheet of paper was a list that was only slightly shorter. "These served their time or were paroled."

"The asterisks?" Shara asked.

"Those who threatened me or seemed to harbor a grudge," he said, then shook his head. "It's only the tip of the iceberg." Then he brightened somewhat. "LeBrea's detectives are checking out those with the asterisks. You know, are they at work or at home? How they react when asked about their movements the past twenty-four hours." He gave Shara two folders. "We haven't been able to locate these two. LeBrea wants Rudy and Cheyenne to track them down."

Shara smiled. "It's what they do best."

All of a sudden, the intercom barked.

"Mind if I get in and we have a chat?" It was LeBrea, Shara could tell. Brash must have nodded. They heard a door open then shut. "May I ask why you're here?" Again, it was LeBrea.

"Same reason you are, Detective. Something's going down. Seems I'm the only one who knows," Brash said.

Shara had never met the man but she had seen his photo besides his column, "Brash Thoughts." The voice didn't mesh with the photo. The photo showed a handsome, confident, even cocky man. His voice was nasally and grating, with a trace of a lisp.

"And what do you think is going down?" LeBrea asked.

"I know, Detective. First you're dispatched here in the dead of night," Brash said. "Heard it on my scanner. You're in there all night. The home of a homicide detective. Curious, isn't it? Then the Feds show up. And your guys are canvassing the neighborhood with some bullshit story. Curiouser and curiouser."

"Bottom line, Brash, you got nothing," LeBrea said. "So why hang around?"

"I got my sources within the department, LeBrea. You know those anonymous twits who always get quoted. I do favors. I'm owed favors. Tough to keep a secret when so many people know, isn't it?"

"You're fishing, Brash—"

"A kidnapping's gone down. How's that for fishing? I'm just dotting the i's and crossing the t's before I file my exclusive. Care to comment . . . Detective?"

"Whose been kidnapped?" LeBrea asked. He still sounded noncommittal.

"My sources tell me it's Briggs's daughter. Care to confirm that for me?"

"You're going out on a limb on the basis of *one* source within the department. I don't believe you're that reckless," LeBrea said.

"Got confirmation from the Feds," Brash said. He sounded smug, as if he'd just been waiting for LeBrea's challenge. "You have no love lost for them or they for you. Makes it easy on a reporter. Still, something's bothering me," Brash said, then went silent.

"I'll bite. What?" LeBrea asked. Shara could hear tension in his voice for the first time.

"I took this photo this morning," Brash said. There was a moment of silence. Brash must be showing the photo to LeBrea, Shara thought. "It's Briggs's daughter opening the front door. Since I *know* someone's been kidnapped, I gotta ask myself who the hell was it and why even my sources are in the dark?"

"Let's continue this discussion inside, okay, Brash?" LeBrea asked.

"Anything you say, Detective. After all, I *do* want my story accurate."

"Fuck," Shara said as she heard the car door open. "He's not going to put Renee at risk," she said to Briggs.

"Calm down, Shara," Briggs said. "LeBrea's not going to let that happen. And your lawyer friend at the *News* can kill any story he writes. Right?"

Shara shrugged. This was getting out of hand. Could she count on Lynn Moody and Carter Hastings to do what was right? Again, the loss of control was tearing her up. "I still don't like it" was all she said.

LeBrea came into the study with Brash. It was the reporter who spoke first. "Detective Briggs," he said, extending his hand. Shara saw Briggs reluctantly shake hands with the reporter. "Congratulations on your reinstatement." Then he looked at Shara. "You've been the busy one," he said with a smile. "You're . . . ?" he asked.

"A friend of the family," Shara said.

"And secretive," Brash said. "Never you mind. If I want to, I'll learn who you are. Nice car," he added. "License plate and all," he said with a smile.

Shara resisted the urge she had to throttle the reporter or verbally put him in his place.

"Sit down," LeBrea said, finally exerting his authority.

On first glance, Shara thought Brash handsome; the rugged, handsome kind who appeared in commercials. He was tall, wiry, and wore a dress shirt one size too small to accentuate his muscular build. Overcompensation for his scratchy, high-pitched voice, Shara thought. Looking more closely, Shara wondered how much the wonders of science played in Brash's appearance. Did he wear a rug? His hair just didn't seem natural. He had a tan of one of those who frequented tanning salons that were in vogue. Shara wished she could see a photo of the reporter in his high school yearbook. She'd bet the house he'd had more than a little plastic surgery. Still, close your eyes and just listen to the voice and you'd cringe. It grated on her already strung-out nerves.

"This is off the record, Brash," LeBrea began.

Brash nodded.

"There *has* been a kidnapping. The abductor thinks he has Briggs's daughter. It's someone out to hurt Briggs. There's been no ransom demand."

"May I ask who was the young lady who *was* kidnapped?" Brash asked.

"You may not," LeBrea said. "I'm not playing games here, Brash."

"And I have a responsibility to tell the truth. Ferret it out anyway I can. It's the public's right to know."

"Even if it puts the victim in danger?" asked Briggs.

"I don't see how," Brash said. "Keeping me in the dark defeats your purpose."

"Once the kidnapper learns he doesn't have my daughter, he can't torment me," Briggs said, leaning forward, his face just inches from the reporter's. "The victim becomes a liability. She dies and he fades back into the woodwork. Spare me the platitudes about the public's right to know. We're talking about a young woman's life here."

"So you want me to sit on the story," Brash said. "What do I get in return?"

"An exclusive," LeBrea said. "When we catch the perp, we tell you first. Before we make his identity public, you'll have at least three hours to dig up all you can on the sucker."

"What about the victim? Assuming she's unharmed. An interview with her would seal the deal," Brash said.

Briggs reached for Shara's arm and gripped it tightly. Shara understood. *Remain silent*, he was telling her. "Out of the question," Briggs said. "You're no fool, Brash. You know what my daughter went through. Who knows the trauma inflicted on this young woman by this sick bastard who has her. The last thing she needs is being in the public glare."

Shara saw Briggs and Brash lock eyes. Brash was the first to break contact. "How about a compromise. I get to talk with your daughter . . . Alexis, after the kidnapper is apprehended. I'm not insensitive," he went on quickly. "Your daughter's perspective is unique. A victim herself, her friend snatched from under your roof. You can be present. And consider this: She speaks to me, and you can deny access to my colleagues."

Briggs gripped Shara's arm tighter. "Deal," he said. "No more digging and no staking us out from across the street. Detective LeBrea will keep you informed without compromising the search. We catch the perp, you get your exclusive. And an interview with Alexis."

"I can live with that," Brash said. His eyes wandered to Shara for a moment then went back to Briggs. "Just don't jerk my chain. You go back on your word, and I dig into the story with a vengeance." He stood. "I'll see myself out," he said and left.

"Do you believe him?" Shara asked. "Or is he playing us?"

"He doesn't know you've got a source at the paper. Two can play his game of anonymous informants," Briggs said. "He goes behind our back, we'll know."

"You were wrong to give him access to Alexis," Shara said. "Her rape and beating will be replayed by the media. She shouldn't have to endure that again."

"She's strong, Shara," Briggs said, shaking his head. "And you know she'd be the first to insist on the interview if it protects Renee. We both know she feels guilty. For no good reason, I know," he said when Shara was about to speak. "It might do her good. And I'll be present. If the questions get out of line, I'll end it." Briggs handed Shara the two folders she had put down on his desk. "Let's stay focused. I have more files to pore over. We've got to locate these two," he said, tapping the folders in Shara's hand.

Shara looked at her arm and saw red welts from Briggs's grasp. She held up her arm for him to see. "Thanks," she said. "My mind said 'Shut the hell up,' but what he was asking . . . ."

"I've hung with you long enough to gauge your . . .

temper threshold," Briggs said with a smile. "Civil with Cleary and silent with Brash. I'd hate to be the person you take your frustrations out on."

Shara scrunched up her nose. "Let me get to work or I'll take it out on you." She looked at LeBrea, who must have felt like an interloper. "Look Paul, I want you to know I appreciate everything you're doing," she told him. "I tell it like I see it. Briggs will tell you when I leave. I'm not one for platitudes, and I don't idly toss out compliments. You're good. I'm glad Briggs brought you in." Feeling slightly foolish for gushing such praise on the detective, Shara hurried out before he could respond.

Chapter Nineteen

Norman set his alarm for 6 a.m. Three hours of sleep would recharge his batteries. Alexis wasn't quite what he had expected, he thought, when he awoke and went about his morning ritual. He showered, shaved, brushed his teeth, flossed, gargled with mouthwash, then put on a fresh pair of slacks and a white dress shirt. No, Alexis had most definitely startled him. She looked chaste and pure, unlike his own daughter. It shouldn't have come as a surprise. Briggs wasn't the type to allow a slut in his home. It pleased him that, other than earrings, she had no other piercings. No tattoos. No burns . . . *brandings,* Rose had called them. All were both signs of rebellion and cries for attention, Norman knew. Fashion statement my ass, he thought as he remembered Rose's words. Alexis was certainly no rebel, not with Briggs around to patrol after her. And her hero worship for her father seemed to indicate her father didn't ignore her. It saddened him all the more when he contrasted Alexis to his Rose.

Norman went into the kitchen and made a peanut butter and jelly sandwich for himself and one for Alexis, making sure to cut off the crust. He had taken out a can of concentrated orange juice before he'd napped and after adding water poured a glass for himself and one for his guest.

Norman was more than a little intrigued by his captive. He thought of nothing else. Not what he would do after he killed her. Not how he'd dispose of her body. Not whether he would simply go home when the deed was done, as if nothing had occurred, or whether he would flee. His mind was fixated on Alexis and only Alexis in the here and now. There was a toughness about her he hadn't anticipated. It made him wonder just how much influence her mother exerted on the girl. Yes, she was very much her father's child. And the mouth on her, he recalled, and laughed aloud. He knew she must be both terrified and humiliated, yet she had hid it well. She hadn't cried when he'd cut off the buttons of her blouse to expose small but firm breasts. She hadn't yet begged or pleaded. She was feisty, he had to grudgingly admit. *Yes*, like the father he detested.

He had planned to put Alexis out of her misery that morning. Quickly. Humanely. But now he decided he couldn't kill her until she gave into despair. He had to break her. Only when she caved would Norman know Briggs's spirit could be likewise crushed. He so wanted Briggs to feel the despondency he had felt when he lost his family.

Norman went downstairs. Walking toward the cabinet, he smelled something he couldn't immediately identify. Norman had a keen sense of smell. He couldn't abide anything foul or rotten. He smelled chicken and hamburger before he cooked it. Stores *said* their poultry and beef were fresh, but for them, the bottom line was the only line. Day-old chicken or meat passed off as fresh-cut was the norm. Who would be the wiser? Norman *was*. Out it went into the trash.

Norman opened the closet, and the smell assaulted him. *Urine*. Alexis had urinated on herself. Norman thought it crass how so many referred to urine as *pee* or *piss*. Those who had to *tinkle* were just as absurd, if less boorish. And what kind of upbringing did one have to call a bowel movement a *crap* or a *shit*.

Norman was furious with Alexis. *Urinating* on herself. *Fouling* herself. A complete lack of discipline. He put the plate with the sandwich and glass of juice on the table and locked eyes with Alexis.

"Don't you have any self-control?" he yelled at her. "You sicken me. What's wrong with you?" he asked.

Alexis mumbled and Norman closed his eyes for a second. He hadn't removed her gag. He did so now. "Where is your willpower?" he asked anew.

"I hadn't gone to the bathroom since before you snatched me," she said, not sounding the least bit apologetic. "What was I supposed to do?" She paused a moment. "Can I at least bathe? Shower?" Another pause when Norman remained silent. "Wash myself off with a cloth?"

Norman replaced the gag and left. He couldn't release her from her bounds, he knew. She had probably urinated on herself intentionally. He'd let her shower, she assumed, and she'd concocted a scheme to escape once she was untied. How she underestimated him. Yet he couldn't abide the stench. She had to learn it would do her no good to soil herself. He filled a basin with water and Ivory soap. Cold water. *Ice cold water*. She wanted to play games. She had a lesson to learn. He came downstairs with the basin, a washcloth, and some paper towels.

First he cleaned the floor of the cabinet with paper towels and a bottle of Mr. Clean he kept in the cellar, where Alexis's urine had dried and left a stain.

Now it was time for Alexis's lesson. Norman ripped off her panties and smiled inwardly as he saw her startled expression. He put his hands into the icy cold water and lathered up. With the washcloth in one hand, he lathered Alexis's thigh with the other. She began to struggle, then shiver. He looked up at her and smiled. He wiped her with the washcloth. He slowly moved his hand up, lathering, then rinsing, then wiping, lathering, then rinsing, then wiping.

Her privates were surrounded by a bush of black down. It was gentle, not coarse like Jan's. His ex-wife had liked to talk dirty when they made love. She referred to her privates as her *pussy* or *twat*. Norman couldn't tolerate such crude language. More than once he'd lost his erection because of Jan's vulgarity. Privates or genitals were appropriate. *Never pussy*. He lathered Alexis's privates as she continued to struggle. He noticed he was breathing heavily, but he was too occupied to care. She was a pretty young thing, he had to admit.

With all the urine washed off, he considered stopping, then decided to give her a complete body wash. She had been in the foul-smelling trunk of his car. Who knows when she had last bathed. He pulled her blouse open and began lathering Alexis's breasts. Her nipples became engorged, and Norman was suddenly aware he had an erection. Disgusted with himself, he abruptly stopped. He tossed the water from the basin onto Alexis's torso to remove the soap. He went to the sink at the other end of the basement and came back with a plastic bucket. He saw the girl shivering.

"You feel the need to urinate or defecate, use this. No more soiling the cabinet." Without another word, he left.

Upstairs, Norman paced back and forth, his anger at himself building. She *had* concocted a scheme all right, but it wasn't to escape. It was to humiliate him. He had been aroused. He was disgusted. Not at himself but at Alexis for manipulating him. Sixteen years old and already a tease. Hadn't her father taught her better? One doesn't use sex to get what you desire. It's vulgar. Profane. *Intolerable*.

Alexis had wanted a bath or shower. She wanted privacy when she washed. It had been denied to her, so she'd used her sex as a weapon. She thought his embarrassment at being aroused would force him to relent. "Silly bitch," he said aloud. She was sorely mistaken. Every time she fouled herself, he'd bathe her. But he wouldn't again be lulled by her sexual wiles. She would never arouse him again. What a fool she was to think he'd be taken in.

She *was* just like her father. She would degrade herself to get what she wanted. Fifteen years earlier, Briggs had likewise bent the rules in an attempt to get Norman to confess to a crime he didn't commit. Briggs had hit Norman in the stomach repeatedly without leaving any telltale bruises. Norman hadn't broken then. He wouldn't allow Briggs's daughter to manipulate him now.

Norman forced himself to go back downstairs. He would feed Alexis, possibly chat with her. He would educate her to act like a lady, not a whore. He would show her that debasing herself had been for naught.

Chapter Twenty

When Shara arrived at Cheyenne's home, Cheyenne was outside pruning a tree Shara vaguely recalled from her last visit. It seemed taller. Also fuller, even though it was December. Then again, she'd seen it in the evening the last time. *Focus*, she scolded herself. Your mind is wandering again.

When Shara had left Briggs, she'd first gone to Rudy's. Driving, she grabbed the steering wheel so tight her fingers began to cramp. Rage and frustration filled her. Rage at Brash. Fury at the kidnapper. Frustration with the slow pace of the investigation as well as having to passively react rather than take the offensive.

Rudy had comforted her and promised speedy results. Now she had to rely on Cheyenne's professionalism to quickly determine whether they had a solid lead or another dead end.

For December it was warm. Not quite Indian Summer-warm, but a beautiful day to nevertheless.

"So this is how you get your tan," Shara said to Cheyenne. "You're into gardening."

"Into *nature*," Cheyenne countered. "I don't grow flowers to clip them, stick them in a vase, and watch them wither and die. I don't grow vegetables to consume. Trees, bushes, even the grass intrigues me. You prune a tree to improve its health," Cheyenne said, demonstrating. "You remove the small, weak shoots that steal nutrients from the more vibrant." She bent down and turned over a stone. Ants scurried about. "Nature living in harmony," she said with a smile.

Shara pulled a small branch that had fallen into Cheyenne's brown hair. The sun made her hair appear slightly red. Showing the branch to Cheyenne, Shara had brushed against Cheyenne's face. It was drier than it looked. "Aren't there . . . fungi and insects that kill trees? You know, disrupt the harmony you speak about?" Shara asked, curious despite her need for haste.

Cheyenne took the branch and rose to her feet. "No different than the humans who kidnap young women." Cheyenne scowled in thought for a moment. "I take that back. There is destruction in nature, but it's seldom permanent. Lightning starts a forest fire. A forest is leveled, but not destroyed. It grows back eventually. Not so with man. A child shot in a drive-by is gone forever."

"I can't argue with you," Shara said, thinking what would be forever lost if Renee wasn't found safe.

"You've got someone for me to find?" Cheyenne asked.

"My mind's scattered," Shara said.

"You need some sleep," Cheyenne said.

"I took a nap. *Really*," she said when Cheyenne gave her a look of disbelief. "Okay, forty-five minutes, but I don't need a lot of sleep."

"With the stress you're under, forty-five minutes isn't nearly enough," Cheyenne said. "Forget it," she said with a laugh. "It's not my place to give advice. You know your body. So what do you have for me?"

Shara handed Cheyenne a photo along with a printout Briggs had provided. "He's one we can't locate. See what you can find out about him. Does he still harbor a grudge against Briggs? Where he might be? Track him down if you can. He either becomes one of our primary suspects or you eliminate him."

"Done," Cheyenne said. "I'll get right on it."

Shara decided to stop at her home before going back to Briggs's house. She needed a change of clothes. Several actually. Despite a refreshing breeze, she felt clammy. Soon she'd smell rank.

Once home, Shara packed a bag with several changes of clothes and other necessities. She recalled what Cheyenne had told her. She *had* been under stress. Her earlier nap had hardly been invigorating, what with her fever dream. Maybe an hour. What could she do at Briggs's home other than be in the way? She set her alarm and lay down.

Shara awoke as she had earlier, coughing as if she had a bird's next lodged in her throat. Her skin was dry just as it had been after her first nap. Brittle, she thought. If she touched it, she feared her skin might crumble. Nonsense, she thought as she fully awakened. It was the product of her second fever dream. She sat on the edge of the bed gathering her strength. Her cough remained persistent. She walked to the bathroom and drank four glasses of water before her throat cleared. She took a twenty-minute shower, feeling like a tree soaking in water during a storm.

Her wits finally about her, Shara analyzed the dream. She was in the same cellar or basement as before. The body she inhabited was identical. Not a clue as to who it was. But through her eyes, she saw Renee. A bucket was between her legs and her panties were gone. Shara grimaced. *What the hell had he done to her?* Would *that* fragment appear in a future dream? Renee still had her blouse on, though it remained unbuttoned. Renee looked haggard, but her eyes still showed defiance.

Then Shara's eyes surveyed the room. What was she looking for? She had no idea. But Shara took notice of the room's layout. If—no, *when*—she found this cabin or cottage, Renee's abductor might be with her. If Shara charged in blindly, she might only imperil Renee. So Shara noted where the stairs were, how many there were in case it was dark, and where the single light bulb was that only slightly illuminated the darkened room. And that was it. The fragment hadn't produced a hell of a lot, but still it was another piece of the puzzle. Shara vowed to take another nap that afternoon. This time the fever dream was unfolding far more rapidly than usual. It was as if the dream itself was aware time was short. Speaking of time, she had best get back to Briggs's house to see if there were any new developments.

Chapter Twenty-One

Renee had refused to let herself cry until her captor left. She had almost vomited in disgust when he had gone upstairs. She swallowed it down. Gagged, if she threw up, she'd drown in her own puke.

Renee wondered how much more she could take. She could handle physical punishment. The man's slaps stung but left no permanent damage. She could accept verbal abuse. But his hands on her body . . . it was asking too much of her. He'd lingered on her genitals far longer than was necessary. His fondling her breasts when he washed them paled in comparison. And then he had stopped abruptly and tossed the freezing basin of water on her and left. Why, dammit, why? It was important, she knew. She closed her eyes and, still shivering from the cold water, replayed the entire scene over again. No, she thought, she *relived* it a second time, which made her shiver all the more.

What had she missed? He'd touched her breasts, and the frigid water had engorged her nipples. He'd looked down then. To avoid seeing her tits? No, that made no sense. He'd . . . he'd looked down at himself. He'd had an erection. *The fucker had had a hard on.* Renee almost laughed despite her discomfort. That was what had infuriated him. He'd been aroused and was embarrassed. She could use that against him.

She heard him coming down the stairs. She wondered what new horrors awaited. Make him angry, she thought. Don't let him see your fear.

Renee saw him approach almost cautiously. He took off the gag.

"I can't breathe with that on," Renee said.

"Not my problem," he answered without emotion.

"The cold water made me feel queasy. I almost vomited. Keep the gag on and you'll come down and find me dead. Is that what you want?"

"Without the gag, you'll yell, not that it will do any good," he said.

"So why the gag, asshole?" she asked.

He smacked her. Harder than was necessary. Yes, she thought, he was still upset with himself, and possibly her, for becoming aroused. She was bleeding again. He took out his handkerchief—a new, clean one, she saw—sighed, and wiped the blood from her chin. "Why do you make me hit you?" he asked in a far softer tone than he had used just a moment before.

Renee said nothing. She expected another whack in the face but none came. "What is your name, asshole?" she asked, knowing she was goading him to strike her again.

"None of your concern," he said, his voice calm.

"I'll call you Asshole, then," Renee said.

He shrugged. "Does your father allow you to use profanity in his house?" he asked, his voice getting more animated.

"My father doesn't keep me tied up. He doesn't play with my privates. He doesn't fondle my breasts," Renee said.

"I was washing you," he said.

There wasn't much conviction in his voice, Renee thought. She'd touched on a raw nerve. She *had* aroused him. He was having trouble dealing with it. Exploit it. Rub that nerve raw. Accept the physical abuse. It was far better than additional sexual torture.

"You got off on it," Renee said. "Admit it. My father

may have done you wrong, but he doesn't play with the pussies of teenagers."

"You know *nothing* about how your father ruined my life," he said.

"Then tell me, Asshole. It's not like I've got someplace to go," Renee said.

"You want to know? You *really* want to know?"

"Tell me or not. Makes no never mind to me," Renee said. "He probably arrested you for molesting a young girl. Or was it a boy you fondled?"

"*Nothing of the sort*!" the man shouted. "How dare you accuse me of exploiting children. I should beat you for your insolence," he said, touching his belt. "That's what you deserve."

"Better than your fingers—"

"Your father thought he had all he needed to put me in jail for life," the man cut her off. "I was convenient for him. He never looked at any other suspects. And he was wrong. *Proven* wrong. I rotted in jail for three months awaiting trial for a crime I didn't commit. The scum who killed the girl, he . . . he bragged to his new girlfriend. She went to the police, fearful for her own safety. *He confessed to your father*. And fine man that your father was, he never apologized to me for doing me wrong. Lamar Briggs couldn't look me in the face and admit he'd made a mistake. I was forgotten the moment he had the real killer. He didn't give a damn what shambles he'd made of my life."

"So you're mad at him because he didn't say he was sorry?" Renee asked. "You really are an asshole." She saw him start to swing at her, then stop.

"You want me to hit you, don't you?" he asked. "That's why you're so crude. I won't hit you . . . now. Maybe later. With my belt. That will wipe that smug look off your face." He paused. "Your father *should* have been man enough to have apologized to me, but that's insignificant. I was a publicist, and nobody wanted to be represented by an alleged murderer."

"But you were cleared," Renee said, genuinely interested.

"Tell that to the firms that refused to hire me. Know what I do now?" he asked, then went on before Renee could answer. "I'm a sales associate at a Barnes & Noble bookstore. A cashier with a fancy title. I lost my house, two, three times the size of your puny home. I lost my family."

"All because of my father," Renee said sarcastically. "That's bullshit." She saw him look at her with loathing. "Look, I believe you. My dad arrested you for a crime you didn't commit. You lost your job. But he's not to blame for every bad thing that's happened to you since. If your wife left you because you weren't bringing home big money, it doesn't seem to me you lost much at all—"

"That's not why she left," he said. "I started drinking. I became verbally abusive. It was the liquor."

"So first you blame my dad and now you blame alcohol for your problems. My father didn't force that alcohol down your throat. You take no responsibility for what your life became. That's a cop-out," Renee said.

"Your damn father was given a second chance. He screwed up big time, when I had done *nothing* wrong. Why should he get a second chance when I was denied one?"

"I guess life ain't fair, Asshole," Renee said.

"Ain't that the truth," he said. "I guess you're being here proves that. You've done nothing wrong, yet you're suffering because of your father. Life ain't fair, Alexis. A sad epitaph for both of us."

He took out his knife and rested the blade against Renee's face. "I could cut you, Alexis. Would that be fair? I could make you look so ugly people would avert their eyes. Is that fair? I may. See, I get these urges. You're beautiful and you know it. Boys like to look at you. You get asked out on dates. You get to pick and choose because you're one of the pretty ones. But a slice here," he said and rolled the flat edge of the knife down Renee's cheek. "And one there," he said, demonstrating on the other cheek. "Then you're not so pretty. Boys no longer want you. Oh, some desperate boy will use you for your body. Pity sex. Is that fair? You'd have to put out or be desperately alone. You act so tough, like your father. Tell me to cut you, Alexis. You know I will. What? Silence." He paused, put the knife down, then quickly raised it again. "Or maybe I cut out your eyes," he said, the knife point an inch from Renee's eye. How would you like spending the rest of your life in the dark?" he asked. "I'm god down here. Just remember that."

"Is god going to feed me or do I starve to death?" Renee asked. She tried to put as much conviction into her voice as possible. He was scaring her, and she couldn't allow him to see her fear. She didn't like the look in his eyes at all. They were glazed over again, as if he were in a trance. Her question seemed to bring him back to reality.

"One tough cookie, aren't you, Miss Alexis Briggs," he said, shaking his head and putting his knife away. "Are you going to say please?"

Alexis remained silent.

"Suit yourself," he said. He picked up the sandwich and took a bite.

"Please, Asshole," she said, the first word in a whisper.

He held the sandwich to her mouth, then pulled it back when she tried to take a bite.

"Beg," he said.

"I said please. I won't beg. Do what you want with me. I'll never beg."

He shrugged and held the sandwich to her again. This time he didn't pull back when she took a bite. He fed her the sandwich, then the glass of juice. "Now what do you say?" he asked when she had finished.

"Thank you," Renee said.

"That wasn't so hard," he said. With his handkerchief, he wiped crumbs from her mouth. "Do as you're told and you won't bring out the beast in me. I don't want to cut you, but he does. Get him riled and there's no telling what he'll do." He picked up the towel he used for a gag.

"I'm not going to yell," Renee said quickly.

He looked at her, then the towel. "You don't get a second warning. Understand?"

Renee nodded.

He put the towel on the table and left. He hadn't closed the doors of the cabinet this time. Had he forgotten? She was exhausted. She had to measure every word she uttered. She could go just so far with this crazed lunatic. She truly believed he had a split personality. Part of him feared what that beast within him might do. And she had to digest every single word he voiced. A sentence, a single word, could mean the difference between life and death. But it was physically draining. She wanted—*needed*—sleep. Before she closed her eyes, a thought struck her. He had threatened to cut her face, to gouge out her eyes. He was truly terrifying. But . . . he was still embarrassed that her naked body had sexually aroused him. He wouldn't rape her, she now knew. Little comfort, since she knew he planned to kill her. She'd take every morsel of hope she could. She was too exhausted to analyze him anymore. She closed her eyes and was soon asleep.

Chapter Twenty-Two

Renee opened her eyes and there was a woman sitting outside the cabinet staring at her. Renee had no idea how long she'd slept. Morning, afternoon, evening? She had no clue. It was terribly disorienting and added to her feeling of powerlessness.

The woman was staring at her as if she had been scrutinizing Renee in her sleep. The woman was naked, which made no sense at all to Renee. Her knees were drawn up to cover her breasts. She was tawny, far darker than Renee, but her features were Caucasian. She had thick, brown curly hair which made its way past her shoulders.

"Who are you?" Renee asked.

"I'm here to help you," the woman said, ignoring Renee's question. She shifted position and now sat cross-legged, totally comfortable with her body exposed. Renee now saw her breasts were full, firm, and rode high on her chest. She had a thick mound of brown pubic hair, which covered her genitals, as her captor had referred to them.

"Do you live here? I mean around here?" Renee clarified. If this beautiful woman was her captor's girlfriend, his anger at Briggs wasn't enough to jeopardize such a relationship. Old . . . well, *older* men like her kidnapper didn't often get the pick of the litter. Here was a stunning woman half his age. Renee knew intuitively she had no relationship with her tormentor. "How did you get in?" she asked when her companion remained silent.

"Is that really what you want to talk about? It's not like I can spend the entire afternoon with you," she said.

"Is it afternoon?" Renee asked. "I have no sense of time."

"I'm here to be your clock?" the woman asked. "What a waste of time," and she laughed at the clever play on words.

"Set me free. You can do that, can't you?" Renee asked.

"Afraid not. I'm here to help you, but there's a limit to what I'll do."

"You're *me*," Renee said, the truth finally dawning on her. "A part of me. I've conjured you up so I won't go mad. That's why you can't free me."

"If you say so."

Renee laughed. "I must already be insane having created you, naked and all."

"Maybe that's how you feel. You know . . . *exposed*," the woman said.

"Which is why you're naked," Renee said, nodding. "I feel vulnerable. That . . . beast can do whatever he wants with me. And he's so unpredictable. One moment gentle, as if he regrets snatching me. Another part of him seems to get off on being cruel, showing me how impotent I am. The two vie for control. His darker half seems to be getting the upper hand."

"I won't let him kill you," the woman said.

"How can you stop him?" Renee asked.

"Fight him as you have been doing," the woman said, not answering Renee's question. "Shara will be here for you, but you must give her the time she needs. You've only slept a short time. You must conserve your strength. Sleep. You'll need your wits about you to keep him off balance."

Renee wanted to talk to this figment of her imagination

longer, but just the thought made her admit to herself that this ordeal was taking a horrible toll on her. She shut her eyes. She remembered when she was a child telling her father she was just resting her eyes when she was about to fall asleep in the car after a long drive. Later he'd tease her about it. "You took a nap," he'd tell her. "No, I was just resting my eyes." She did so now and slept.

Chapter Twenty-Three

Entering Briggs's house, Shara frowned at the sight of Claire Cleary. Sitting in a chair smoking a cigarillo, the agent had a smirk on her face.

"Sam Brash is dead. *Murdered*," Cleary said just as Briggs and LeBrea entered the room.

"We just spoke with him—" Shara started, stunned by the revelation.

"Two hours ago," Cleary cut in. "Detectives Briggs and LeBrea told me of the meeting. A heated discussion was how they referred to it."

Shara looked at Briggs and LeBrea, who both seemed solemn. "Are you accusing me?" Shara asked. "Where was he killed? How was he killed?"

"Let's talk in Detective Briggs's study," Cleary said.

Shara saw Briggs carried a number of file folders. "Can you work while we talk?" Shara asked.

Briggs nodded.

Shara walked into Briggs's study. She was too wired to sit. She paced. Brash dead. *Murdered.* And Cleary believed she had killed him. It dawned on her that both Briggs and LeBrea thought she might be culpable. Most definitely capable in her current state.

Cleary entered and sat at Briggs's desk as if it were hers. "How did you get jurisdiction of this case?" Shara asked.

"I'll ask the questions, if you don't mind," Cleary said, taking out a tape recorder and turning it on.

"I do mind," Shara said. "Answer my question or I walk."

"Fine," Cleary sighed. "Sergeant McGowan caught the case and assigned it to homicide detective Chompsky. I believe you've met him."

Shara said nothing. Chompsky had looked into Deidre's murder. Shara had spoken to him once.

"After Sergeant McGowan was told there may have been a connection between the Brash murder and a case we were involved with, they deferred to us. They are far more cooperative than your Detective LeBrea. Now I have some questions I'd like you to answer. Please sit."

Shara ignored Cleary and continued to pace. "I'd like my attorney present," Shara said.

"You're not under arrest, Shara," Cleary said, her tone softening. "Look, tell me what happened now while I can still help you. We have evidence you were at the Brash apartment. You went over to have a chat after this morning's discussion. You were worried. With reason, I grant you. You quarreled. Things got out of hand. I know how much pressure you're under. It wasn't premeditated, but you killed him in the heat of passion. I take that to the District Attorney and you're a sympathetic figure. No one would blame you. But . . . once we get attorneys involved, well, my hands are tied."

Shara laughed. "Jeez, Claire, right out of *Law and Order*," she said referring to a television police procedural where the police tried to persuade the perp that it was in his best interest to cooperate and spill his guts without an attorney present. "You really need to get out more. Using television as a training tool doesn't work for you." Shara stopped pacing. She came up to the desk and looked down at Cleary. Shara was seething. "I work the system, Lady. Your line . . . it's a crock of shit. You *do* want to help me, Claire. Right into a prison cell for a hell of a long time.

I've already said I want my attorney present when I give a statement, so don't ignore my request like they do on TV. I'm outta here unless you want to arrest me. I *do* know my rights, and I choose to exercise them."

Cleary said nothing.

Shara walked to the door.

"Be at my office in Center City at three today . . . with your attorney, if you so desire. Be there or I *will* issue a warrant for your arrest."

Shara walked out without saying a word. A moment later, Cleary exited. Cleary said her goodbyes to Briggs and LeBrea. She noted Cleary was particularly cordial to them.

When Cleary was gone, Shara looked at the two detectives. "You think I killed Brash," Shara said, shaking her head. "What the fuck is wrong with you?"

"You were upset with Brash," LeBrea said. "He could have put Renee in immediate jeopardy."

"I understand your concern, Paul. You don't know me." She turned to Briggs. "You, Briggs, know me all too well. Tell me you think I'd pull a stunt like that. Tell me that even if I went over to talk with Brash, which I didn't, I don't have the self-control not to off the fucker."

"I want to believe you, Shara. You were gone for two hours . . . " he said and trailed off.

"Fine. You want proof. You'll have your proof, but nothing Cleary or even LeBrea will believe. Where's Alexis?"

"In her room," Briggs said.

"Get her," Shara said. "I'd go up, but you'd think we were conspiring behind your back."

Briggs sighed and went upstairs. Shara paced. Briggs came down moments later with Alexis.

"Your father thinks I killed that reporter who threatened to go public. Read my mind. Tell them," Shara said.

"Shara, Alexis is no longer psychic," Briggs said. "You know that." Shara could hear real concern in Briggs's voice. He thought she was losing it. *No, had lost it.*

"No, Briggs, she still is psychic," Shara shot back. "She has an . . . an on/off switch. She can read minds when she chooses. She lied to you because her psychic abilities made your wife so uncomfortable."

"Is that true, Baby?" Briggs asked Alexis.

Alexis nodded. "I'm sorry," she said. "Mom was so freaked out . . . I thought it best to keep my powers secret from her. I can control it now, like Shara says. I haven't pried into your thoughts or mom's since."

"You can tell if Shara killed that reporter?" Briggs asked.

Alexis nodded.

"Did she?" Briggs asked.

Alexis walked over to Shara and touched her hand. She looked at Shara sternly before answering. "The thought crossed her mind but only if Brash wrote a story a released a photo that put Renee in danger," she said, looking at her father, then at LeBrea. "But she didn't. She didn't see him after she left here. She met with Rudy, then Cheyenne. She went home and slept for an hour. She has a bag with a change of clothes in her car."

LeBrea looked at Briggs. "This isn't some stunt, is it Lamar?" he asked.

"Give Paul your car keys, Shara," Briggs said. Shara flipped her keys to LeBrea. "Go see for yourself," Briggs said.

"Do you believe me now?" Shara asked Briggs when LeBrea left.

Briggs nodded. "I apologize. I'm frustrated. I'm exhausted. I'm worried for Renee. I wasn't—"

"Apology accepted," Shara said. "Now before LeBrea gets back, I need a favor. Cleary wants to hang me out to dry. At best she'll tie me up so I won't be of any help. At worst she'll arrest me even if she has no case. Just for spite. We both know her. I need to know what happened to Brash. Can you ask Rios to poke around?"

Briggs shook his head. "I won't put her in that position, Shara," he said. "She'll do it out of loyalty to me, but if caught, it'll cost her her job."

Shara closed her eyes.

"I will call Morales," Briggs said. "If he agrees, it won't be out of blind loyalty. When LeBrea comes back, tell him I'm in the study working on the files." He looked at his daughter. "I understand what you did," he said with a smile. "I won't tell your mother. No more secrets, though, between us. Okay?"

Alexis nodded.

"When LeBrea returns, impress him," Briggs said to Alexis. "Make him a believer. I need time to convince Morales to get what Shara needs."

LeBrea returned with Shara's bag and a perplexed look on his face.

"Sit down, Detective," Alexis said. "Let me tell you about yourself." She signed a smile to Shara.

Shara went outside and sat on a chair on the front porch. She hadn't killed Brash. The thought hadn't crossed her mind. But . . . she knew there lurked a darkness within her which would have surfaced if Brash had become a threat to Renee. She would have killed him without an ounce of remorse. She wondered if she could control that part of her that had killed before when she came face to face with Renee's abductor. Briggs was unaware of her dark side, which was why Shara had been shaken that he could even suspect Shara of cold-blooded murder. She recalled the look Alexis had given her before telling the others Shara hadn't killed Brash. Yes, Shara thought, Alexis was aware of what lurked within her. She knew

Shara was innocent, but also knew Shara capable of murder to protect Renee.

Shara shook her head. *Don't dwell on it. Focus.* Who the hell would murder Brash? She hadn't a clue.

Chapter Twenty-Four

At three-twenty, Shara was ushered into the office of Claire Cleary with her attorney Arnie Winkler. They had arrived at 3 p.m. Showing who was boss, Cleary kept them waiting for twenty minutes.

Shara had two lawyers she used when necessary. They were polar opposites. Douglas Frazier, who had helped Shara with J'aime's problem, would be her choice if she ever went to trial. His expertise was not needed now. A confrontation with a vengeful Claire Cleary clearly called for the pit-bull mentality of Arnie Winkler. He wasn't a trial lawyer and seldom appeared in court, yet opposing attorneys were loathe to go up against him. Winkler had no scruples if he believed in his client's innocence. He used the media, skirted around gag orders, threatened, cajoled, and was as bombastic as they come. Simply put, he was cunning, conniving, and calculating. He could plea bargain a murder down to a traffic violation. At least that was his reputation and it served him well.

He operated below Claire Cleary's radar. And Cleary didn't have the intelligence to leave the room for a few minutes to find out just who Arnie Winkler was. It was what Shara had counted on. To Cleary, he was an attorney, plain and simple. A necessary evil provided to alleged felons like Shara. As a matter of fact, Shara saw a smirk on Cleary's face as she gave Winkler a quick once-over, then dismissed him and focused on Shara. Arnie Winkler didn't look to be in Cleary's class.

The impression he gave was intentional. He certainly didn't look intimidating. He was grossly overweight and his suits appeared purchased off the rack. His tie was stained with custard from a donut he had eaten earlier that day. His thinning black hair was disheveled. He also sweated profusely. Those meeting him the first time assumed it was nerves. The assumption, Shara knew, was a fatal error.

Shara had told Winkler what Morales had found out about Brash's murder and why Shara was the prime suspect. He told her before they walked into Cleary's office that he was there simply to take Cleary's measure. Shara's answers should be concise. Volunteer nothing, he told her. And don't answer questions until he nodded his approval.

Without uttering a greeting, Winkler gave Cleary his card. It was bent in one corner. It looked intentionally amateurish, as if he'd printed it off his home computer.

"I have just a few questions for your client, Mr. . . . Winkler," Cleary said, glancing at his card. "It would have been so much simpler if Miss Farris had answered them earlier."

"You weren't asking questions then, Agent Cleary," Winkler said. "You accused my client of murder."

"A misunderstanding on Miss Farris's part, I assure you," Cleary said.

"Which is why I'm present. No further misunderstandings. So let's not fence. Ask your questions."

Cleary shrugged. "Can you account for your whereabouts between 10:30 and 12:30 today?" Cleary asked after she had turned on a tape recorder.

Shara waited for Winkler's nod, then succinctly answered. She'd met with Rudy, Cheyenne, then gone home for a nap, shower, and change of clothes.

"You forgot to mention your visit to Sam Brash's apartment at 11:45," Cleary said. "The Presidential Towers on the Parkway," she added.

"I was never at his apartment," Shara said.

"Then how do you explain your fingerprints on his computer," Cleary asked, bending closer to Shara. It was her smoking gun. But, unbeknownst to Cleary, it came as no surprise to Shara. Morales had told Briggs of the existence of Shara's prints at the crime scene. Shara honestly couldn't explain them away.

"I was *never* at his apartment," Shara repeated.

"Fingerprints don't lie," Cleary said.

"My client has answered the question. Don't badger her. Move on," Winkler said.

Cleary obviously wanted to pursue the matter. She tried again and Winkler objected. Move on or they would leave was his ultimatum. Cleary nervously looked at her list of questions.

"You didn't want Brash to publish the photo of Alexis Briggs, did you?" she asked.

"No," Shara said when Winkler nodded.

"You were certain he was going to do so anyway, according to Detectives LeBrea and Briggs."

"What Detectives LeBrea and Briggs might have thought is irrelevant," Winkler interjected, not allowing Shara to answer.

"Brash took a photo with a digital camera. He brought you, Briggs, and LeBrea a print. We found no copies of the photo in Brash's apartment. The hard drive of his computer was destroyed with a virus," Cleary said.

"Is there a question coming?" Winkler said.

"Brash's prints were on the computer. The only other set was yours," Cleary said, looking at Shara. Did you destroy the data on his hard drive?"

"I was never in his apartment," Shara repeated.

"Then explain the prints," Cleary said, her voice rising.

"Asked and answered," Winkler said. "How did Mr. Brash die?" he asked.

Shara knew the answer and had told her attorney. She watched Cleary carefully as she answered.

"He was strangled with a tree vine," Cleary said.

"Any prints on the vine?" Winkler asked sarcastically.

"No," Cleary said.

"Did anyone see my client enter or leave the apartment?" Winkler asked. "Any security camera footage of my client?"

Cleary shook her head.

"Any hair, fibers, or other physical evidence that could tie anyone to the murder?" Winkler asked, already knowing the answer.

Cleary shook her head.

"Odd," said Winkler. My client was somehow careless enough to leave her prints on Mr. Brash's computer, yet there is no other physical evidence at all at the crime scene. Yes, quite odd," he said, as if to himself, then took out a soiled handkerchief and wiped his forehead. "Was my client's car spotted in the area? Maybe she got a ticket," Winkler said.

"No," Cleary answered. "Would your client agree to a search of her car and apartment?" Cleary said before Winkler could go on.

"Not without a warrant," Winkler said.

"We can readily obtain one," Cleary said. "We have motive: the threat by Brash to go public with the kidnapping. We have opportunity: your client has no substantiated alibi when the murder took place. And we have her prints at the apartment."

"And I have the results of a polygraph test taken half an hour ago," Winkler said, placing the report on Cleary's desk. "It says my client's telling the truth."

"These are highly unreliable," Cleary said waving the report.

"Arrest her then," Winkler said.

Cleary seemed taken aback. "We're . . . we're not prepared to do so at this juncture."

"Then this interview is over," Winkler said, rising. "Come, Shara." They left the office with Cleary sitting at her desk as if she were trying to think of a way to drag them back in.

"How did we do?" Shara asked Winkler when they were on the street outside.

"Without the prints, they have nothing. How do you explain the prints?" Arnie asked.

"I honestly can't. I didn't lie to you, Arnie. I was never there. Someone had to have planted them. Who, why, and how, I don't know."

"Cleary will use the prints to harass you," Winkler said. "She won't arrest you. Not yet. But she'll be a thorn in your side. Can you live with that?"

"I can't have that, Arnie. Not right now." Shara said. "Normally, I wouldn't give a shit. Cleary can hound me to death, but she doesn't have enough to arrest me. But . . . there's the kidnapping. My total focus has to be on Renee. I'll deal with this lunacy after Renee is found. I need Cleary off my back, plain and simple. Can you do that for me?"

"If we go on the offensive," Winkler said with a smile. Shara knew her attorney had a plan. Knew, too, that he was enjoying himself. "Let's go back in and see Fred Dearborne, Cleary's boss. Follow my lead. Say nothing unless I tell you. And don't look so glum. It's not like you."

"I don't like being framed," Shara said. "Other than Cleary, nobody has it in for me. I'm missing something, and for the life of me, I can't grasp it. Who would kill Brash and then frame me? Only Briggs and LeBrea knew

Brash and I clashed. Yet it's not something I can think about right now."

"For now, let's assume it's two different people. Someone killed Brash," Winkler said. "And Cleary is intent on pinning it on you, regardless of what she has to do."

"Cleary framed me?" Shara asked

"Precisely," Winkler said. "We blame the frame on Cleary."

Fred Dearborne greeted Winkler warily when he and Shara entered his office. Unlike Cleary, Dearborne, based in Philly, was keenly aware of Winkler's reputation.

"Fred, my client just gave Agent Cleary a statement," Winkler started after the two men shook hands. "Though it was more of an interrogation, I'm afraid. I'm frankly baffled by Cleary's hostility. It's clouding her judgment and compromising your case."

"Cleary's a professional," Dearborne said. He looked from Winkler to Shara, then focused on the lawyer. Shara thought Dearborne looked more like an aging businessman than a Fed. His brown hair was thinning. He combed it forward to cover his receding hairline. His buttoned suit jacket prominently displayed a bulging waistline. He looked to be about fifty. Unlike Cleary, Shara didn't get the feeling he had any aspirations other than retiring with a full pension. "She may come on strong. That's our Claire, but she harbors no grudge against your client."

"I beg to differ, Fred," Winkler said. "You weren't in Philly at the time, but Cleary blames Shara for her demotion. Cleary ended up with egg on her face when she failed to heed the warnings of Shara and Lamar Briggs."

"I wasn't aware," Dearborne said, looking glum. Shara was certain he was aware. She didn't think Dearborne a fool. It wouldn't have taken much probing to learn the reason for Cleary's fall from grace.

"I have it on good authority that Agent Cleary was at the scene of the Brash murder before forensics arrived," Winkler went on. He took out a second copy of Shara's polygraph test and handed it to Dearborne. "Since my client was never at the Brash apartment , I believe Cleary planted her prints on the victim's computer. The prints, after all, are the only evidence she has. As I told Agent Cleary, I find it odd someone would leave fingerprints that could be so easily found, yet there was no other physical evidence. The fingerprints scream of a frame-up against my client. After all, other than the prints, everything else is speculation."

"That's an awful big leap," Dearborne said.

"My client is willing to submit to a polygraph administered by your people, if need be," Winkler said.

Dearborne looked at the printout Winkler handed him, then shook his head. "It won't be necessary. You're many things Arnie, but you don't play loose with evidence. I'll accept the results of your polygraph."

"Then the harassment must stop . . . *now*," Winkler said. "Shara is under immense stress. Her presence and peace of mind are pivotal if her ward's kidnapping is to be resolved with Renee's safe return. Cleary will continue to badger Shara, and that's unacceptable. If any harm comes to Renee, the FBI will be held responsible." He paused. He locked eyes with Dearborne and spoke coldly and slowly. "I give you my word I will make it my personal crusade to crucify *anyone* who may have obstructed Renee's safe return."

Dearborne closed his eyes and rubbed his temple with the back of his right hand. Shara knew Winkler wasn't bluffing. So did Dearborne. He didn't need Arnie Winkler all over his ass.

"I'll make sure Cleary keeps her distance until Renee is found," Dearborne finally said.

"Not good enough, Fred," Winkler responded. "Cleary's a loose cannon. Promise all you want, you can't control her. She's off the case and out of town. That's non-negotiable. Your people will have total access to Shara and our cooperation as soon as Renee is found. I have no desire to impede your investigation, but Renee takes precedence. Cleary's history here or I go on a rampage. You know I don't make idle threats."

Winkler didn't have to elaborate. Dearborne took all of five second to come to a decision, then looked from Winkler to Shara. "You're right. Renee's safety is our primary . . . our *only* concern right now. I'll personally be the Bureau's liaison with your people in regards to the kidnapping. Cleary will return to D.C. immediately."

Outside, Shara embraced Winkler. "How can I repay you?" she asked.

"I know a pastry shop on Market Street. My stomach's growling," Winkler said. He talked food as they walked to the store. Shara laughed despite herself. With Cleary gone, Shara could again concentrate solely on Renee's abductor. No Brash. No Cleary. No interlopers. She paused in mid-thought. No interlopers *unless* Brash's murder was related to Renee's kidnapping. Cleary was many things, but Shara didn't feel she had the audacity or cunning to plant Shara's fingerprints on Brash's computer even though it had been Winkler's strategy to to intimate the fingerprints had been planted by Cleary. Someone had. Someone out to cause Shara grief. But who? She tucked the question in the back of her mind, hoping it wasn't somehow related to Renee's disappearance.

Chapter Twenty-Five

Norman had been staring at Alexis for a good fifteen minute before she awoke. She had looked so peaceful at first as she slept. As always, Norman was conflicted. Kill her in her sleep. Be merciful, one part of him demanded. But then he remembered her resistance. Kill her before she cracked and Briggs would have prevailed yet again.

Then Renee's face contorted. She pursed her lips, squeezed her eyes shut, and seemed to convulse. Would she die in front of him? It would expose her weakness. Briggs's frailty, too. But, then she urinated and awakened. Repulsive, Norman thought. Fortunately, other than soiling herself, her urine dripped into the bucket.

Norman stared at Renee, sure she would avert her eyes at her humiliation. But she locked eyes with him, and he could feel his rage return.

He went upstairs to fill a basin with water. Another sponge bath was in order. His hand reached out for the cold water faucet and an idea struck him. He filled the basin with hot water instead. Keep her off balance, he thought to himself.

He came downstairs and lathered his hands. The water stung. He smiled. When he began washing Alexis's thighs, he kept his eyes on hers. He saw her eyes widen in shock, saw her face contort with pain. He suppressed a burst of laughter.

The water was merely tepid by the time he reached her genitals. He gently brushed a finger against her clitoris to see how she'd react. Jan had called it her *honey spot*. Much as he had loved his wife, when they made love, he was often disgusted at her demands and crude language. He recalled when she had first suggested they have oral sex. Only she had been far coarser. "Go down on me, Sweetheart," she'd pleaded. When he didn't comprehend, she continued. "Eat me, Norman." He still wasn't certain what she wanted. "*Suck my pussy*," she'd yelled in frustration, pushing his head from her breasts to her privates. Norman couldn't do it. The mere thought made him lose his erection. Jan had grudgingly accepted that the best she could get was a finger on her clitoris—her clit, she called it, making the term sound vulgar to Norman.

Norman's touching Alexis was clinical. An experiment. He'd learned from his last encounter and wouldn't allow Alexis to arouse him now. With his soapy hands Norman touched Alexis's clitoris several times.

"Tell me you're just washing me," Alexis said with distaste. She didn't seem the least bit intimidated nor embarrassed.

"I think you really want me to make love to you," Norman said to mask his disappointment.

"I knew you were a perv," Alexis answered.

"Let's say for the sake of argument that I'm not going to let you go," Norman said, ignoring her. "You're going to die. I'm not saying that's going to occur, but if your father doesn't pay the ransom. Well . . . do you want to die a virgin?" It was a purely academic question. Not even the beast within Norman could rape this child. Though a young woman, Norman constantly compared Alexis to his daughter. To *his* child. He would never have sex with a child.

"Die a virgin or have you fuck me?" Alexis asked sarcastically.

Norman ignored her vulgarity. So like Jan, he thought. Why not say intercourse, he thought, then went on. "You could do far worse. Boys your age care solely about their own needs and desires. Me, I'd try to please *you*."

"I'd rather die a virgin," Alexis said dryly.

Suddenly angry, Norman took out his knife and put it to Alexis's throat. "Right here? Right now?" he yelled.

"I won't beg for my life, Asshole. I won't cry. You do what you must. I die now, I die with dignity. I win. You lose. There's a lot worse," Alexis said.

Incensed at Alexis's willingness to die, Norman unfastened his belt and began thrashing her. He struck her thighs, her stomach, her shoulders, and finally her breasts. And his efforts finally brought tears to her eyes and Alexis began sobbing.

"I thought you said you'd never cry," Norman yelled in triumph as he finally stopped beating her.

"You really are an asshole," Alexis said between sobs. "Crying out in pain doesn't mean you've crushed my resolve. You hurt me. I cried. But it's a hollow victory. Beat me all the fuck you want. It's the only way you'll get tears out of me."

Norman said nothing. He went upstairs and lay in bed, deflated. He had made her cry, but she was right. Her determination had been strengthened, not crushed. He sometimes detested that part of him that lost control. Crying and being spiritually vanquished were not one and the same. He'd been a fool to gloat, and Alexis had put him in his place. Norman was as resolute as ever to prevail. After all, there was only so much Alexis could tolerate before she crumbled. Yet the thought of victory brought no joy.

He kept finding himself comparing this girl to his Rose, and his daughter was always found wanting. Even when he brought Alexis to her knees, which was inevitable, his admiration for her would remain. She had proven a worthy adversary. A product of her father, did that mean he would also have to alter his opinion about Briggs? To grudgingly respect the man? The thought appalled him, but Norman couldn't push it away.

This battle of wills was taking its toll on him. Norman closed his eyes. Just a short nap, he thought.

He awoke seven hours later, just after midnight.

Chapter Twenty-Six

Shara returned to Briggs's house at 6 p.m. to yet another crisis. Carter Hastings, Sam Brash's editor at the *Daily News,* had just arrived. He and LeBrea were engaged in an argument when Shara entered. She felt the urge to turn and flee. She fought it and offered a weak smile.

"*You!*" Hastings said to Shara without greeting. "I've wanted to speak to you, and all I get is the runaround. Where have you been?" Hastings demanded in a thick South Philly accent.

"Around," Shara said. She didn't mean to sound flip, but she didn't know how much Hastings knew. She'd have to tread carefully. Carter Hastings was not the lightweight Claire Cleary had been. And he was also no great fan of Shara's. A product of South Philly, by sheer tenacity he had worked his way to editing one of the city's two major papers. He now dressed Main Line and hobnobbed with the elite. His accent, though, was a badge of honor. He knew he would never be totally accepted by Philly's monied gentry. They would invite him to their exclusive country clubs. They'd court his goodwill. But he was still an outsider. Though wealthy, he was new money, which somehow tainted him. He not only knew it but relished their discomfort at having to kiss his "big Italian ass," Shara had heard him say on more than one occasion.

Shara had done some investigating for Deidre Caffrey, Hasting's most prized reporter. More than once Shara had played Deidre, though only once by design. The last time it had cost Deidre and the paper an exclusive, which earned Shara Carter Hastings's antipathy. With Deidre's murder, an uneasy truce had followed.

Hastings now approached Shara so they would have been face to face if Shara were taller. Hastings was himself no more than five foot nine, but still he towered a good six inches above Shara.

"Look, Farris, I *know* Brash was down here working on a story. *You* called Lynn Moody, remember, to rein him in. What Brash found out, I can, as well. I *do* have an army of reporters at my disposal. One of my reporters is murdered, and we come off as fools with no idea what he was working on. Detective LeBrea has stonewalled me. I can see your footprints all over this, Farris. What gives?"

Shara shot a glance at LeBrea, who shrugged. He looked exhausted. For good reason, Shara thought. He was running a sensitive investigation while putting out brush fires on all sides at the same time. He probably hadn't gotten any sleep all day, either.

"Come with me," Shara said and walked up to Alexis's room. Shara stopped before entering. "I'm going to level with you. I hope you'll use discretion because a life hangs in the balance. I know that sounds overly dramatic, but you make the call."

Shara knocked on the door, and Alexis told her to come in. The kidnapper's message remained scrawled on the mirror. Hastings looked at it and then at Shara. The color had drained from his face.

"Someone *thinks* they've kidnapped Briggs's daughter," Shara said, pointing to Alexis. "It was actually a friend of hers. Renee LeShay. If it rings a bell, it's because Renee's father killed his wife—Renee's mother—while Renee and her mother were at a shelter for battered women."

"I remember," Hastings said, clearly intrigued. "He pled to manslaughter. He'll be out in a few years. It never sat right with me, but we couldn't dig up anything."

"It's complicated and not for public consumption. Suffice it to say, Mr. LeShay was more a victim than his wife," Shara said. "In any event, I'm Renee's legal guardian." Shara explained the need for secrecy and how Brash could have compromised the search for Renee, hence the call to Lynn Moody. She told Hastings of the deal they'd made with Brash. She told him everything *except* the one thing she couldn't herself explain: how her prints had gotten onto Brash's computer. By the time she was finished, Hastings had regained his composure. Shara did tell him the FBI had asked her for a statement. She told him he could contact Fred Dearborne for confirmation.

"I know the awkward position this puts you in," Shara concluded. "It's bad enough Brash has been murdered, but do you want to blow the whistle now and be responsible for yet another death? Keep your pit bulls leashed and I offer you the same deal Brash accepted. When we find the fucker who kidnapped Renee, you get a three-hour exclusive window. You also get an interview with Briggs—the only one he'll give."

Hastings stroked his chin in thought. Shara saw his five o'clock shadow. This wasn't the Carter Hastings invited into the homes of Philadelphia's monied aristocracy. This was the Carter Hastings who had exposed the drug dealings of one of Philly's warring crime families while having the commonsense not to implicate the real powers that be. They owed him. Many others owed him, too.

"We'll look like asses until the truth comes out," Hastings said, as if thinking out loud.

"And heroes when it's learned you killed a story to protect a life," Shara said. "Your restraint would make for a good editorial. The rest of the media will pick up on it. "The Editor With a Heart," Shara said, reciting what could be a competitor's headline.

"You got balls, Farris, I'll give you that," Hastings said. "We take a hit for a few days for a pat on the back for our compassion when our true motive is revealed. I can live with that," he said, his decision made. He looked at Alexis. "It was supposed to be you, huh?" he asked.

Alexis nodded.

Hastings looked at Shara. "Brash would have wanted an interview with the victim, which you would have refused. He would have accepted one with Alexis as compromise. Not one with Briggs." He put up a hand before Shara could speak. "Brash could be a prick," he went on. "I know my reporters, Farris. I'm not going to throw this child to the wolves for the sake of a story. The exclusive and interview with Briggs will suffice. Plus you owe me one. And you know I'll collect."

"Thanks, Hastings," Shara said. "Deidre spoke highly of you. I can see why now."

"Laying it on kinda thick," Hastings said with a laugh. He paused. "I miss Deidre. Good people. Far more than I'll miss Brash, but you didn't hear that from me." He then looked at Alexis again. "Don't be beating up on yourself, young lady. I see it in your eyes. Some freak abducted your friend. You're not at fault." He extended a hand to Shara, who shook it. "I'll hold you to your promise," Hastings said. "Tell LeBrea to call me. And I won't forget that favor you owe me," he added with a wink.

Chapter Twenty-Seven

Renee had again cried herself to sleep after her captor had abruptly left. Battered and bruised, she knew she wasn't just fatigued. And hunger had little or nothing to do with her frequent naps. No, she realized, when she slept, she escaped her tormentor, even if just for a little while. She didn't have to ponder his next atrocity. Dwelling on that *would* have crushed her resolve. There was a part of the man that was capable of anything. She didn't want to contemplate all the ways he might persecute her. The Norman Flowers who had an embarrassing erection when he'd touched her breasts was not the same man as the one who had just touched her clitoris and talked about making love to her. *That* Norman Flowers was capable of rape . . . and far worse. Renee didn't want to think what was next in store for her. She couldn't run away, so her body shut down and she slept.

She awoke to find her visitor from earlier in the day again staring at her, her face not able to mask her anxiety. She was naked, as before.

"He beat you something awful," she said. Renee could hear genuine sadness in the woman's voice.

"It hurt . . . hurt bad, but if that's the worst he does to me, I'll be grateful. It's just a dull throb now," Renee said.

Suddenly Renee felt something on her thigh. No, something *crawling up her thigh*. She looked down and saw a hairy spider the size of a quarter. She began to shiver uncontrollably. She hated insects, spiders most of all. It crept up past her genitals and nestled for a moment in her pubic hair, then continued its upward ascent. Was the spider poisonous? Renee wondered. She didn't know much about spiders. She only knew that some were deadly. Had she endured the torment of her abductor only to die from a spider's bite? It crawled up to her breast and settled on her nipple, its legs exploring as Renee's nipple engorged, almost in welcome. Renee bit her lip to keep from screaming. If her captor knew of her fear of spiders, Renee knew he would use it against her. She tasted blood. She didn't realize how hard she had bitten down.

The woman—her other self—stood up and removed the spider from Renee's breast. She placed it gently in the palm of her hand for a moment then placed it on the ground and it scuttled away.

"Why didn't you kill it?" Renee asked. "It might return when you're not here."

"It's not dangerous," the woman replied. "Kill all spiders and you'd regret it. You want to live in a world filled with insects?"

Renee shook her head. What the hell was going on? She wondered. How could this creature she had conjured in her mind remove the spider that had been on her? The spider must have been her imagination. Was she losing it? What would she imagine next? Looking around, though, Renee was aware there were any number of spider webs on the ceiling of the basement. She might have imagined the one that had crawled on her, but there were certainly real spiders that could torment her.

The woman approached Renee, climbed into the cabinet, and straddled Renee. Their breasts touched, and Renee was aware her other self was far more endowed than she was. Just like her to conjure someone with big tits, she thought to herself. Renee could also feel the body heat from the woman. Renee was about to ask the woman what the hell she was doing.

"Shush," the woman said, as if she anticipated Renee's question. With her fingers, she touched the cabinet above Renee's head and ran her fingers down around the contours of Renee's body. She lowered herself as she did so, her lips brushing against Renee's pubic hair. Finally, the woman had completely outlined Renee's body.

"What did you do?" Renee asked.

"I've . . . staked out my territory, I guess you'd call it," the woman said. "Like lions peeing around the perimeter of land they claim as their own so other lions won't encroach. You have nothing more to fear from the spiders."

Renee yawned and dozed. It must not have been long. When she woke up, the woman was sitting in front of her. Maybe the spider had been a dream after all, Renee thought. Obviously something her imagination had created couldn't have done what Renee had . . . dreamed. There was no way her other self could have removed the spider. No way Renee could have felt the heat from someone she had created to keep herself sane.

"You're something else," the woman said. "There's quite a bit of Shara in you. It's now time to help you."

"You'll free me?" Renee asked, trying not to build up her hopes. She had to remember, after all, that this woman *couldn't* really set her free. She was a creation of Renee's imagination. A protector of her sanity, but capable of nothing more. Not even protecting her from spiders.

"I can't," the woman said. "This has to play out. But you can't give in to despair—"

"I won't," Renee said, but she could hear the lack of conviction in her voice. His atrocities seemed endless. She felt beaten down, her confidence in herself ebbing. And now her mind was playing tricks on her. Soon would she be able to tell the difference between what was real and what she imagined? Had she already gone insane? If so, it wouldn't be long before her captor realized and decided to kill her.

"You've got to play for time," the woman continued, as if reading Renee's mind. Her long hair now covered her breasts. Renee wondered why the modesty, then decided it unimportant. "You need a distraction to give Shara the time she needs to find you. Something to keep him away so you can regroup."

"And pray tell what can I do that I already haven't?" Renee asked.

The woman smiled and told her.

Chapter Twenty-Eight

At 11 p.m, Shara emerged from Briggs's study. Over the years Briggs had made an awful lot of enemies. It seemed the number was endless. Shara had four more names for Rudy and Cheyenne to check out.

Shara saw a dejected and exhausted LeBrea sitting in an armchair in Briggs's living room, his eyes focused on nothing, his body tense. Shara went into the kitchen and returned with two beers from the fridge. When she handed one to LeBrea, he offered a weak smile.

"How do you do it?" Shara asked, taking a chair facing the detective. "The pressure of kidnappings," she added.

"It's no easy task," LeBrea said, taking a gulp of his beer. "You try to remain detached. There's the kidnapper and the victim. Only problem is, the victim has a name and a face. And no matter how hard you try to distance yourself, the victim becomes a real live human being who just might never return home alive. You, Alexis, Briggs all talk about Renee, and I can't tune it out. The ones cops like myself lose haunt my dreams. We could have done more. We all replay it endlessly looking to see where we fucked up."

"Bullshit," Shara said. "I've seen you in action. You're the fuel that keeps this engine running. No easy task with all the added distractions."

"Thanks for the vote of confidence," LeBrea said. "The logical me agrees with you. Still, I'll second guess myself," he said with a shrug. "I always do." He paused and took another swallow of beer. "I envy Briggs. In homicide you begin after the fact. The victim ain't coming back. Me, I make a mistake and a kid dies. The only job more stressful is a hostage negotiator. They're on the scene. An error in judgment and a hostage dies," he said, snapping his fingers. "If there's more than one hostage, you have to put your error behind you. You've got to be on . . . at your best until the siege is over. I've talked with a number of them. It's not like in the movies. The toll it takes is incredible. Suicides, divorces, nervous breakdowns, and all around self-destructive behavior is what's in store no matter how good you are. The good ones—the lucky ones—get out before they're consumed. Before they become victims themselves."

"You're talking about yourself," Shara said.

LeBrea shook his head. "Fortunately I've been involved in just three other kidnappings. Only one turned out badly. The one that haunts my dreams. I'm tapped now because of my experience and so-called expertise, but it's not my calling. I'm just about burnt out. My sarge will understand when I tell him I can't handle it anymore. It's become too personal," LeBrea said, finally making eye contact with Shara.

"You married?" Shara asked. She was suddenly aware she knew little about the man. He intrigued her.

"I've been engaged to the same woman for five years off and on. It's kind of a safety net for both of us," LeBrea said. "We'll never marry. We'd be divorced within six months. But when I want, I have someone to go home to and we're a couple for three or four months. We each go our separate ways but always return to one another. She has no desire to marry, either. She's been through one bad marriage to a cop already. When asked, we say we're engaged, but it's a sham. It allows us to steer clear of serious relationships." He paused a moment. "I'd ask about you, but Briggs told me you don't let anyone in except maybe Renee and Alexis. So I won't pry." He looked at his watch. "Time for you to get some sleep. I'll relieve Briggs, then you, me."

Shara nodded, rose, and walked up to Alexis's room, where she'd crash. When this is over, she thought, maybe someone like LeBrea was what she needed. No long-term emotional commitment. She didn't think a lasting relationship was possible, what with the baggage she carried around. She was in a serious but long-distance relationship for a year and a half. Clay Fluery, a sheriff's deputy in Dismal, Virginia had become her first lover. He loathed big city life as much as Shara savored it. Neither seemed willing to budge. As a result, they hadn't taken their relationship to the next logical step. Shara had gone off to be with herself for a week, shortly before Briggs returned to the police department. She'd slept with Roger McCandless, a sheriff in a small town in the Poconos. She had met him on another case. Going to bed with McCandless just happened. She didn't regret it. Clay had had his share of women *before* Shara. He was faithful now, but she had made no such promise. As much as Clay satisfied her, Shara had no reference to compare her lover. McCandless had been far different than Clay as a lover. Certainly not better. Just different. Shara wondered what LeBrea would be like in bed, then shook her head. At some point she'd have to level with Clay. Their relationship was built on mutual trust. He might not be able to accept Shara's experimentation. Her *becoming*, she smiled, thinking of Lysette. And the current status of their relationship was unfair to both of them.

Shara slept on a rollaway cot Briggs had brought into Alexis's room. Alexis was tossing and turning in her sleep when Shara entered. Still feeling guilty, Shara thought.

Shara fell asleep immediately and woke up crying. She saw Alexis staring at her. "A fever dream?" Alexis asked.

Shara nodded, then composed herself. She started coughing just as she had with the other two dreams. She signed to Alexis for a glass of water. She drank it, then went into the bathroom herself and drank several more glasses before the cobwebs in her throat became dislodged. She splashed water on her face. She'd shower later. She wanted to talk with Alexis now.

Alexis didn't pelt her with questions. She and Renee were so similar in many ways, Shara realized. Alexis would wait until Shara was ready to share.

"I had another fragment, but this one was far different from the others." She replayed the dream in her mind. Relived the images that had assaulted her, and then shared. "I was in the same body I told you about, but she was even more detached than before. My throat's not quite as dry. She was like a camera, allowing me to see events as they might unfold. Like before, she wasn't emotionally involved herself. At some point I'll figure out her identity. Maybe it's not important that I know who she is. In any event, what I saw now was like a preview of what *might* occur."

"You mean it hasn't happened yet?" Alexis asked. "That's a departure from *any* dreams you've had in the past."

"Part of the curse of these dreams," Shara said. "There is no formula. There are no rules." She paused, closed her eyes in thought, then went on. "This was more of a warning. What might happen, like I told you. A worst-case scenario. I saw the kidnapper to go the window. The one I told you about before."

"You *saw* the kidnapper?" Alexis asked with excitement.

"Just his back. He was in shadow. No way I'd know him if I saw him or a photo of him," Shara said. "Anyway, something was going on outside. The police and the FBI had the cabin surrounded." Shara closed her eyes and wiped away a tear. "Renee was still tied up. He looks out the window, then goes over to Renee and slits her throat. Blood was spurting everywhere. His back to me, he takes out a gun and shoots himself in the head. Then the police and FBI storm in. LeBrea was with them."

"But it hasn't happened," Alexis said.

"And it won't," Shara shot back. "This was an admonition directed toward me. The bastard won't be taken alive if the police corner him. And he'll take Renee with him."

"The alternative?" Alexis asked.

"You know damn well," Shara said. "I've got to find him. Surprise him. Confront him before he has a chance to take the easy way out . . . and Renee with him. And do it alone."

The phone ringing startled them both. Shara, for one, was glad for the interruption. She knew Alexis's next question. Would she take the kidnapper alive? Shara had no answer, which would certainly disturb Alexis. Alexis was in many ways like her father. There was a code to adhere to. Courts decided guilt or innocence and meted out punishment to the guilty. Alexis was no fan of vigilante justice. Shara, a born cynic, knew the justice system was hopelessly flawed. Rapists and murderers got off on technicalities. The wealthy could afford the best attorneys in combat with overworked, underpaid, and often inexperienced prosecutors. Witnesses could be coerced, bribed, even killed. All three had occurred in Philly recently. Juries could be bought. Often the guilty escaped punishment entirely or received a mere slap on the wrist. Judges were far behind the times when it came to punishing certain crimes. Those accused of domestic violence seldom received the sentences they deserved. And the justice system seemed unaware that rape, for a woman, was worse than being killed. The victim relived the incident endlessly. The life of someone raped was altered irrevocably. And victims of rape who testified in court were raped, figuratively, yet again, often accused of lying because they felt guilty after consensual sex. Those who accused males of date rape were often encouraged not to press charges. Many young women knowing what they faced in court refused to press charges or made poor witnesses. Things were changing slowly . . . far too slowly, as far as Shara was concerned.

Shara had firsthand proof how the legal system could be manipulated. Arnie Winkler. Cleary hadn't stood a chance against him. Sure, Shara knew she was innocent, but it was Winkler who had rid her of her nemesis. There hadn't been a level playing field. Much as Alexis might abhor it, sometimes another form of justice was necessary.

When Shara and Alexis got downstairs, LeBrea was standing outside Briggs's study. He put up a hand, then his finger to his lips. *It was the kidnapper*, Shara knew. A call at two in the morning, close to twenty-four hours after the abduction itself. It could be no other.

LeBrea, Briggs, and Shara had planned for such a contingency earlier that evening. How to widen that forty-eight to seventy-two hour window was the focus of the discussion. What should Briggs say to make the kidnapper think twice about killing Renee?

The phone conversation lasted less than forty-five seconds, not long enough for a trace.

Briggs was visibly shaken when he hung up. He hit the rewind button on a tape recorder without saying a word and they all listened.

"How does it feel, Briggs, to be on the top of the world one moment then free falling without a parachute the next?" The voice was calm. He didn't try to disguise himself. He was someone who lived in Philly, Shara was certain, but was neither Italian nor Irish. There was no thick accent. Educated, Shara felt, not poor white trash. All potential clues.

"What do you mean, on top of the world?" Briggs asked.

"You were reinstated. I don't know how you pulled that off, but you got the second chance I was denied." Shara heard his anger mounting. "It's not right. You're going to pay."

"By killing my daughter?" Briggs asked.

"You'll have to live with that forever. You'll never forget what it cost becoming a cop again. It'll tear your family apart." The kidnapper now sounded bitter.

"I'll grieve, but I'll move on," Briggs said. "Seems I fucked with you and you're the one who went free falling. Those with faith and inner strength accept life's heartaches and move on." Shara nodded. This was the tactic they agreed to follow.

"You're saying I didn't?" the kidnapper said. "I tried, Briggs. Faith and inner strength can take you just so far. I've lost it all because of you. Now it's my turn to inflict pain."

"It hurts. It hurts bad, I'll grant you that," Briggs said. "Each time I think of my daughter being terrorized by you, it eats at me something fierce. I know you plan to kill her. When you do, she'll finally be at peace. I'll mourn her, but then I'll be able to move on. She's suffering now, and that's what's haunting me."

"You want your kid to die?" the man asked. He sounded confused to Shara. Good, she thought. Get him to thinking. Keep him off balance.

"I want her torment to end," Briggs said, raising his voice. "We both know you don't plan on letting her go."

"Don't start mourning just yet," the man said. "You'll suffer. Long and hard."

The phone went dead.

"Renee's alive," Shara said, breaking a long silence. "You did good, Briggs. You caught him off guard."

"Play it again," LeBrea said. "This time to learn more about the kidnapper."

They listened, all jotting down notes. Earlier LeBrea had fastened blank paper to the walls of Briggs's study. The chalkboard was already filled. "What do we now know?" LeBrea asked when the tape ended. He had a magic marker in hand."

"He has a grudge against me personally," Briggs said, "but that we knew."

"Yes, but now we know for sure we're not dealing with a friend or relative," Shara said. "This *is* the guy you wronged . . . at least in his own mind. That *does* narrow our search. You got a second chance, though," she said, looking at Briggs. "Which means he feels he was denied one."

"Meaning?" LeBrea prodded.

"He never recovered from what he perceived Briggs took away," Shara said.

"He's lost his family," Alexis said. All eyes turned toward her. Alexis hadn't been present at the other strategy sessions. She seemed suddenly jazzed, as if the veil of guilt had finally been lifted. "They've left him," she elaborated. "He said my death will tear our family apart. What happened to him to destroy his family?"

"Why did he lose his family?" LeBrea asked. "Feel free to speculate." He looked at all of them, but had said the last for Alexis's benefit as she was a new participant to their brainstorming sessions.

"He lost his job and couldn't get another with the same pay and status," Briggs said. "That second chance he said he didn't get. I got my job back. He never got his."

"He lost his house," Alexis said. "No job. No ritzy house."

"He turned to booze or drugs," Briggs said.

"He lost contact with his family," Shara said. "Self-absorbed. Self-centered. Bitter. Angry. Temper tantrums.

He drove his family away. He's alone now. He's got nothing but his rage to fuel him."

They went on for another ten minutes before LeBrea summed up.

"Okay, first and foremost, I think we've bought ourselves some time. That forty-eight to seventy-two hour window I mentioned was optimistic. We've got him thinking now. He may be reconsidering his options. We know he's white, middle class, someone who had a good job. Now he's either unemployed or he has a job that's unsatisfying and doesn't allow him to maintain his former standard of living. He *had* a family but is probably alone now." He paused and looked around to see if anyone had anything to add. "Let's get this into the computer and refine our search. Briggs, search your memory . . . and your files. Go with your gut. I'm gonna catch some shuteye. Briggs, you've got two hours and then you sleep. Don't argue," he said when he saw Briggs about to protest. "You make an error in judgment due to fatigue, you'll second guess yourself the rest of your life. None of us can go non-stop."

Briggs nodded.

"We've bought ourselves time, people," LeBrea said. "Let's use it wisely."

Day Two

Chapter Twenty-Nine

Norman came downstairs with a sandwich and a glass of juice for Alexis and found her again asleep. He smiled inwardly. Within she must be suffering, he thought. She had to be fraying at the edges. Soon her false bravado would collapse, which would mean Briggs had also given into despair.

Neither spoke as he fed her.

"Would you like another sandwich?" he taunted her. He'd make the offer. She'd let down her guard and acquiesce. Then he'd tell her she wasn't deserving, yet again squashing her hopes.

". . . my father."

Norman had been so into himself he hadn't realized Alexis had spoken.

"What?" he asked.

"I said, why don't you call my father?"

"Why would I want to do that?" he asked disdainfully, but she had aroused his curiosity.

"I'd think you want to hear him distraught. You know, at the breaking point," she said. "See if he was desperate enough to beg for my life." She paused. "Or are you afraid to talk to the man himself? He did you wrong. Fifteen years you've suffered, but to my father you don't exist. You haven't *once* confronted him. You're not even an afterthought. Well, you're finally in the driver's seat. This is your big chance to rub it in, but I see you passing it up.

You don't have the balls to face him even over the phone. That's pathetic. *You're* pathetic."

He slapped her. "Watch your mouth, young lady," he said.

"Hit me all you want, Asshole. Even now my father intimidates you. The thought of just speaking to him terrifies you. That voice from fifteen years ago. You *can't* confront him . . . even over the damn phone."

"You think I'll call him from here and he'll trace me," Norman said, proud he could see through her ploy. "There's no phone service in the cabin, so you lose again." He paused. "Oh, that second sandwich. You can forget about it."

Norman went upstairs. As he cleaned the kitchen sink, he found himself drawn by Alexis's suggestion. It was risky. On the other hand, if he drove an hour toward Philly, even if the call was traced, there was no way to ascertain his whereabouts. And short conversations couldn't be traced. He'd watched enough reality-based cop shows to know not to fall for any delaying tactics. It would be sweet to hear Briggs grovel, to hear him plead for his daughter's life. A pitiful hat-in-hand, Briggs was worth a little risk. And if Briggs *was* at the breaking point, Norman could rid himself of Alexis. With the knowledge Briggs had fallen apart, Norman would be victorious. He laughed aloud. Maybe the daughter was stronger than the father.

His decision made, Norman went downstairs, gagged Alexis without telling her why, then shut and locked the cabinet.

An hour later, he spotted the perfect pay phone. It was outside and to the side of a Wawa convenience store. He wouldn't have to go inside to use the phone, so nobody would see him if the call was traced. There was also parking behind the store. He saw no security cameras. This wasn't the city, after all, where a store that *wasn't* robbed was an aberration. No one would spot his car or record his license plate number. He congratulated himself on this thoroughness.

Hanging up after speaking with Briggs for less than a minute, Norman was both furious and despondent. The call hadn't been the satisfying experience he'd envisioned. Driving back to the cabin, he replayed the conversation over and over, analyzing—overanalyzing—each phrase, every word, each pause. Briggs hadn't sounded crushed. Norman had heard no despondency in the man's voice. He didn't plead for his daughter's life. On the contrary, he almost welcomed her death. He spouted some garbage about faith and inner strength seeing him through this harrowing experience. He'd mourn his daughter then move on. He'd implied that was something Norman hadn't been able to do.

Norman had never been particularly religious. He'd forgotten the importance of religion to Blacks. He now remembered reading an article where two pictures were prevalent in many Black homes. One was Martin Luther King, the other, Jesus. Even dwellers of roach-infested, crime-ridden, gang-controlled high-rises paraded to church every Sunday thanking the good Lord for their blessings.

Norman had totally ignored the possibility Briggs would lean on religion to see him through his greatest challenge. *Mourn and move on.* Briggs expected his daughter to die. Having accepted that inevitability, the sooner the better, as far as Briggs was concerned, so Alexis would suffer less. Meaning Briggs would suffer less. Norman wouldn't give Briggs that satisfaction. Alexis would remain captive until she broke. A day, two tops. Then Norman would call Briggs again and let him know his daughter had suffered more than necessary because of her father's arrogance and blind faith. Yes, if he destroyed Briggs's faith in God, that would be one less crutch for him to lean on.

Chapter Thirty

Renee had heard her abductor start his car soon after she challenged him. Her inner self *had* been right. That was why he'd gagged her and shut the doors to the cabinet. Renee didn't know how long he was gone. She'd tried to count to herself at first to keep track of time, but she had dozed twice. Still, she was proud of herself, and her spirits were buoyed. She'd bought time. And as a bonus, while uncomfortable, he couldn't abuse her or debase her when he was gone.

While Renee knew Briggs was upset she had been kidnapped, she wasn't his daughter. He'd feel guilty and frustrated, but she was certain it would have been far worse for him if Alexis had actually been this man's captive. Renee could use that knowledge when the man returned.

She heard him return, heard the door to the cabin shut, then heard his steps on the stairs. She had lived in the hustle and bustle of the city all her life. The silence of the cabin was deafening. Earlier she could hear when her captor paced upstairs, turned on the water, even when he opened a refrigerator or cabinet. So when he returned now, she wasn't taken by surprise. He came downstairs almost immediately. He was eating a candy bar. Renee almost salivated at the sight. She hadn't dwelled on her diet of peanut butter and jelly sandwiches and orange juice, but now seeing something different made her crave a bite.

"Want some?" he asked, as if reading her mind. He

held the candy bar close so Renee could smell the chocolate but couldn't take a bite. Renee hesitated, not wanting to seem desperate. "Have it your way," he said and took another bite.

"Yes . . . I'd like some," Renee said. She was asking, *not* begging.

"I don't think so," he said. "I ask, you answer. You go stubborn on me . . . you get *nothing*. He paused. "On second thought, why not?" He opened her blouse to expose her breasts and wiped the chocolate goo on them, then laughed. "At least you can smell it. It's a Milky Way Midnight. You must think it commonplace, but when I was your age, we didn't have near the choices you do now. There was but *one* Milky Way. Now you can choose between regular and Midnight, and this is ever so much better than the original. When I was growing up, you had Pepsi and Diet Pepsi, Coke and Diet Coke. Now there's all sorts of variations. Pepsi One. Pepsi Max. Pepsi Natural. Pepsi Next. I don't even know what Pepsi Natural or Pepsi Next is. Something for everyone, though."

He took a bite of the bar he had wiped across her nipples and smacked his lips. "Your father sends his love," the man said, matter of factly. "Actually, he considers you already dead. No, that's not quite right. He knows you're still alive. He thinks you'd be *better off* dead. Imagine that, a father wanting his only child's death. Maybe it's because he's falling apart at the seams. Or maybe you disappointed him. Is he one of those men who wanted a son and was disheartened when you came out of your mother's womb without a penis?" He took another bite, finishing off the candy bar. "See, I took your advice and gave your father a call. We had a nice chat. He didn't seem nearly as intimidating as he was fifteen years ago when he had *me* at his mercy." He paused again. "Cat got your tongue, Alexis? Don't want to hear the wreck your father's become. I almost pity the man. *Almost*." With his finger, he wiped some of the chocolate off Renee's breast, then licked it off his finger. "Tasty," he said and laughed.

"I'm supposed to accept what you say as truth, Asshole?" Renee said.

He swatted her in the face. "That was for calling me a liar. I've never lied to you, Alexis. I'm a man of honor."

"You're full of self-pity and self-loathing," Renee said. She had to make him believe emotionally she was as strong as ever. She'd be belligerent and endure the pain of his beating, which she was certain would follow. She wouldn't let him know her humiliation when he touched her breasts to wipe the chocolate from them. "You blame all that's wrong with your life on a single incident. You let that define you. In school they call it a self-fulfilling prophesy. Since my father fucked you, you expect to fail, so you make sure you do."

"Dime store psycho-babble," he said, but Renee could see her words stung. He was fiddling with a ring on his finger. A wedding ring. He was divorced but still wore his wedding ring, Renee had noticed. He would use his thumb to twist the wedding band on his ring finger whenever Renee got too close to the truth or disturbed her captor.

"You could have moved to another city and started over," Renee said, "but you wallowed in self-pity. It was so much easier, wasn't it, than accepting responsibility for your failures. You lost your family. You took a dead-end job. *You* decided the path you'd follow. Unhappy with how your life's turned out, you blamed your failures on my father. There's no honor in that. So pardon me if I don't believe a word you say about my father."

She must have struck a chord because he said nothing in return. He left, then returned with the now familiar basin of water. This time he simply wanted to inflict pain. He used no soap. He just dipped the washcloth in the frigid water and rubbed her raw. He lingered at her breasts, where the washcloth felt like a Brillo pad, producing welts that wouldn't soon disappear. When tears fell from her eyes, he smiled.

"You can hurt me all you want," Renee said, biting down on her lip. "I'm not too proud to cry, Asshole. I've already told you that. You haven't accomplished a damn thing other than make me cry from pain . . . and you know it."

He said nothing but continued to rub the coarse washcloth across her nipples until they bled. Then he left.

"Why couldn't my Rose be more like you," she heard him mumble when he was halfway across the room. She wasn't sure what that meant, but she felt a sense of victory just the same.

Fatigue again washed over Renee. These mental contests were excruciating. It seemed she had correctly guessed that her captor's conversation with Briggs hadn't gone the way he had anticipated. She'd called him on it, and his response proved her correct. But she had no plan. She was making it up as she went along. She didn't know how far she could push him before he didn't give a damn anymore. How far could she go before he totally lost it and killed her, even if inadvertently? She had to measure each word with that knowledge. She had almost gone too far just now. It sapped her of what little energy she had. She slept…

. . . And awoke to the sight of her inner-self looking at her with concern. "You frustrate him," the woman said. "You don't cower before him. It's the only reason you're still alive. But his anger grows and the pain he inflicts on you escalates."

"Tell me something I don't know," Renee said. "How long can I keep it up?"

"As long as necessary," she said.

She sat cross-legged now, her nakedness fully exposed.

"At what point do I go too far? You know, say something so he loses it completely and kills me . . . maybe without meaning to do so?" Renee asked. "He's becoming devoured by that beast within him. And that monster knows no limits. He—"

"Shara will rescue you. Don't despair. When she does, you have a decision to make."

"Pizza with pepperoni or sausage," Renee said, feeling giddy.

"It's not something to be taken lightly. It's literally a life-or-death choice," she said.

"What are you talking about?" Renee asked. "I can't take any more of your riddles."

"If I gave you a gun, would you shoot the bastard or spare him?"

"I couldn't—" Renee started.

"Don't be hasty," the woman said, cutting Renee off. "If he's taken alive, you have to testify in court. You have to describe in detail, first to the police, then to a prosecutor, and then in court—a public forum—all the horrors you've been through. A defense attorney will say you lied or that you brought it upon yourself. All lies, but you'll feel violated again. It would be all over the media." She paused. "I know what you're thinking. Your name would remain confidential because of your age. Don't be naive. Your name will come out. Count on it. And it's not over with the trial. You go back to school and what? You get looks. There's talk behind your back. You can't escape what he's done to you. Maybe you get counseling and have to rehash it to yet another stranger."

"I get it," Renee said. "Not a pretty picture."

"If he's dead, you tell only the police and you can leave out his greatest atrocities. So, do you shoot him or spare him?"

"You're telling me to kill him," Renee said.

"You conjured me, or so you say. I ask questions. You provide the answers. Consider this, too, before you answer. Even if he's found guilty, he hasn't killed anyone. Maybe his lawyer will plea bargain to spare you the humiliation of testifying. Your father killed your mother . . . with reason, granted. A plea bargain was struck for your father. Why not with this monster? Maybe he gets fifteen years. With good behavior, he could be out in ten. Remember Shara and her half-brother? Alive, Bobby haunted Shara. She was free only when she killed him. Ten or fifteen years from now you'll still be a young woman. Will he seek revenge? Do you dare take the chance? Do you want to go to sleep each night thinking of the day he's freed? That is *if* you can sleep."

"I want him out of my life. Out of my mind," Renee said.

"You want him dead," she said.

"I didn't say that," Renee countered.

"Think on it," the woman said. "You'll have to live with the consequences for the rest of your life."

Renee closed her eyes. She didn't want to have this conversation. She didn't want to think of all she'd gone through to survive only to be the centerpiece of a media circus. When she opened her eyes, the woman was gone, back inside of her, having given Renee yet something else to torment her mind.

Renee did want him dead. That realization rocked her entire belief system. She recalled how angry she had been with Shara for what she had done to Denise. Shara had promised not to kill Denise. Technically, she hadn't. But she had convinced Deidre's sister the forest was her salvation knowing full well the forest would swallow Denise whole. Denise was alive, but she was a prisoner of the forest being driven mad as she saw herself kill her lover again and again and again.

Shara had called it self-preservation. Denise would have turned on Shara, and Shara couldn't risk exposure. Renee had condemned Shara's vigilante justice. Renee loved Shara as much as ever but didn't know if she could ever trust her completely again. Shara had broken a promise she'd made to Renee. It was as simple as that. And, even though Denise was alive, Shara *had* taken her life. Renee had forgiven Shara, yet even now she dwelled on the deceit. Only now, knowing what she wanted to do, did Renee comprehend she was a self-righteous hypocrite. She had never been in Shara's position, so she could take the high road and be indignant at Shara's decision. She wanted even more to survive her ordeal so she could tell Shara she understood what she had done to Denise. Tell her that she now knew that self-preservation could bring out the beast in a person, but that didn't mean Shara was evil or had given in to her dark side. Tell Shara she truly forgave her and understood why she had deceived her.

Now the same choice might be thrust on her. Renee's inner self had pulled no punches. A public trial. Humiliation. Accusations by the bastard's attorney. And worse, the possibility her abductor would one day be set free. It went against all Renee believed in to pull the trigger of the gun her inner-self had figuratively placed in her hand. Yet in her mind's eye, she saw herself pull the trigger. Saw the man fall. And felt relief wash over her.

Chapter Thirty-One

Shara was napping at 10 a.m., when she heard a commotion downstairs. LeBrea had lit a fire under them after the kidnapper's call to Briggs. It was like an adrenaline rush. But a crash was inevitable without tangible results. The brainstorming the night before had eliminated dozens upon dozens of suspects, yet by morning they were no closer to identifying the abductor than they had been before the call.

Shara had slept, less because of fatigue, more to see what the next fever dream brought. Oddly, there had been no dream at all. Shara was in a foul mood when she came downstairs. She saw LeBrea laughing at one of his detectives, who was red-faced with embarrassment.

LeBrea looked at Shara, shook his head, and told the other man to assist Briggs. "There was a neighbor we couldn't interview yesterday. An old lady across the street three houses down. She got back an hour and a half ago. Carrera goes over, walks on her lawn, and knocks on her door. She greets him in a walker and tells him to go to hell. Something about stepping on her lawn, disrespecting her. He tried to apologize, but she said if he didn't get the hell off her property—using the sidewalk, not the grass—she'd clobber him with her walker."

Briggs had emerged from his study, stretching, his eyes bloodshot. "Andrea Dawson," he said. "She was a court stenographer, then a crossing guard when she retired. She must be pushing eighty. Emphysema has slowed her down, but she doesn't want anyone's pity. She does demand respect, though."

"Anything Carrera can do to make it up to her?" LeBrea asked.

"First impressions are lasting ones with Andy," Briggs said and smiled. "When Alexis was young, she couldn't say Andrea. She called her Andy. Andrea ate it up. Sad to say, Carrera's worn out his welcome with her. She'll speak to Shara, though."

"Me?" Shara asked. "Why me?"

"She had two sons and a daughter," Briggs explained. "Her daughter, Lisbeth, died from sickle cell anemia when she was seven. From what I gather, Andrea was never the same. There's a bond between most mothers and their daughters. Andrea Dawson pines for the relationship she would have had with her daughter. She doted over Alexis when we moved here, but since the rape . . . ."

"Alexis couldn't communicate other than by sign language for four years," Shara finished for Briggs.

Briggs nodded. "And since she's recovered, Alexis has had so much catching up to do, there hasn't been time for Andrea Dawson. What I'm getting at is, she might respond to a female."

Shara took a quick shower then put on a clean pair of jeans and a sweater over her top. She looked in the mirror. She looked like . . . a bounty hunter. It would have to do. That and her natural charm. She laughed at the thought. She wasn't much of a charmer. However, as a bounty hunter, she had learned to take on a variety of personas. It was like playing a part in a play. Shara was a damned good actress who could become just about anyone. Rudy had dubbed her Chameleon because of her ability to become a Hispanic cleaning lady, a homeless bag lady, or a Mainline socialite. For Andrea Dawson, she decided to play the part of a confidant, the daughter she longed for.

Shara walked across the street to Andrea Dawson's

house, carefully avoiding the grass. After Shara introduced herself, Andrea Dawson quickly appraised her, smiled, then invited her in. "I recognize you," she said. "You spend a lot of time with Alexis," Dawson said, her voice a wheezy rasp. "Poor child. She's been through so much. You've been a friend to her?" she asked.

"We've grown quite close," Shara said. "In some ways, I'm the big sister she never had, I guess. Someone she can confide in and know I'll never repeat anything she tells me."

Andrea Dawson let Shara into a living room. It was clean but cluttered with memories. There were photos everywhere. Shara walked over to a mantel. The old woman followed in her walker. Andrea Dawson was short—even shorter than Shara—dark-skinned, with thinning white hair. Shara saw a photo of a young woman with a devilish smile next to a man in an army uniform. "You were beautiful," Shara said. "And you knew it, Mrs. Dawson," she added.

"Andrea, please," she said, smiling. "Perceptive thing, aren't you. That's my husband Nicholas. He fought in Vietnam, though he didn't have to. He was in his thirties, but enlisted just the same, the old goat. He wasn't particularly patriotic, but he sure did love a good fight."

"And you were a handful for any man," Shara said. "The photos say it all."

"Before I met Nicholas, I did sow my oats," Dawson said. "Oh hell's bells, even after we married, it took me some time to settle down, if you get my drift," she said, then went into a coughing fit. "Nicholas passed ten years ago. He was in the garage tinkering. He was forever tinkering. Getting nothing much accomplished, mind you, but he didn't care. He didn't come in for lunch. It was a heart attack."

"I'm sorry," Shara said.

"Spare me," Andrea said, then laughed. "We had a rich,

full life. I miss the laughter he brought to this house, but it's been ten years. One can't live completely in the past." She pointed out a picture of her two sons and told Shara one was living in Houston and the other in Los Angeles. She had numerous pictures of her seven grandchildren. "I don't get to see them as much as I'd like. My boys were always closer to their father. When he died, they visited far less frequently. And I don't get around like I used to." She put a mask to her mouth and breathed deeply. "Emphysema. I smoked too much for far too long. Not that I regret it for a moment. I know plenty of people who never smoked, seldom if ever drank, ate all the right foods, yet are pushing up daisies while I'm still alive and kicking. You only live once. No time for regrets."

Shara picked up a picture of a young girl she knew was Andrea's daughter.

"Lisbeth," the old woman said. "My baby. She died when she was seven. Her, I miss the most." She paused, as if recalling time spent with her daughter, and sighed. "You didn't come over to look at old pictures, though, did you?"

"Lamar Briggs has been receiving some harassing phone calls," Shara said. "I'd like to ask you a few questions, if it's not too much of an imposition."

"It's not at all, long as you show manners," Andrea said. "It's not like I have anyplace to be. Company is nice, but I've learned to live with myself quite nicely. You, you're not rude. You indulge an old woman." Shara saw a twinkle in Andrea's eye. "That other one strolled across my lawn like it didn't exist. Got no use for them without manners. You . . . I know you're bursting to ask your questions. Still, your interest in me and my family was genuine. I can spot a phony a mile away." She paused to take another whiff of oxygen. "I'm quite fond of Lamar and his family. Of course I'll answer your questions. Don't mind if I sit, do you?"

she asked and walked to an overstuffed armchair near the window without waiting for Shara to answer.

"Can I get you something?" Shara asked when Andrea had sat down.

The old woman smiled. "You needn't—"

"I know," Shara interrupted. "I do have questions, but I don't have to be rude. Now, can I get you something?"

"A feisty one, you are," Andrea said. "A little tea would be nice. And I baked some cookies when I got home. Chocolate chip. But only if you join me. Not to would be rude," she said. Shara noted that same devilish smile from the photos.

Shara came back ten minutes later with two cups of tea and a plate of cookies. They drank in comfortable silence. The cookies were still warm. Soft and chewy like Shara liked them. Also cooked from scratch. Shara hadn't realized how hungry she was.

"I spend most of my time by this window now," Andrea said when Shara had taken the tray back into the kitchen. Shara saw a pile of books on an end table next to the chair. There were best-sellers, non-fiction titles, and a number of mysteries. Conspicuously absent was a copy of the Bible, which made Andrea Dawson even more intriguing. Someone her age not clinging to religion. "Once I sit, I only get up to pee," Andrea said with a laugh, then put the oxygen mask to her mouth and breathed deeply. "Old is fine as long as you got your health. Me . . . I indulge in the little pleasures. A good book. Some television. Seeing people coming and going. You can tell a lot by how people walk. I watch for the mailman, young'uns walking home from school, mothers with their strollers. And I go to Atlantic City with a group of seniors once a month. That's where I was yesterday. I play the slots. Gonna hit the big one, then live the high life," she said, rubbing her hands together. Again she laughed. Shara liked the woman. She didn't take herself too seriously.

"I don't imagine many cars come by," Shara said.

Andrea shook her head. "The people who live on the block, of course. UPS. Fed-Ex. The mailman. It's a quiet street."

"Did you notice anything out of the ordinary recently? A car that didn't belong?" Shara asked.

Andrea Dawson paused a moment in thought. She was so still Shara though she might have fallen asleep. "Now that you mention it, there was one. About a week ago. Yes, he came by real slow, like he was searching for an address. It was around one o'clock. I was watching for the mailman. He comes one-ish." She paused. "I thought it odd because he passed by the next two days around the same time."

Shara leaned forward in her chair. "Didn't it make you suspicious? Did you call the police?"

"Well, he didn't stop. And there were no children outside. If there had been children out, I would have been concerned. You know what I mean. A man cruising for children. Anyway, with Detective Briggs on the block, I wasn't too worried. There's nothing like a policeman across the street to discourage hooligans. I don't get no eggs on my window at Halloween. No vandalism at all on this block. No groups of teens smoking, drinking, or horsing around. I would have called Detective Briggs, but the car stopped coming by."

"Do you recall what kind of car it was?" Shara asked, holding her breath in anticipation.

"A green Saturn," Andrea said without hesitation. "I seen them on TV. *A different kind of car. A different kind of company* or something of the sort is what they say they are. The commercials haven't been on for years, but I still remember them. Something about them just caught my attention." She paused a moment. "They made it seem the company was owned by the workers, and you don't have that much these days." She paused again. "I don't know much about cars nowadays. When I was young, there were far fewer brands. And each had a unique look. When my father drove down to the shore, we'd play a game. Guessing the types of cars. Now it's hard to tell one from the other. But that Saturn commercial, it kinda personalizes the company *and* the car. So I recognize one when I see it. It could have used a wash."

"Did you get a look at the driver?" Shara asked.

"My eyes aren't what they were, child," she said. "Eye doctor wanted to fix me up with these newfangled glasses that adjust for reading *and* seeing far away. But you gotta bob your head up and down to focus," she said, moving her head to demonstrate. "More trouble than they worth. I stick to my reading glasses and take them off when I look outside."

"Can you tell me *anything* about the driver?" Shara asked, politely waiting until Andrea was spent. "Black, white?"

"He was white. I can tell you that. Not much else, sad to say."

"You didn't happen to notice his license plate number?" Shara asked.

Andrea pointed to her eyes and shook her head. "They were Pennsylvania plates. I know that from the color. But letters or numbers, that I can't help you with."

Shara got up. "Thank you very much, Mrs. Daw—Andrea. I appreciate your taking the time to talk to me. Not just about the car either," Shara said.

"Why, thank you, child," Andrea said. "Odd how you got me talking and I know nothing about you," she said. "You're a good listener. You keep people talking so they can't ask about you. Am I right?"

Shara nodded. "You're very perceptive yourself."

"Before you go rushing off, take a dozen of my cookies with you," she said.

"I couldn't," Shara said.

"Nonsense. Give some to Lamar and Alexis," Andrea said. "None to that fool who walked on my lawn, though," she said and laughed. "I shouldn't hold a grudge at my age. Life's too short. But . . . old habits die hard. None of my cookies for that clown."

Shara got the cookies, said goodbye, and left.

Chapter Thirty-Two

"Thought you were going to make a day of it," LeBrea said when Shara returned. Shara saw Cheyenne's car parked on the street. LeBrea would have told her if Cheyenne had found anything important.

"You get more bees with honey," Shara said. "One of my strengths as a bounty hunter is becoming the person I create for a role. Andrea Dawson wanted someone to talk to. I became that person. Immersed myself in the character. She's sweet. I indulged her, but I also left with something we can use."

LeBrea looked at Shara expectantly.

Shara handed him a chocolate chip cookie. "Try it. They're delicious."

"*This* is what you came away with?" LeBrea asked, irritated.

"I'm jerking your chain, LeBrea," Shara said and laughed. She told him about the green Saturn.

"Is she . . . reliable?" LeBrea asked.

"She's old and her health's nothing to brag about, but she's not senile," Shara said. "She's sharp as a tack mentally. She doesn't put on airs. She recalls the car from a commercial. She was upfront with why she couldn't tell me more about the driver or the license plate. But she's a one-woman neighborhood watch. Had he come around when school let out, she would have called Briggs or the police. I'll vouch for her credibility. Bet Briggs will, too."

"Then let's add this to our search," LeBrea said, sounding excited. "Though if it's him, he might have used someone else's car."

"No, he wouldn't," Shara said. "First, he's a loner, remember. And from what we've learned, he came out here on impulse. He didn't think it out. Didn't rent a car. It's his car, Paul. And this is our guy. Call it gut instinct, but we might have finally caught a break."

Shara went to find Cheyenne. She was in the backyard with Alexis next to a sickly-looking tree. Cheyenne was laughing. The sun was on Cheyenne's flowing brown hair making it look even more red and radiant than the day before. Shara also noticed that Cheyenne dressed in earth tones. Alexis said something Shara couldn't hear and signed to Cheyenne. To Shara's amazement, Cheyenne signed back. Then it dawned on Shara. She was jealous of Cheyenne. Shara didn't want Cheyenne in Alexis's life. It was selfish, even immature, but her relationship with Alexis was unique. Cheyenne was an interloper.

Cheyenne turned as if reading Shara's mind. She waved a greeting, and both she and Alexis walked toward Shara.

"I brought LeBrea information on the two guys you had me check out. Both dead ends, sad to say. I got a chance to meet Alexis, though," Cheyenne said. "She's everything you told me and more."

What have I told Cheyenne about Alexis? Shara wondered. She tucked the thought away. This wasn't the time. The clock was ticking on Renee. "We may have a new lead," Shara told them both. She told them about the green Saturn Andrea Dawson had seen. "She sent over some cookies, by the way," Shara said to Alexis.

"Chocolate chip?" Alexis asked.

Shara nodded.

"They're to die for," Alexis said.

"You might want to tell her that yourself," Shara said, sounding peevish and regretting it.

Alexis looked at her without seeming to comprehend.

Drop it, Shara told herself, but ignored the warning. "When is the last time you spent time with her?" Shara asked.

"I've been pretty busy since I recovered," Alexis said.

"Self-absorbed," Shara said. "Justifiably so," she added when she saw a flash of hurt in Alexis's eyes. "She just seems really fond of you and pretty lonely."

"She taught me how to bake brownies from scratch," Alexis said. "I'll make some for all of us and bring her a plate." She paused. "Thanks for setting me straight. I have been into myself lately. Like you said, rightly so. So many changes occurring so quickly." She looked at Cheyenne. "Shara doesn't treat me with kid gloves. She says what's on her mind. Sometimes it stings, but her brutal honesty is what I often need." She smiled. "My parents still treat me like a porcelain doll. Shara treats me like a rag doll. Tosses me around when I'm too full of myself."

Shara rolled her eyes, both embarrassed by the praise Alexis had heaped on her and feeling foolish for the pang of jealousy she'd felt earlier. Cheyenne was no threat to Shara. And Alexis needed to forge new relationships.

"Have you seen the war room?" Shara asked Cheyenne, referring to Briggs's study.

Cheyenne shook her head. "Briggs was taking a break when I arrived. We spoke in the living room."

"Let me show you and see if Briggs has anyone else for you to check out," Shara said.

Cheyenne seemed mesmerized by the notes on the chalkboard and paper on the walls. All the raw data was there. On one wall, however, LeBrea had organized the most pertinent information. Cheyenne ignored that. She was drawn to what had been discussed in their brainstorming sessions.

"Mind if I underline a few things and offer my two-cents?" Cheyenne asked LeBrea.

"Knock yourself out," LeBrea said. "We've been staring at the same material for so long, we could use a fresh perspective.

Cheyenne roamed around the room, seemingly taking everything in. Then she came back to the chalkboard. Cheyenne underlined the word a*mateur*, then *impulsive*. She stood back a minute then underlined the word *trigger*. "Have you isolated the trigger yet?" she asked.

"The trigger is Briggs's reinstatement to the police force," LeBrea said.

"But how did the kidnapper find out about it? *When* did he find out about it?" She paused. "Okay, he's impulsive, right. He didn't plan this out. He got the urge and just did it. And he acted like a rank amateur. But why now? There was no major announcement when Briggs was reinstated. You haven't been involved in any headline-grabbing case, have you?" she asked, looking at Briggs.

Briggs shook his head.

Alexis, who had been observing, went to a corner of the room where a stack of papers lay. She looked through them for several minutes then held up the front page of the *Inquirer* that had a major article on scandals that continued to rock the police department. "Two weeks ago," she said, then showed them a second article buried deep within the paper. "It mentions your reinstatement," she said, looking at her father.

"So we have someone who's pissed that Briggs got a second chance when he didn't," Cheyenne continued, underlining the word *second chance*. "This guy who never got his second chance for some wrong blames Briggs. He's learned about Briggs's good fortune from the paper. He stews for a couple of weeks. He even drove by Briggs's house on several occasions," she said, underlining the words *green Saturn*, which LeBrea had added when Shara went outside to find Cheyenne. "And finally he acted on impulse. He just couldn't take it anymore." She paused, then underlined *amateur* again. "What if he was arrested but never charged? Or tried and acquitted? Or the case was dropped for lack of evidence? The point is, the guy's life was ruined by the charges themselves. You know the accusation made page one, but when the case was dismissed or whatever, it was buried with the obituaries, if it was mentioned at all. You've been looking for felons who served time. Maybe this guy didn't. He would have learned how to be a more accomplished criminal in prison, not the amateur he appears." Cheyenne shrugged. "Or maybe not."

"Forget the maybe not," LeBrea said. "It's another avenue to explore. Briggs, you recall anyone fitting that profile?" He circled the word *amateur* that Cheyenne had underlined. "This has always bothered me. What if your alarm system had been activated? What if you had a dog? It's not someone you know or anyone who has been stalking you over a period of time. Otherwise Renee wouldn't have been snatched. So our perp on impulse breaks a window, saunters in, goes to your room, and *only then* stops to decide what the hell he wants to do. Kill you or . . . a light bulb goes off in his head, and he decides to grab your daughter. About as amateur as it comes. If this guy had served any time in prison, no way would he enter a cop's house as he did."

"But, like you said, he acted impulsively," Briggs said.

"Even a fool learns in prison," LeBrea said. "Like Cheyenne said, he would have learned to be a better criminal. Not this guy."

Briggs leaned back and closed his eyes. Three times he opened them and jotted down a name on a pad. The phone rang as he was writing. Picking it up, he mouthed to them it was Rios. They talked for a minute and he wrote down a fourth name. He went to a wall where there was a blank piece of paper and wrote down three names then left a space and wrote a fourth.

"These first three fit Cheyenne's profile. Three good arrests. Only they were innocent."

"And the fourth?" LeBrea asked.

"A parolee with a grudge. We hadn't gotten to him yet," Briggs said. "He's white, graduated high school, and . . . owns a Saturn. That was what Rios was calling about." Briggs returned to his computer. After a moment, he looked up. "Cheyenne, cross out the first name," Briggs said. "He's in prison *now* for manslaughter." Two minutes later Briggs sighed. "Cross out the second. Died two years ago. A suicide." The third name took longer. "Hmmm," Briggs finally said. "This last one has never served time. He's alive and in Philly." Briggs picked up the phone and called Nina Rios. He asked her to check with the Department of Motor Vehicles to see what model of car he drove and his current address. "Oh," he mentioned just before disconnecting. "I've got a file on him. I'll send someone over for it. Thanks a lot, Nina." He turned his attention to the others. "Who wants my parolee? Earl Bartram," Briggs said, after finding his file.

"I'll take it," Cheyenne said.

"Tread lightly," LeBrea said. "We don't want to spook him."

"Gotcha," Cheyenne said and left.

The phone rang three minutes after Cheyenne had left. It was Rios. When Briggs hung up, he looked from LeBrea to Shara to Alexis. "Drives a Saturn and lives in town. Like the other, we don't know the color of the car.

The DMV has just so much information. Shara, want to give this to Rudy?"

"I'll take this one myself," Shara said. "I've been cooped up here, a couch potato, reacting to what's gone down. Time I did what I do best."

"Nina has a file on him. I remember the case, but there are some particulars that escape me that you may need," Briggs said.

"Tell me about him, Briggs," Shara said. "Why does he hate your guts?"

"I'd forgotten all about him," Briggs said. "He was an infinitely forgettable man. Let me see. He was around thirty-five years old. Married with two young daughters. This was fifteen years ago, give or take. We caught a body of a stripper in Fairmount Park. A jogger found her. There had been no great effort to hide the body. Nude. Raped. Beaten to death. The perp kept beating her long after she was dead, according to the M.E. Lots of anger. And the M.E. said it was personal. You don't beat someone that bad out of blind rage unless you know that person and feel wronged.

"Norman Flowers was a successful publicist at an up-and-coming Center City PR firm," Briggs went on. "Good family man, but he was a regular at a strip club in Pennsauken, New Jersey, just across the Walt Whitman Bridge. That's where the girl worked. Gina Meloni was her name, but she was Gigi when she worked." Briggs paused. Shara thought he was trying to remember the details.

"She was his *special* girl," Shara said. When Briggs looked at her, she elaborated. "I managed an upscale strip club when Lysette was ill, remember? Some girls cultivate regular customers. They feel special and reward the dancer with bigger tips and sometimes other presents."

Briggs nodded. "It's all coming back to me in a rush," he said. "So many cases, but each one is tucked away. It's like taking out a file. Now that it's out, it's like it was yesterday. Gigi was a pretty young thing, no more than twenty. She was beaten something fierce, now that I recall. Seemed Flowers gravitated to her and eventually frequented the club only when she worked. Gigi told friends Flowers was her Sugar Daddy. Aside from the good tips you mentioned, yeah, he lavished her with gifts."

"Did they have a relationship outside of the club?" Shara asked. It was frowned upon by management at most clubs. Most girls kept their personal and professional lives separate, but it wasn't unheard of for a deeper relationship to form.

"No, it was all at the club. But he was possessive. More and more he'd monopolize her time, then get angry when she spent time with other customers. More than once he was warned to behave or he'd be excluded from the club. Gigi or Gina was no angel herself. She got greedy. Flowers made good money, but he exaggerated. She extorted him. Threatened to tell his wife they were having an affair if he didn't buy her silence. Then she was offed."

"Did she keep a diary?" Shara asked. "How did you find all of this out?"

Briggs tapped his head. "She wasn't the brightest girl in the world. She kept no diary, but she told one of the other girls. She showed off her expensive jewelry. Bragged how Flowers had become putty in her hands. Later she told this co-worker she was sick of his presuming she was his and only his. Said she wouldn't have gone to his wife. If he paid her off that would have been a bonus, but one way or the other, she would be free of him.

"When her body was found and we talked with her co-workers, well, Flowers was a logical suspect. He didn't have an alibi. He admitted being at the club the night she was killed. And, yes, she had extorted him. He'd gone driving trying to figure out what to do. He had abrasions on one hand. Said he'd punched a wall in anger at being played by the bitch. He couldn't remember where, though. He said he'd been in a blind rage but he hadn't gone back to the club after her shift. He had a history of violence. Nothing major, but there had been a few bar room brawls when he was younger and an altercation with a roommate while at college. And he punched out a guy he thought was coming onto his wife in a restaurant. It seemed like a slam dunk. We . . . I arrested him. It made the front page of the papers and was the lead story on the evening news."

"But he was innocent," Shara said.

Briggs nodded. "He was remanded without bail. It was a pretty heinous murder. Three months later, a girl walks in and says her boyfriend bragged to her about killing this dancer. Turned out it was Gina's old boyfriend. The new girl was also a dancer. She got scared and dropped a dime on him."

"He hadn't been a suspect?" Shara asked.

"For a New York minute," Briggs said. "He had an alibi. Let's see," Briggs said and closed his eyes again. "He was watching a basketball game at a friend's house. He had no history of violence. No record whatsoever. I fucked up. What can I say? We brought the boyfriend in and he caved almost immediately. Before we brought him in, we talked to his buddy, and he admitted he lied about the alibi. The boyfriend had killed Gina in a jealous rage. He hadn't liked her baring her pussy to strangers, especially this one dude she'd told him about. Flowers. She'd show him the gifts he'd given her, gifts the boyfriend could never afford. No way the boyfriend could compete with Flowers. He worked for a messenger service. She said if he really loved her, he'd buy her gifts like her Sugar Daddy. When they made love the night she was killed, she called him her Sugar Daddy. He went ballistic."

"Didn't you find his semen?" Shara asked.

"You Flowers defense attorney?" Briggs asked.

"It's just not like you to be sloppy," Shara said.

"He wore a rubber," Briggs said. "He really thought she screwed this guy and others at the club. He told us he didn't know what diseases they carried and he wasn't about to get the clap or something worse. So he wore a rubber when they fucked."

"You let this guy slide because you were certain Flowers was the perp," Shara said.

"Maybe, but we *did* interrogate the boyfriend initially," Briggs said. "I pushed him hard, but he came off as being accepting of Gina's occupation. He didn't come by the club and hover like some boyfriends. Gina hadn't told anyone he had a problem with her profession. Hell, maybe she wasn't even aware. He agreed with her that it paid well. When they had a nice nest egg, they'd marry and she promised to quit. With his alibi, no priors, and no history of violence, he was in the clear."

"So Flowers never went to trial," Shara said.

"It's like Cheyenne said. When the boyfriend copped to the murder, it didn't make the front page. I remember reading the *Inquirer*. You had to turn to something like page twenty before Flowers was even mentioned."

"Was his life ruined?" Shara asked.

Briggs shrugged. "I have no idea, though from his new address I would tend to think so."

Shara took the paper he handed her with his address and looked at Briggs.

"He had a home in Lower Merion when he was arrested. Now he's living on 11th near South. Quite a come down. He *could* be our guy," Briggs said. "But he's stayed out of trouble for fifteen years. I don't know if someone could harbor such resentment for that long a period of time. It might be a wild goose chase."

"I'll let you know," Shara said. "Look, I gotta get out and do something even if I come up empty. The waiting is eating me up. It just makes me dwell on what Renee could be going through."

As Shara headed for the door, Alexis stopped her.

"What if it's him?" Alexis asked. "You catch him with Renee. What then?"

Shara knew what Alexis meant. "I'll cross that bridge when I come to it," Shara said.

"You could end up in jail," Alexis said. "Think of Renee before you administer your own brand of justice."

"That's dirty pool," Shara said. "Making me focus on Renee."

"You were by my side in my time of need. Without you, I'd never be whole. Don't you owe the same to Renee? She'll need you when this is over."

"You've made your point," Shara said. She gave Alexis a hug. "Thanks for forcing me to look at the big picture. I can't promise I won't hurt the fucker if I find him, but I'll return him in one piece."

Driving to Center City, Shara had no idea what she would do if Flowers was her man and she found him with Renee. She knew Alexis was right. But deep within her was another Shara Farris, one who had been tormented for years after her half-brother had brutalized her. That Shara was an avenger, a murderer. If that part of her surfaced again, she might be uncontrollable.

Shara stopped briefly at the Roundhouse, the central headquarters of the Philadelphia Police Department. Nina Rios gave her a file on Flowers.

The reclamation of South Street into a tourist attraction didn't extend to housing south of South Street. Norman Flowers lived only a few blocks from The Haven, a shelter for battered women where Shara had met Renee. Flowers's three-story building hadn't been renovated and was a sad sight.

It was still unseasonably warm for December in the low fifties. A solitary man, as decrepit as the building, sat outside on a folding chair reading the sports section of the *Daily News*. He winked at Shara as she entered. The stairs groaned as Shara climbed. The walls were covered with graffiti. The stench of fried fish was strong. There were two doors on the third floor. 3B was Flowers. Shara knocked. No reply. She removed a pick from her jeans pocket and in less than thirty seconds was in Norman Flowers's apartment.

It must have come furnished was Shara's first thought. The furniture was mismatched. A red arm chair was threadbare and stained. It faced a twelve-inch RCA TV. A card table and folding chairs sat in the kitchen. The refrigerator looked ancient, yet it was amply stocked. Shara picked up a half gallon of milk. It wouldn't expire for another two weeks. Flowers had bought it no more than a week before. *Impulsive*, Shara thought. If he were the kidnapper, he had gone on with his daily routine and had acted without premeditation.

In a cramped bedroom, there was only a bed and a dresser. The only photos on the top of the dresser were of Norman Flowers from fifteen years earlier—the same Norman Flowers in the mug shot in the file Nina Rios had given her. There was a photo with Flowers, a woman Shara assumed was his wife and two young girls, his daughters, Shara was certain, taken at Sears. A formal family portrait. Additional photos of his wife and children littered the dresser top, but all were from some distant past. Shara lifted one photo that seemed out of place. The frame was new. A girl, maybe eighteen, stared at Shara solemnly. No time to dwell on it now, Shara decided.

Next, it was into the bathroom and what Shara sought. Over the sink, next to the mirror, was taped the news article Alexis had showed them earlier. Highlighted in yellow was mention of Lamar Briggs's reinstatement to the Philadelphia Police Department. Shara could imagine Norman Flowers staring at it daily as he shaved. Norman Flowers had kidnapped Renee. But where the hell was he? Shara expertly searched the drawers of the dresser in Flowers's room, a bureau in the living room, and all drawers in the kitchen for clues but came up empty.

She left the apartment and carefully made her way downstairs. Maybe he had Renee in the basement, though Shara doubted it. She believed in her fever dreams. There were no trees surrounding the building. This wasn't a cottage or cabin. The door to the basement opened as easily as the apartment above. Just a storage facility, Shara saw. Spider webs near the entrance told Shara nobody had been down in months. There were no windows. There was no set of stairs like in her dream.

What now? Shara thought. She should call LeBrea. The combined resources of the police and FBI could be mobilized to locate the cottage or cabin where Flowers held Renee. But she hesitated as she recalled the final fever dream. Renee's throat slit. Flowers killing himself as the police and Feds surrounded his lair. Involve LeBrea and the FBI now and Renee would die. She'd try to locate the cabin on her own. For the first time since the kidnapping, Shara felt she had gained a semblance of control. She was in her element. She could stalk the bastard. She had the tools. Bring in the cavalry and she was back where she started. Helpless. It was time to check the file Rios had given her for clues.

Shara walked outside. The man in the folding chair stared at her. "You're not the police," he said with a hideous smile. He had several teeth missing in both the top and bottom of his mouth. Several others were brown from tobacco stains, one or two almost blackened. He hissed when he spoke. "You don't smell police, walk police, or act police," he continued. "Hell, breaking and entering into Norman Flowers's apartment ain't something the police would do." As he finished, he spat tobacco juice on the ground.

He was short, even shorter than Shara, but his upper body was muscular. His face and arms were deeply tanned, his hands calloused. He looked to be nearing fifty.

"I'm a bounty hunter," Shara said. "I can come and go as I damn well please." Shara hoped he'd buy the line. *If* there had been an outstanding warrant on Norman Flowers, she *could* have entered without permission and without a warrant. What she'd done was breaking and entering; illegal, plain and simple.

"Norman finally got hisself into trouble, huh?" the man asked and stuffed another wad of chewing tobacco in his mouth. "Name's Jack Ciani, by the way. Everyone calls me Money, though. Long story short, I was a jockey. Not half bad either, but after one too many falls, well, I can't ride no horse anymore. I *do* know my horses, though. Make my living betting on the nags. Do all right, especially with exactas and trifectas. Got me the name Money because I'm right more than I'm wrong, and I don't mind sharing my expertise." He paused. "Didn't catch yours."

"Is Norman the type to get into trouble," Shara asked, not answering the man's question.

"Not normally," Money said. "Until recently, he seemed to have the fight knocked out of him. Lived here going on five years now and kept mostly to hisself. Last few weeks, though, he was talking up a storm. Pissed as hell about some cop getting his job back on the police force. Told me how the cop had fucked him up and ruined his life, pardon my French. What's he gone and done?"

"He have a green Saturn?" Shara asked, again ignoring Money's question.

"You're a cool one," the man said, then deposited some tobacco juice on the ground. "Get me to do all the talking, but got nothing to say in return. My mouth's getting parched and my memory's getting kinda hazy, if you get my drift."

Shara kept five twenties in her jeans pocket. She had more money if she needed it, but she wanted her sources to think there was a limit to what she could spend. She gave Money a twenty. "You're memory getting any better?"

"Yeah, he has a green Saturn." Money pointed across the street. "That there's his unofficial parking spot. He'd put milk crates in the space when he left and spot me a ten to make sure they stayed there. Been gone for two days now."

"That unusual?" Shara asked.

"He goes someplace once a year. For four or five days. But he tells whoever's out here ahead of time. Not this time, though."

"So he has a second home. Maybe a cabin for vacations?" Shara asked.

Money shrugged. "Know nothing about that."

"He see his wife and kids often?" Shara asked.

Money laughed. "You don't know a hell of a lot about him, do you? His wife up and left with his two girls . . . I don't know, some fifteen years ago, I think. Leastwise, that's what he says. She's someplace in the Midwest. And it's his ex-wife."

Shara was going to thank Money and check out Flowers's files when she saw the man smile."Norman does see one of his girls, though. She's a student at Temple. Betcha didn't know that, didya Miss Bounty Hunter?"

"You wouldn't happen to have an address on her at school, would you, Money?" Shara asked.

Money extended his hand. "I can do better than that. I can tell you where she works. Ain't far away either."

Shara gave him two more twenties. He stared at the remaining two bills in Shara's hand, then shrugged. "She works at CondomNation on South Street. Know where it is?"

Shara nodded. She described the girl in the new picture in Flowers's apartment.

"That be her," Money said. "Only been by once or twice lately, though. Don't say squat to the likes of me. Not even a 'hi' or a nod of the head."

"Maybe she's shy," Shara said.

"She's got that pissed-at-the-world look, if you ask me," Money said.

Shara gave the man one more twenty and her card. "If Flowers returns, call me at that number, okay, Money. I'll make it worth your while."

"Who am I to turn down a sweetheart like you," he said and spat some more juice on the ground.

Shara held out her last twenty. "And I was never here," Shara said.

"Who was never here?" Money said, took the money, and let out another belly laugh. "Take care of yourself, Sweetheart. You bet on the nags, come on by and I'll give you a tip."

"I just might do that, Money. Thanks for your help," Shara said and made her way to South Street.

Chapter Thirty-Three

Shara knew she had no more than an hour before she'd have to call LeBrea. She would have to stall for time when she did call, mislead him if necessary. If she told him the truth, the last fever dream could become a reality. Mislead him, she thought. Just like she had done with Deidre. It was the right thing to do, but the thought didn't comfort her. LeBrea deserved better. But Shara's fever dream guided her actions. To do otherwise could mean Renee's death.

Toward the east end of South Street was CondomNation, a sort of sex toys superstore. If a woman wanted a vibrator, for instance, there were literally dozens to choose from. Shara couldn't see their allure. In the dozen years from the time of her feigned suicide when she was eleven until Clay Fluery had entered her life, in more ways than one, she had been perfectly content to let her fingers do the walking. But to each her own, she thought.

Walking into the store, or boutique, as it was referred to as if the word added class, Shara spotted Rose Flowers stocking one of the aisles. Nina Rios's file told her little about the girl and it was obviously dated. The girl stocking, though, was the same one as in the photo in Norman Flowers's apartment. She was pasty, anorexic-looking, a plain girl with straight shoulder-length black hair. Shara walked over to her.

"Rose Flowers?" Shara asked.

"Melissa Flowers," the girl shot back, her face turning red.

"Really," Shara said sarcastically. The girl had changed her name, Shara thought. Why?

"Rose *Melissa* Flowers," the girl said with a sigh. "My parents felt Rose Flowers sounded . . . quaint," she said with a shrug. "I was the butt of jokes until I was nine. Then it was Melissa. What's it to you anyway?"

Shara knew she had to gain the girl's trust. Rose Melissa Flowers might protect her father even though they might still be estranged. Shara would lie if she had to. She didn't give a damn about Flowers's daughter. Renee was her priority. Rose Melissa Flowers clearly had issues. Shara would play on them.

"The piercings, tattoos, and brandings, are they because of your father or mother?" Shara asked, ignoring the girl's question. Melissa Flowers was a walking pincushion. Her lip was pierced with a small, round ring. When she talked, Shara saw her tongue carried a stud. There were rings in her right eyebrow and left ear. Shara wondered if they helped balance her head and almost laughed aloud.

The girl wore a transparent plastic dress with a white swatch of cloth covering small breasts and another cloth strategically placed to cover her pubic area and ass. When she bent down to pick up an enormous black dildo, her breasts were exposed. A ring adorned one of her nipples. There was another in her navel. She must have known what bending down exposed, but she seemed unfazed.

Melissa looked at Shara, knowing she was being scrutinized. She tugged at her dress. "Both my parents are a piece of work," she said. "Who the fuck are you anyway?"

"Your father's fucked up big time," Shara said. "With your help, I might be able to save his sorry ass. So, the decorations, who is responsible?"

"It's a fashion statement, not a form of rebellion," Melissa said.

"Have it your way," Shara said. "Seems like you don't give a damn what happens to your father." Shara turned as if to leave.

"I didn't say that," Melissa said a bit too quickly. "What has he done?"

"Why did your mother leave your father?" Shara asked.

"Do you always answer a question with a question?" Melissa asked.

Shara pointed to her watch. "The clock's ticking on your father. I don't have time for a get-to-know-you chat."

"How will knowing why my parents split help my father?" Melissa asked.

This time, Shara did answer the question. "To help him, I need to understand him. The more I know, the better chance I have to reach him. My knowing about your father improves his chance of survival. Or do you want him dead?" It was as close to the truth as Shara would admit to this stranger. As a bounty hunter, Shara usually had plenty of time to learn what made her quarry tick, what he was capable of, his habits, and his strengths and weaknesses. With Norman Flowers, Shara had hours. Something Melissa told her now could be crucial later.

Melissa shook her head. "I hardly know my father, but I don't want him dead. I came back to Philly for college in part to reconnect with my dad. Why do you care whether he lives or dies?" she asked.

"He was fucked over by the police once," Shara said. "Doesn't seem right that it happens again. You ready to talk?" Shara asked.

"Not here. Over lunch. I'm starving," Melissa said.

"Where to?" Shara asked.

"McDonald's, of course," Melissa said. "I know I don't look like it, but I get off on fast food. A Big Mac, fries, and a shake. You pay, I'll talk."

Melissa's greeting by the staff when she walked up to the McDonald's counter was like the character Norm walking into the bar at Cheers on television. Everyone who worked there knew her by name, and her presence seemed to brighten their day. Maybe she had more depth to her than Shara had first assumed.

Melissa didn't nibble nor even eat her food. She attacked it voraciously. You couldn't honestly say she had ketchup with her fries. It was more like fries with her ketchup. She emptied a dozen of the plastic ketchup packets onto her fries, then went back for another half dozen. She answered Shara's questions with her mouth full. After all, she got just half an hour for lunch so she could leave CondomNation at three for a 4 p.m. class at Temple.

"So why did your mother leave your father?" Shara asked. Her own burger was dry and tasteless, the fries a little too limp for her taste. She sipped a cup of watered-down Diet Coke.

"I was only three," Melissa said between bites. "Most of what I know I heard from my mother. My older sister was only five, so her memory isn't too good either."

"Your sister April," Shara said.

"Yeah, another one of my parent's great ideas. *April Flowers*. She kept her name, though," Melissa said.

Shara wanted to kick herself. Give this girl an opening and she had a story to relate. Shara didn't want to sidetrack her any more than necessary. "So your mother left because . . . ."

"My father lost his job after his arrest. Even though he was vindicated, nobody seemed to want a publicist tainted by the murder of a stripper. He looked for work for something like three months, eating up all of our savings. My mother had to get a job as a secretary, and he became Mr. Mom. He began drinking. My mom says he was a pretty heavy social drinker before his arrest. Now he woke up to a beer and worked his way up to hard liquor before dinner. He was an angry drunk. He never hit any of us, but he yelled and argued often with my mother. *That* I remember. Not what they argued about, but just that there was a lot of yelling. He went to bars at night. Someone would usually drive him home at closing. He was too drunk to find his own way home. From what my mother told us, he was forever bemoaning his fate. That was her word—*bemoaning*. She eventually had enough. She had married a successful up-and-coming businessman. Now we were on the verge of losing our home. She moved to Michigan and soon after divorced him. We lived with her parents while she worked so she could rent a decent apartment for us."

Melissa looked down and saw she had no more food. She looked up at Shara with big blue eyes, a bit out of proportion with the rest of her face. Shara could read her mind. "Here," Shara said, holding a ten-dollar bill. "My treat as long as you keep talking." Shara had been wrong to think Melissa was anorexic. She had some metabolism, though. From the looks of her, she didn't exercise a hell of a lot.

Melissa returned with seconds of all she had already eaten along with a stack of ketchup packets.

"So you blame your dad," Shara said, looking at Melissa's many facial and body ornaments.

"A fashion statement," Melissa said, her mouth full. "I already told you *both* my parents were a piece of work. I grew up with my mom, so I *know* her shortcomings firsthand." She paused while taking a bite from her burger. "You know how some people can't be alone?" she continued. "They break up and rebound to some other guy a few weeks later?" Melissa said.

Shara nodded.

"Well, my mom did that one better. She kept getting married. Two months after she left her parents' home, she remarried. Divorced him two years later. Then within three months, she married yet again. April and I didn't factor into her decisions. It was all about *her* needs. The third marriage lasted a little less than three years. After she divorced, she wised up. She began having affairs with married men. It was far safer. There was no fear of commitment. These men were married. She was never alone again. She had three affairs, one lasting five years. Can you believe it, some stupid bitch not knowing or not caring that her husband was bedding another woman for five years?"

Melissa asked Shara if she would get her some more ketchup. Shara was glad for the distraction. It was time to cut to the chase. Melissa, though, had other ideas.

"My mom told me and April *all* about her men friends," Melissa said, pouring ketchup on what remained of her fries. "And did I tell you how loud she was in bed? She'd be making love, and the noise echoed through our apartment. Is it any wonder I lost my virginity at twelve?" She suddenly stopped and looked at Shara. "Why the fuck am I telling you all this? It's not relevant."

"Maybe because nobody else ever asked or cared for your opinion," Shara said. "And I'm a good listener." Wanting to move on, Shara decided against asking about the piercings again. She knew it was a cry for attention. She didn't need Melissa's validation. "Did you really come back to Philly to reconnect with your dad?" Shara asked.

"My mom wasn't any great role model, right," Melissa said. "So maybe she had bad-mouthed my father. You know, exaggerated. Maybe he didn't know where we were, which is why he never contacted us. So, yeah, I decided to go to Temple so I could spend time with him."

"How did it work out?" Shara asked.

"The first two months were totally awesome," Melissa said, polishing off her shake. "I located him in the phonebook and just knocked on his door one day. It was all awkward and shit for a while, but we were getting along real well until a few weeks ago." She paused. "You think I can have some apple pie?" she asked. "It's to—"

"Die for, I know," Shara said with a smile. She handed Melissa two singles. Melissa returned with a pie and her third shake.

"What happened the last few weeks?" Shara asked.

"He turned angry and sullen all of a sudden. He began talking about this cop who was the cause of all his heartache. He'd been kicked off the police force and then allowed to return. It was just plain wrong, my father kept saying. I went over to his place less and less. He didn't call. It was like he no longer cared."

"Like he was obsessed," Shara said.

"Yeah. *Obsessed*, that's the word. He forgot all about me. I saw him last week, but he was going out somewhere and gave me the bum's rush. Then I got pissed when he called to apologize and told him I was going to transfer at the end of the semester. To tell you the truth, I've been thinking about it, but I really hadn't made a firm decision."

Shara waited a minute for Melissa to finish her pie and shake, then hoped she'd have Melissa's undivided attention. That is if she didn't want something else to eat. "This is important, Melissa," Shara said, then paused until the girl was looking at her. "Your father had to sell his house in Lower Merion. Was there any place you remember him taking you when you were young? You know, a second home? A summer cottage?"

Melissa scrunched up her nose. "My mom told me once that every summer we'd go to Dorney Park and Wild Water Kingdom. I was only three, but I *do* remember going at least once. April used to tell me about it. We'd *did* have a cabin. We'd get up early before the crowds arrived. We'd stay late after most others had left. At times we had the place almost to ourselves. Then we'd go to a cabin my dad had bought to spend the night."

"Did April tell you where it was?" Shara asked, holding her breath.

Melissa looked stumped for a moment, then brightened. "My mom talked about it once when I was ten. She and her . . . man friend were going to bring us east for a vacation. My mom thought my dad might still have the cabin. She was telling me and April about a road leading to the park after you got off the turnpike. If you took a left, you'd get to the park. If you took a right . . . went down two, no *three* lights, there was a road . . . the third right after the third light," she said excitedly. "I remember it because of all the threes. She even mentioned a spare key in a birdhouse my father had built."

"You never took the trip, though," Shara said.

"Mom's man friend broke up with her," Melissa said. "I think the thought of a full week with my mom scared him off. Like she was asking for a commitment he couldn't or didn't want to make. Funny thing is, my mom just wanted to go on a vacation." Melissa looked at her watch. "Shit, I gotta get back to work. Was I any help?"

More than you can imagine, Shara wanted to say, but shrugged instead. "It's a long shot, but I'll check it out."

"You'll try to help my dad?" Melissa asked.

Shara wondered why Melissa hadn't asked what trouble her father was in. Maybe she didn't want to know. "I'll do what I can," Shara said noncommittally. Shara had one other question and felt a fool for even wondering about it. But her curiosity got the better of her. "I see you have a navel ring. Uh, do you have one—"

"Through my clit?" Melissa said with a laugh. "I get asked that all the time. I thought about it. I almost went and did the deed when I got here. The *ultimate* fashion statement," she said with a laugh. "Once I got here, a lot of my anger left me. Things with my dad were cool. College is great. I've got loads of friends. It seemed a little much.

And where do you go after that? Even with things with my father souring, I think I'll leave a piece of me metal free." Melissa got up, again looking at her watch. "Come by the store anytime," she said. "Maybe we can . . . you know, talk again."

"And have lunch," Shara said with a wink. Melissa laughed and dashed off. The last had been a lie. Melissa reminded Shara a bit of Deidre Caffrey's sister, Denise, and J'aime, whom she had met just a few weeks before. Denise, in particular, talked about herself as if no one else existed. It was exhausting. Shara felt the same way talking to Melissa. She was very into herself, as were most eighteen-year-olds. And Melissa seemed to need someone to open up to. She had led one very fucked up life. Melissa might one day mature and let someone get a word in edgewise. It wouldn't be Shara, though.

Chapter Thirty-Four

Shara had what she needed. Now she had to play for time. A call to LeBrea was in order, but what should she say? She'd been gone almost two hours. Any further delay would raise suspicions. She made the call from her cell phone once she'd gotten onto the Schuylkill Expressway. In less than two hours, she'd be at Norman Flowers's cabin.

Shara could hear LeBrea's anticipation when he answered the phone. "Give me some good news," he said.

"Did Cheyenne come up with anything on Bartram?" Shara asked. Inquiring about other suspect, would help keep LeBrea off the scent.

"Only that he's been cheating on his wife and there will be hell to pay," LeBrea said, sounding deflated.

"Did Briggs come up with anyone else?" Shara asked.

"I never knew a man who had so many enemies," LeBrea said. "We have three more possibles, but I'm not optimistic. Was Flowers a dead end?" he asked, sounding tired, almost defeated. Shara felt guilty, but the fever dream kept her from saying anything.

"Don't get too excited, but don't cross Flowers off your list," Shara said. "He hasn't been to his apartment the past two days. Someone I talked to says he still harbors animosity against Briggs. And he's still got the Saturn, and it's green."

"Any idea where he could be?" LeBrea asked.

"I'm going to Barnes & Noble on 18th and Walnut now to see if he's at work. Rios added that to the file she gave me. Meanwhile, you might want to get a search warrant for his apartment."

"On what basis? Us cops need probable cause," LeBrea said.

"He hasn't been home, the Saturn, and his grudge against Briggs," Shara said. Send one of your detectives to speak to a guy named Money. He'll be right outside the building. He was the one who told me Flowers was still pissed at Briggs. Then find a friendly judge."

"I can get it done," LeBrea said after a moment's pause. Shara could hear his excitement building. "What's your gut say?" he asked.

"He *could* be our man, but I don't want to jump the gun," Shara said. "If we put all our resources into Flowers and it turns out we're wrong, that window we have might disappear on us. Let's see what the warrant turns up."

Shara heard some commotion in the background, and then Briggs was on the line. "I'm alone in my study, Shara," Briggs said. "Level with me. Is Flowers our man?"

"It's like I told LeBrea: it's possible," Shara said. "LeBrea needs to search Flowers's apartment."

"You know that will take time—getting that warrant," Briggs said. "An hour, maybe more."

"Yeah, but he needs to search Flowers's apartment," Shara said.

"And you didn't," Briggs said. "It wasn't a question."

Shara remained silent.

"I've worked with you for almost two years, Shara," Briggs said. "You searched his apartment. You found something. Tell me I'm full of shit."

"Nothing definitive," Shara said, but she knew she sounded lame. She could easily fool LeBrea, who didn't know her, but Briggs was another story. He knew her all too well.

"I know you, Shara," Briggs said, as if reading Shara's mind. "You're onto something. I can hear it in your voice. That crap about a search warrant. You've been in Flowers's apartment. You found something or you wouldn't have asked LeBrea to get a warrant and do it legal. You're stalling for time. Flowers is our man. What are you holding back? And why the hell do you want to do this solo?"

"You gotta trust me on this, Briggs," Shara said.

"Not good enough," Briggs said. "You're too emotionally involved. Will you be able to live with yourself if you make a foolish mistake?"

Shara turned onto the Blue Route, which would take her to the Pennsylvania Turnpike. She had to get Briggs off her back. "Talk to Alexis. Tell her I said it was okay for her to tell you about the fever dream I had. But *only* you."

"Fever dream?" Briggs asked. "What are you—?"

"There's no time to explain," Shara said. "Just talk to Alexis. I'll call you in an hour, ninety minutes tops," she said, then disconnected.

Chapter Thirty-Five

Renee was awake when her captor returned this time. She saw he was cradling a cat. He had a saucer in one hand, the cat in the other. Renee didn't know much about cats. She had had only one pet in her life. Her father had bought her a turtle when she was seven. When he asked her to name it, she had shrugged. "Let's just call it Turtle," she said. Her father had shrugged. "Turtle the turtle it is then." Only Turtle didn't hang around very long. Renee kept him in a shallow turtle bowl her father had bought along with some food. Turtle spent a lot of time doing nothing, and Renee quickly tired of him. One day she looked in his bowl and he was gone. She and her father had searched all over for an hour.

"Where the hell could he have gone to?" her father had said.

"He must be a smarter turtle than we thought," Renee had said. She'd smiled. "He was just waiting, and when nobody was here, he made his escape. He'd probably had it all planned out for weeks. You know how patient turtles can be."

Her father had laughed.

So Turtle the turtle had been quickly forgotten. Renee had never wanted another pet. It had been too upsetting losing her turtle. Well, it had bothered her a few days, at least.

Over a year later, Renee's mother had moved an armchair when a knitting needle had fallen under it. She just couldn't reach it. Renee had heard a scream and came running. There where the armchair had been was Turtle the turtle with a thick layer of dust covering him. Renee almost cried. She wondered if he had suffered. Of course he had. He had starved to death or died from lack of water. Regardless, it could have taken him days or even weeks to die. She cringed at the thought.

Her mother went to get a dustpan and came back to find Renee sobbing.

"I'm sorry, Baby," her mother told Renee. "We'll give him a nice funeral. I'm sure he's in pet heaven with friends and relatives."

Renee's mother had been holding Renee, but she was no longer listening to her mother. Turtle the turtle *was moving*. Renee almost peed on herself. It didn't seem possible. "Mom . . . Turtle's moving," Renee said.

"Nonsense," her mother had said, then looked at Turtle and let out another scream.

Seems that Turtle had somehow managed to stay alive for over a year. Renee was never sure if Turtle had lived under the armchair for a year or had only recently made it his home, but he was very much alive. A bit afraid of him, Renee had asked her father to find Turtle another home. He'd given it to a relative. Renee had never asked about Turtle after her father had given him away. She hadn't thought about Turtle until she saw this man with the cat.

The cat was tan with a white patch of hair over its nose. And oddly, its tail seemed bent. When it held its tail out, a portion was definitely at almost a right angle to the rest of its tail. Renee had no idea how that could happen.

Norman put the saucer down near the cabinet, and Renee could see it was filled with milk. He put the cat down. The cat immediately began licking at the milk.

"A stray," Norman said. "I found her under the steps of the cabin. Shivering. People can be so cruel," he said calmly, looking from the cat to Renee. "If someone's going to buy a pet, they have a responsibility, don't they, Alexis?" He didn't wait for an answer. "But what happens, they tire of the pet, and instead of accepting responsibility and taking care of the pet, even if they no longer want it, they abandon it. Worse, they toss it out like it was trash. That's what must have happened to this one. She doesn't seem to be very good at self-preservation in the wild."

"She's alive, isn't she?" Renee said. "Maybe she wasn't quite ready to give up and die."

"Well said. I hadn't thought of it like that," he said. "I thought you might like the company." He picked the cat up and brought her close to Renee. "I cleaned her up." The cat licked Renee's face. "Whatcha know, she's taken a liking to you." He put the cat down. "I gotta go upstairs. Why don't the two of you get acquainted. Oh, what should we call her?" he asked. "Your cat, your choice."

"Call her Cat," Renee said.

The man looked at her strangely, then shrugged. "Just as good as anything else, I guess," he said then left.

Renee was intrigued by the cat. It looked older than a kitten, but she thought it only a couple of years old. Maybe it was because it was so scrawny. She wondered how long it had been in the wild. It was a survivor, though. Just like her. After finishing the milk, the cat slowly made its way to the cabinet. Its eyes seem focused on Renee's. "You must have had a real shit taking care of you," Renee said aloud. "Or *not* taking care of you. The way you're so cautious, I imagine you got kicked around quite a bit when you were no longer wanted."

The cat seemed to respond to Renee's soothing voice. She brushed against one of Renee's legs, tickling her. Renee laughed, despite herself. Here she was, possibly spending her last day on earth alive, and she was laughing at the antics of a cat. The cat purred as if in answer. After a while, the cat stretched, snuggled by Renee's foot, and went to sleep.

The man came down perhaps an hour after he had left Renee with the cat.

"She was tired, huh?" he said. "Can't sleep too well in the wild. Lots of predators out there." He looked at Renee. "I read someplace that giraffe's never sleep. They may take a cat nap, but they're so fearful of predators, they never really sleep. Can you imagine that? This little critter must have been like that. Lots of big, bad animals in the woods who would want to make this one its meal."

He picked the cat up, who mewed in protest at being awakened. "Seems this fella's taken to you right quick. Funny thing, though," he said and paused a moment. "You know what would happen if I tossed him into your cabinet and shut the door? She'd panic, and, say, after an hour when I opened the door, I imagine you would be much the worse for wear. So friendly one minute, an animal the next. She might scratch your eyes out. Want to test out my theory?" he asked.

"What kind of game are you playing, Asshole?" Renee asked. "Are you just bored?"

"Curious, not bored," he said. "More to the point, what you're missing is that here I'm god. Literally. I hold your life in my hands," he said, cradling the cat. "Tossing this creature in with you would be like god experimenting. I'm your god, Alexis. I could keep you here for months. We're in the wilderness. I can do with you as I please. Just like god."

"A pathetic god," Renee said, confused by the man's sudden change in demeanor. Was this the man who tried to keep the beast within him at bay or was this a different manifestation of the beast? Or, could the two have merged into a new menace?

"God has the power over life and death, Alexis," the

man said. He put a hand around the cat's neck. "Such a bony thing, I could crush its throat with just one hand. Just like I can do whatever I please with you, trussed up as you are. I could rape you if I wanted . . . but I wouldn't do that. It's so crass. I can't even grasp the mind of a pedophile. I mean, how does someone get off molesting children? I could disfigure you. We've already had that discussion, haven't we? Tell me I'm your god, and I'll spare the cat's life."

"You won't kill that cat," Renee said. "She hasn't wronged you like my father. You'll only hurt me because I'm an extension of my father. But the cat is an innocent."

"True, I *don't* want to hurt this cat. But its life is in your hands. I ask just one thing of you, Alexis. If you comply, the cat lives. If not . . . well, have I really killed the cat or would you be responsible for its death? That's our conundrum, isn't it? Call me your god, even if you don't mean it or this creature's death is on your hands."

Renee remained silent, but she felt panic building within her. She didn't want to be responsible for the cat's death. But if she gave into this vile monster, he would take it as a sign of weakness. Would he consider this surrender enough so he could kill her and end this game of cat and mouse? What the hell should she do?

The man began to squeeze a bit harder, and the cat began to struggle in the man's grasp. Weak as it was, she was no match for him.

"Okay, you're my god," Renee whispered. "Now let the cat go."

"I couldn't quite make out what you said. A little louder please," he said.

"You're . . . my . . . god," Renee said, spitting out each word one at a time. "You heard me that time. Now keep your word."

The man kept squeezing.

"*You bastard*," Renee shouted. "You gave me your word. I thought you were a man of honor. *Let the cat go!*"

He squeezed until the cat went limp, then dropped it on the floor. "See, I *am* a god, though not a very merciful one. I made you bend to my will, Alexis, but it wasn't enough. As god, I set the rules."

Renee bit down on her lip so she wouldn't cry. He'd planned this all along. She almost heard her inner-self again ask the question whether she could kill the bastard if given a gun. The debate still raged within her, but he hadn't done his cause any good with his callous disregard for life.

"Ask me and I'll take this poor little thing outside and give it a proper burial," the man said.

Renee said nothing.

"Going stubborn on me again. I'll just toss her in with you, otherwise. You can smell her as she begins to decay. She'll heap scorn on you for not allowing her the dignity of a decent burial because you're so pigheaded. So, ask me to bury it. Ask nice, and I *promise* I will."

"I don't believe you for a moment," Renee said. "I won't play your fucking game. Do whatever the hell you want with it. I'm not asking you for anything."

"We'll see about that," the man said. He took out his knife. "Remember the talk we had about your face? Are you so stubborn you'd let me cut the skin off your face so you'd look grotesque? Peel it off like the skin off a cooked chicken. Or would you ask me not to? Don't answer now. That's for later."

He tossed the dead cat at her left foot. "Enjoy your company," he said and left.

Renee felt like she wanted to puke, but she couldn't allow herself. That would mean another sponge bath, and the last had been terribly painful. If Shara was going to rescue her, it had best be soon, she thought. This man was losing his battle with his darker side. Vicious as he was a day ago, he would never have killed the cat. It hadn't wronged him, and he had had some perverse sense of justice when he'd first abducted her. But now to kill another living creature just to prove he had the power to do so . . . that meant he was losing the battle with his beast within. And that animal who had brutalized her and killed this cat would soon become the dominant personality. When that occurred, she was dead, and there was nothing she could do to prevent it.

Chapter Thirty-Six

Once upstairs, Norman cleaned the kitchen. He had cleaned the kitchen after lunch, but he really didn't have much else to do and wanted to keep his mind occupied. He was too agitated to nap or read a book. The cabin had no television. He had brought a transistor radio with him, mainly to listen to the news. He was certain Briggs wouldn't go to the media, but Alexis had proven to him that Briggs was far more complex than the man Norman had learned to loathe. Maybe . . . just maybe, after the phone call, Briggs had decided to use the media to help locate his daughter's abductor. But there hadn't been anything on KYW-AM, Philly's all-news radio station.

Norman was also tired of his battle with Alexis. She had proven far more resilient than he'd imagined, which meant that Briggs, too, might not crumble, even with the death of his daughter. Time was running out. Norman knew a far more vengeful part of himself had surfaced; one not at all like the refined Norman Flowers. Norman had controlled what he called his *other self,* but he felt that control waning. Norman hadn't wanted to kill that cat. He hadn't intended to kill the cat if Alexis did as she was told. But even when she acknowledged he was her god, his other self refused to keep his word and spare the creature. What would he do next? Killing Alexis—which he knew he had to do or spend his life in prison—was inevitable. It was simply a matter of self-preservation. But his other self might want to first rape and sodomize Alexis. His other self might want to torture and mutilate Alexis before he killed her. Norman couldn't let his other self gain such control. Even if Norman was never caught, he could never live with himself if he raped, tortured, or mutilated the youth in his basement.

Norman knew what had to be done. After midnight, when there was virtually no chance of anyone prowling around, he would slit Alexis's throat. No chatting, no threatening, no playing games giving his *other self* time to emerge. A quick and painless death. Then he'd bury her and return to the city. Having his revenge, he might even move out west and try to resurrect his life. Briggs would be a beaten man. His daughter's body would never be found. Briggs could never be sure Alexis was dead, much as his mind would scream that she couldn't possibly be alive. He would never have the closure he'd need to move on. Norman was sure Briggs would eventually curse the god he had leaned on. Maybe a few years down the line, Norman would call Briggs. Maybe feed him some hope. He'd taken Alexis with him, he would tell Briggs. After a long period of adjustment, she came to understand that Norman was more worthy to be her father than Briggs could ever be. Then he'd hang up before the call could be traced. That would be a hoot, Norman thought. For now, Norman just wanted to finish the job he'd started before his *other self* made it impossible for Norman to live with himself.

The decision made, Norman was suddenly hungry. He made himself a sandwich and poured himself a glass of orange juice. He'd have to clean the kitchen yet again, but if you're going to do something, you do it right, he told himself.

Chapter Thirty-Seven

Norman Flowers's cabin was just where Melissa said it would be. During the ride, Shara considered what her options were once she arrived. First she replayed each of the fever dreams, memorizing all the details she had been shown by the unknown dreamer.

She considered a simple frontal approach. Knock on the door. When Flowers answered it, stick a gun in his face, *then* get Renee. Simple and direct. It appealed to her until she considered the drawbacks. What if Flowers was in the cellar with Renee when Shara knocked? She didn't know enough about his mental state to predict how he might respond. And what if, regardless of where he was, he ignored the knock on the door. The element of surprise would be eliminated.

Shara could take a peek through the window of the cellar. If Flowers wasn't with Renee, it might make more sense for Shara to first free Renee, then pursue Flowers. If he was upstairs, from what she had been shown, there was only one way for Flowers to get to the cellar without going outside—the stairs. Definitely a plan to consider.

Shara also considered the possibility that Flowers might be in the cellar with Renee. In that case, rather than knocking on the door, she could simply pick the lock and be inside the cabin without Flowers's knowledge. That opened up numerous possibilities. She could wait for Flowers to come upstairs then take him down. If Flowers was harming Renee, the noise might mask Shara coming down the stairs.

Added to the equation had to be Renee's mental state. Could Shara expect any help from Renee? Or was she so traumatized that she wouldn't recognize Shara or, worse, consider Shara another source of torment.

Approximately half an hour from the cabin, Shara intentionally turned her focus to something else. There were too many options, too many variables. She'd wait until she got to the cabin, try to gather additional information, and then decide which of her alternatives was most sensible.

To take her mind off what awaited her, Shara turned her attention to LeBrea. She would have a lot of explaining to do when this was over. She hoped she would be able to mend fences. She recalled how her deceit had finally alienated Deidre to the point Deidre terminated their friendship. Deidre might be alive today if Shara hadn't betrayed Deidre just one time too often. Shara wondered why she didn't want to alienate LeBrea. The simple answer was that without LeBrea's cool head, organization, and determination, Shara may never have located Norman Flowers. Renee owed her life to LeBrea's cool professionalism. Shara was repaying his faith in her with duplicity. Deep down, though, she knew there was more to it than that. LeBrea intrigued her, and Shara wanted the opportunity to get to know him better. And she thought he felt the same toward her. Relationships, though, were built on trust. Could Shara make him understand the significance of her fever dreams? Would he even give her the chance to explain her actions?

By the time Shara got to the road that led to Flowers's cabin, she had a throbbing headache. She parked as soon as she made a right onto a road at the third right after the third light. She sat for a few minutes to again consider her options. She walked a quarter of a mile down the road and spotted the cabin. It might have been a decent retreat when Flowers had bought it, but it was a dilapidated shack now.

Shara saw what she was sure was the cellar window from her fever dream. She had decided that before she did anything else, she would have to determine if Renee was alone in the cellar or if her abductor was with her. She carefully made her way to the window. Looked through. Saw Renee tied up just as in her dream. She heard the crack of a branch behind her. Before she could turn, she was hit on the back of her head.

Chapter Thirty-Eight

Shara woke up to a pounding headache. Her hands were bound behind her back, and her feet were tied with rope. While she had been unconscious, she had had another fever dream. As before, her mouth was dry, but she would be unable to get water. She began coughing, then willed herself to be silent. She didn't want Flowers to know she had awakened. She knew soon the dryness would subside.

The fever dream was of another possible future. In the dream, Shara lay tied as she was now. Norman Flowers stood over Shara with a knife in his hands, his eyes that of a madman. Shara looked to where Renee had been tied and saw she was free. She had a gun in her hand, pointed at Flowers. He turned and looked at Renee, then laughed. Renee's hand shook as she tried to pull the trigger. She couldn't. Killing another human being was something Renee couldn't do, not even after all Norman Flowers had done to her. Flowers bent close to Shara and slit her throat. As the life ebbed from Shara, she looked at Renee. The youth raised the gun, pointed it at her own head, and pulled the trigger.

No, Shara thought, this was not the way it would end. *Couldn't end this way*. She had found Renee's abductor. She had found where he'd stashed her. She was so close to freeing Renee that there was no way it would end in both their deaths. Just like the other dream with the police storming the cabin, this dream was of a possible outcome. Shara couldn't allow this one anymore than she could the first.

The dream receded, and Shara stared at Renee tied spread-eagled in a cabinet. Renee stared at Shara, her eyes filled with despair, tears coursing down her face. Shara *was* in the cellar of her fever dreams, that she knew. Renee had withstood God-knows-what monstrous treatment at the hands of Norman Flowers, certain Shara would save her. And now Shara was just as much a prisoner as Renee. Shara knew it was more than Renee could take.

Before Shara could say anything, she made out another figure in the shadows, close to Renee, but not in the cabinet itself. It was Cheyenne, her hands and feet bound like Shara's. What was Cheyenne doing here? Shara wondered. Something wasn't right, but Shara didn't have the luxury to dwell upon it now.

Shara could also sense a figure lurking near her. She turned her head and was staring at the crazed eyes of Norman Flowers, the same eyes as the man in her fever dream. He'd lost it, Shara knew instantly. Whatever humanity had existed when Melissa tried to reconnect with him had been overwhelmed by his hatred for Briggs. He had fallen into the abyss. There could be no reasoning with this man. He stood above Shara with a knife in his hand. *The knife he would use to slit her throat*, she recalled from her last fever dream. *The knife that would have killed Renee had the police and FBI become involved.* There *had* to be a third outcome, but Shara was damned if she knew what it was.

"Who are you?" Flowers asked, his voice quiet, yet full of venom.

"A friend of Mel— of Rose's," Shara said, knowing Flowers's daughter might be the only way to reach him. As she spoke, she saw Cheyenne struggling to free herself. *Play for time*, Shara's mind screamed. What could she say that would focus his attention completely on her?

"How did you get here?" Flowers asked.

With that question, Shara had her answer. "Rose told me," Shara said, using the name this man and his wife had bestowed on their daughter. She saw Flowers visibly taken aback by Shara's revelation.

"Liar," Flowers yelled. "Rose doesn't know where this cabin is."

It looked to Shara like Cheyenne was succeeding in freeing her hands.

"Her mother told her," Shara said. Keep him off balance. Pique his curiosity, she thought. "Rose is worried about you. She doesn't want to lose you again."

"I'm already lost," Flowers said, sounding resigned and almost rational.

Cheyenne was free. Instead of attacking Flowers from the back, Cheyenne silently made her way to a table. Shara saw Cheyenne take a gun from the table. It was Shara's. Flowers must have taken it from her. But again Cheyenne did the unexpected. She went over to Renee and looked as if she had a knife and was slashing at the ties that held Renee. Shara spoke to mask any sound.

"That's not true," Shara said, her eyes meeting Flowers's. "I won't lie to you. You'll serve time in prison, but there were mitigating circumstances. Harm Briggs's daughter and Rose is lost to you forever."

Renee was now free, and Shara saw Cheyenne had given Renee Shara's gun. What was Cheyenne up to? Shara wondered. Shara recalled the fever dream she had just had. Renee couldn't kill Flowers. They would both die. Possibly Cheyenne, as well.

"Drop the knife, Asshole," Renee yelled. She was sobbing but her hand was steady. Shara had taught Renee how to use a gun. She was lethal, but she had never fired at a human being before. Though crying, Shara saw resolve in Renee's eyes. The prey had become the hunter. But could Renee use the gun in her hand?

Flowers turned toward Renee. "Drop the gun, Alexis, or your friend dies," he said, not raising his voice. He raised the knife. He began to turn toward Shara, as in her dream.

"I'm not Alexis, Asshole," Renee said. "I'm not Briggs's daughter. My name is Renee, Alexis's friend. You accomplished nothing. Put the knife down or your death is meaningless."

Flowers looked at Renee. "Another lie," he said, then turned back toward Shara. She could see a confused look on Flowers's face. He wasn't certain Renee was lying.

He raised his knife and Renee fired once, hitting Flowers in the head. Blood and brain matter splayed over Shara. Flowers fell, and Shara knew he was dead before he hit the ground. Renee sank to her knees, dropped the gun, and, still sobbing, stared blankly into space.

Cheyenne untied Shara. Shara went over to Renee and hugged her. Renee didn't respond. Shara sat down and cradled Renee in her lap. She looked up at Cheyenne, who now stood above Flowers. "Why didn't you take Flowers down?"

"It was Renee's call what to do," Cheyenne said. "After all she's been through being Flowers's captive, I couldn't cheat her."

"How did you get here?" Shara asked. She had so many questions that demanded answers.

"Now's not the time," Cheyenne said. "Renee's in shock and in need of medical attention. You've got calls to make."

"*We've* got calls to make," Shara said.

"I don't think so," Cheyenne said. She went to the cabinet and picked up a cat Shara hadn't seen earlier. It appeared dead. She then walked toward the stairs Shara had seen in one of her fever dreams.

"Where are you going?" Shara asked.

"I wasn't here," Cheyenne said. "Make up any story you want. Alexis can help Renee. That's important to remember." She paused. "You don't want to mention me, I assure you."

Shara looked at Cheyenne. All her questions boiled down to just one. "Who the fuck are you?"

"You know," Cheyenne said. "Or you'll figure it out soon. Sweet dreams," she added, then left.

At that moment Shara knew who Cheyenne was.

Chapter Thirty-Nine

Renee knew she was in a hospital but for the life of her didn't want to awaken. She needed answers from her inner-self but she was alone. She couldn't believe what she had done. *What she had become.* She recalled everything so vividly.

In the cellar Renee remembered being awakened to a commotion. From the cabinet, she saw Shara and her heart raced with anticipation. Shara *had* found her. All she had endured hadn't been for naught. But as her eyes focused, she saw Shara's hands tied behind her back. She'd been captured by the madman who held her captive. Now they would both die.

Renee then saw her inner-self and was totally confused. The woman she had conjured was across the room from Shara, near the cabinet in which Renee was imprisoned. But she, too, was tied hand and foot. And for the first time since Renee had created her, she was fully clothed. It made no sense at all. Her mind must be playing tricks on her.

Then her captor was asking Shara questions. Renee knew she had to be vigilant. Answers to questions about her inner-self would have to wait until later . . . if there was a later. Renee saw Shara's eyes dart to Renee's inner-self, who seemed to be freeing herself from her bonds. Renee wondered how Shara could see something that was a creation of her imagination. *Forgetaboutit. Focus*, her mind screamed.

Renee's inner-self was soon free. Shara continued to talk to the man who had held her hostage so his attention wouldn't wander to her inner-self. To Renee's surprise, her creation slashed at the leather straps that ensnared her. Again, Renee couldn't trust what her mind thrust upon her. The woman she had conjured in her mind had no knife. Her fingers were like razor blades—had *become* razor blades—and *they* had cut the straps. For the first time in . . . she had no idea how long, Renee was free. Then this apparition handed Renee a gun that Renee recognized as Shara's.

Renee had thought long and hard what she would do if given this chance. *What if you had a gun?* her inner-self had asked. She now had that gun. She was assaulted anew by images she would soon face. Public humiliation. Stares and whispers from her classmates. A trial. The media. Her dreams plagued by what would occur when her captor was eventually freed. She knew what she *wanted* to do, but she couldn't shoot this monster in the back. She hated herself for her weakness.

"Drop the knife, Asshole," she yelled. She was aware she was crying.

The man turned and stared at Renee in surprise. Renee tried to squeeze the trigger, but her finger wouldn't obey her command. She would have to face the humiliation, the stares and whispers, the media barrage, and ceaseless nightmares. *Put the knife down*, she told him. *Attack me,* she wanted to plead. Give me the excuse I need. It was then she blurted out her secret . . . that she wasn't Alexis. Maybe the revelation would stop him.

Renee saw momentary confusion in his eyes, but her disclosure seemed to have no effect. He was too far gone. Rather than confront her, he called her a liar then turned away from her. He'd dismissed her. Maybe it was her tears. If so, he had again misinterpreted them for weakness. He hadn't learned a thing about her during their time together.

The fool, she thought. She had provoked him and endured the consequences. She could and *had* done everything necessary to survive another second, another minute, another hour waiting for Shara to rescue her. Now he didn't believe she had the courage to pull the trigger. She had wondered if she did, as well, but now that she saw he was going to attack Shara, she had the motivation she required. It was Shara who needed her now.

Renee didn't hesitate. She fired once, and while her hands ached from being restrained for so long, her aim was true. One shot. That's all she'd needed. A head shot, to *kill*, not to maim. That was how Shara had instructed her. *If you ever have to use a gun, don't ever give the bastard the opportunity to strike back*, Shara had said. While she knew they were fiction, Shara had showed her a number of action films. In each, the villain had been shot numerous times . . . in the body. And each time, when the hero thought the villain dead and had turned his back, the villain had attacked one more time—always to finally face death. Shara had told her in real life a head shot would prevent such an outcome. She'd done as Shara had taught her. And in that moment, she'd become everything she'd abhorred.

So she had to escape within herself to find her innerself, who had now mysteriously fled. Renee was truly alone.

Shara had held her while they were in the cellar after she had been freed. As much as Renee wanted to reciprocate, she couldn't. Having condemned Shara for what she had done to Denise, how could she face Shara now? How could she tell Shara she was glad her captor hadn't dropped his knife. He had made the decision for her. She had consciously gone for the kill shot. Worse, she had wanted him dead. She wanted the bastard out of her mind. Out of her thoughts. Out of her life. Now she had to live with what she had become.

Chapter Forty

Shara jerked awake and for a moment wondered where she was. She saw Renee lying in a bed and everything came rushing back to her. Renee had been brought to a nearby hospital. She'd been in shock and had been dehydrated, but other than some superficial wounds, she was uninjured. She hadn't been raped. As she held Renee in her arms, waiting for help to arrive, Shara's greatest fear was that Renee had been sexually assaulted. Renee had been sedated and intravenous tubes provided nourishment. Shara looked at her watch. It was past midnight. Renee hadn't yet awakened. She hadn't uttered a word even in her sleep.

Renee had been traumatized, a doctor had told her. She had absorbed a good deal of psychological and physical punishment, even if she appeared unharmed. "Give her time," the doctor had said.

Shara knew there was more to it, which she couldn't tell the doctor. Renee had killed a human being. Shot Flowers in the head and seen his brains splatter. She had become Shara for a moment. That was most traumatic of all, Shara was certain. She needed more than simply time. But what? Shara had no idea. She had talked to Renee quietly for the past hour until she'd dozed off herself. She knew Renee could hear her. She had reasoned with Renee. After all she had gone through, Renee could be excused for what would be considered weakness. "You aren't me," she told the youth. "You were driven over the edge. You are not accountable for your actions." When the rational approach hadn't worked, Shara had tried the emotional. "It's not fair, Renee, to cower within yourself when I need you. You're feeling sorry for yourself. Well, shit, girl, you aren't perfect. You're fucking human. Stop being a selfish bitch and open your damn eyes." That, too, had produced nothing. So Shara just sat, holding the girl's hand, waiting for her to awaken.

It had been a taxing seven hours since Shara had made her call to McCandless for help. She had wanted to be with Renee when she was brought to the hospital, but hadn't been allowed to see Renee until after she'd been questioned, grilled, then interrogated by three different law enforcement agencies.

After Cheyenne left, Shara instinctively called Roger McCandless. Epiphany Falls wasn't far from Allentown. She trusted McCandless and knew he would protect Renee from the overzealous Feds and an embarrassed and pissed off LeBrea. McCandless would help Renee and *then* worry about piecing together the puzzle. After she'd called McCandless, she called LeBrea. She told him she had found Renee. Renee was alive. Flowers was dead. She told LeBrea where she was and whom she had called for help. She didn't mention Cheyenne. She spoke her words without emotion. Just the facts, like in an annual report. She then hung up as he pummeled her with questions. Damn, she thought, after all he had done, she had treated him shabbily. LeBrea had become Shara's new Deidre. Use him and abuse him. She felt like a shit.

Having called McCandless and LeBrea, Shara now had to come up with a plausible story. *She* had shot Flowers, not Renee. That was her first decision. Renee had suffered enough. Would *continue* to suffer. While killing Flowers had been justified, Shara saw no reason on top of everything else Renee should be questioned in regards to the shooting.

Leave the girl alone! She would want to scream. This way, Renee was protected. She wiped Renee's prints off the gun, held it, and pointed it at the prone figure of Flowers. She knew she should fire a shot so gunpowder residue would be on her hands. But how could she explain a second shot. She decided to take the chance she wouldn't be checked for residue. After all, Renee was unconscious. No one would suspect Renee had shot the gun. Keep it simple, Shara told herself.

McCandless arrived with three deputies. Within minutes, paramedics were also on the scene. Shara had wanted to accompany Renee to the hospital, but McCandless took her aside. "The shit is going to hit the fan real soon, Shara," he told her. "The fucking FBI called. They're sending a goddamn helicopter with . . . inquisitors, I'd call them. A Detective LeBrea is coming with them. If I'm left in the dark, I'll be shunted aside. I can't help you shackled. You want my help, I gotta know what went down."

Shara nodded. She told McCandless about the kidnapping and how she'd located Flowers. Then she spun the story she had concocted while waiting for McCandless to arrive. Stick as close to the truth as possible, she'd been schooled, so you're not caught in a lie. She did that now.

"Flowers must have seen me approach the cabin," Shara told McCandless. "He surprised me and brought me down here. I was just some meddlesome woman, as far as he was concerned. No threat to him. Hell, he didn't even search me for a weapon. But since I'd seen Renee through the window, he couldn't just send me on my way."

"It's not like you to get taken unawares like that?" McCandless said.

"If it weren't Renee, I probably *would* have been more careful," Shara said. "I didn't know if she was dead or alive. I certainly wasn't at my best."

McCandless nodded. "Go on," he said.

"Well, Flowers tied me up and threw me in the corner, then left for ten or fifteen minutes. He didn't do a hell of a good job tying my hands. I was a distraction, after all. An afterthought. Even while tying me up, I could see his attention focused on Renee. I was still untying the rope that bound my feet when I heard him on the steps. He saw me untied and went for a gun tucked into his waist. I was afraid if we exchanged shots Renee might get hit, so I didn't even pull out my piece. I jumped him. We tussled, he shoved me, and I fell." She showed him the bruise on the back of her head. "He took out his gun but didn't point it at me. He was going to shoot Renee," she said, her voice rising as if she was reliving the memory. "Instinctively, I went for my gun. I shouted to Flowers to drop his gun. He looked at me, but his gun was still trained on Renee. His eyes were crazed. He seemed to suddenly comprehend I hadn't just wandered by. He gave me this sick smile, as if he had come to a decision. He was going to take Renee with him. I had no choice." Her hand was extended, as if she still held the gun. It was shaking. "I didn't come to shoot Flowers, I swear. Especially in front of Renee. I just had no other choice. No other choice," she said, then shut her eyes and shook her head. "No other choice."

McCandless had Shara go over her story a second and third time with his deputies marking Shara's movements as if she were rehearsing for a play. Finally, he seemed satisfied. While Flowers had come at her with a knife, he *had* carried a gun. He probably didn't want to use it, as the noise of a shot couldn't be masked.

It was not too long after that Shara's inquisitors arrived. A very pissed off LeBrea, Dearborne from the FBI, and Briggs were ushered downstairs by one of McCandless's deputies.

"I appreciate all you've done, Sheriff," LeBrea said,

after introductions. "But we'll take over now. This is a kidnapping gone bad. Miss Farris was assisting us."

"It's a homicide, now, Detective," McCandless said, tugging on his handlebar mustache. "I don't want to get into a pissing contest with you, but I'm not just going to walk away and go home to some fishing. Detective Briggs knows me. Before you try pushing me aside, you might want to confer with him."

To LeBrea's credit, he did. He, Briggs, and Dearborne huddled. McCandless looked at Shara and winked at her. He had the same mischievous eyes Shara had first seen when McCandless had confronted Claire Cleary on a case when Shara first met the man. Behind McCandless's easy going exterior was a cop the equal of any in the room. He guarded his turf like a lioness her cubs.

"We'll do it your way, Sheriff," LeBrea finally said. "I do need a statement from Shara as does Agent Dearborne."

"Let's go to the hospital," McCandless said. "I'm sure Miss Farris will be far more cooperative if she's close to Renee. I'll commandeer a couple of rooms there. You'll also have full access to the crime scene here."

Shara hadn't deviated from her story over the next several hours. She almost believed she *had* shot Flowers. With Flowers dead and Renee in shock and unable to answer questions, there was no one to contradict her explanation. And truth be told, neither LeBrea nor Dearborne had truly grilled her. Apparently Flowers's apartment had been searched and the newspaper in the bathroom found. Briggs told Shara that Money had told LeBrea's detectives where Melissa Flowers worked. Her boss had her campus address and she had been questioned. She, too, confirmed her father's obsession with Briggs. They believed Shara's explanation that Renee had been all but unconscious from the moment Shara had seen her. Shara had covered Renee with a blanket she had found tucked in a corner. McCandless had confirmed for them that Renee was wearing only a torn blouse when he arrived. Her torn panties were in the wooden cabinet where she had been imprisoned. There was certainly no sympathy in the room for Flowers when Shara was questioned. They had all seen photographs of Renee's wounds. The cuts and abrasions would heal, but the photographs clearly showed she had been beaten and abused. While not raped, her genitals had been rubbed raw as well as her breasts. Sexual abuse isn't just rape. Renee had clearly been sexually abused.

Shara had been by Renee's bedside for the last two hours and had just dozed off when something awakened her.

Alexis entered the room, looking pensive. Shara had been told Nina Rios was driving Alexis up from Philly. Shara could tell from Alexis's eyes that she'd heard that Shara had shot Flowers. Self-defense or vigilante justice, that was the question on Alexis's mind.

"Read me," Shara said, before Alexis could say a word. "Learn the truth, and then we talk."

Alexis brushed against Shara's arm. Soon Shara saw Alexis's eyes register surprise. "Renee shot him," Alexis said.

Shara nodded.

"You lied to protect Renee," Alexis said. "You're something else. You had me worried, you know." Before Shara could respond, Alexis went on. "Where's Cheyenne? My father told me what happened, but he didn't mention Cheyenne."

"She left," Shara said. "She said she'd never been there. Nothing she did made any sense. I was puzzling it out before I dozed off. I think I know, but I need proof. She said something else I didn't understand. She said you could help Renee."

Again, Shara saw surprise register in her friend's eyes.

"How can she know?" Alexis said. Shara got the feeling she was talking out loud to herself, not to her. Alexis went over to Renee and held her hand.

"A lot of what Renee's thinking confuses me," Alexis said when she let go of Renee's hand. "She thinks Cheyenne is someone she created in her mind to keep her sane. Cheyenne's been with Renee several times during her ordeal." She shook her head in bewilderment.

"It might make more sense than you think," Shara said. "Go on."

"Renee feels guilty for shooting Flowers. For killing him, to be more precise," Alexis said. "That's why she's shut down. She and Cheyenne—Renee never refers to Cheyenne by name, by the way—discussed what would happen if Flowers was arrested. Testifying in court. Knowing Flowers might someday be freed. Even fearing the possibility he might escape from prison and finish off what he'd started. That was . . . tormenting her, I guess. She doesn't believe she killed him to protect you but to rid herself of him for good."

"She's become me," Shara said. Shara had long ago come to terms with who she had been. She embraced her past. It wasn't something she wanted to run away from. But she was no longer that Shara. At least that's what she told herself. She had grown. She had changed. But Renee had taken the decision what to do with Flowers out of Shara's hands. Shara still didn't know if the *old* Shara would have resurfaced and killed Flowers. "Vigilante justice," she went on. "Both you and Renee condemned me for what I did to Denise. Don't deny it," she said with a smile. "I may not have your powers, but I know you all too well. And Renee all but accused me of plotting Denise's demise. Which is probably true. Renee has a conscience—"

"You do, too," Alexis cut in, "much as you might deny it."

Shara shrugged. "The beginnings of one, perhaps,"

Shara said. "But I never felt any remorse over Denise. After all Flowers did to Renee, she still regrets killing him. What the hell do we do?"

"I can alter her memory," Alexis said. "It's what Cheyenne meant, though I have no idea how she knew. I was even afraid to tell you."

"What are you talking about?" Shara asked. "You can alter Renee's memory of what she did?"

"I've got more than just psychic powers," Alexis said. "I didn't know until just recently. Intuitively I knew I could alter someone's memory of an event to help them deal with the trauma. I can't explain how I knew. I don't know where it came from. Possibly the forest. Or maybe with maturity, you know, my hormones kicking in. Something latent residing within me that suddenly surfaced. It was like one day a jack-in-the-box opened up in my mind and let me in on a secret."

"Why didn't you tell me?" Shara asked.

"I . . . I was thinking of helping you," Alexis said. "Of erasing the memory of what your half-brother did to you. With your permission, of course. I didn't know how you'd respond, so I kept putting it off."

Shara looked at her friend for several moments, turning the notion over in her mind. Then she shook her head. "If you could have done so at the time Bobby brutalized me, I would have said yes in a heartbeat. But my entire life revolves around what he did to me when I was eleven. Take that away and everything that occurred since lacks meaning. All that I am stems from that incident." She paused a moment in thought. "You can rearrange Renee's memory of the shooting?" Shara asked.

"Of the entire kidnapping," Alexis said.

"No," Shara said. "We have no right to make that decision for her. She'll have to deal with what happened to her. She can. She will. If she wants it erased later, so be it, but that must be her call. Can you make her believe I shot Flowers? Make the recollection . . . blurry, I guess is what I'm searching for. I don't want her to remember the details. LeBrea and the Feds, even McCandless will want a statement from her. I don't want her contradicting my version."

Alexis nodded.

"Can you get rid of Cheyenne, too?" Shara asked. "Just Cheyenne's appearance when Flowers captured me. Mention of Cheyenne at Flowers's cabin will just complicate matters."

Again Alexis nodded. "When I'm finished, I won't feel well. I don't want you to worry," she added, seeing the alarm in Shara's eyes. "I just want you prepared. It's nothing permanent. I'm absorbing some of Renee's torment, I guess you could call it. I've done it twice before. I'll feel like I've come down with the flu when I'm finished. A good night's sleep is all I'll need."

"You're not bullshitting me, are you, Alexis?" Shara asked. "As much as I want Renee helped, I'm not going to jeopardize your health."

"I'm in no danger. Truth," Alexis said, signing the last word for emphasis. Without waiting for Shara's approval, she grasped Renee's hand again. She sat with Renee for ten minutes, then let go.

"You *do* look like shit," Shara said to Alexis when she was finished. Before Alexis could respond, Renee stirred and opened her eyes.

"Hey, stranger. How you feeling?" Shara asked, hugging Renee. "You gave us a scare." Shara saw Renee glancing around. "You're in a hospital. Flowers . . . the man who kidnapped you—"

"Is dead," Renee said weakly. "You shot him . . . to protect me. My hero," she said with a tired smile. Her eyes began to tear. "I knew . . . knew you'd rescue me. Through it all . . . that's what kept me going. Knowing . . . knowing you would be beating the bushes for me. Knowing no matter what . . . I had nothing to fear."

Shara hugged Renee again. She didn't feel much like a hero. She'd been manipulated. And she hated to admit it, but Renee owed her life more to Cheyenne than to her. Being certain who Cheyenne was just made Shara seethe all the more.

Day Three

Chapter Forty-One

As Shara left the hospital the next morning, Agent Dearborne stopped her. "I'm not going to be a thorn in your side like Cleary, but there's still the murder of Sam Brash to clear—"

"And I'm the prime suspect," Shara finished for him.

"I'm of a mind to toss it back to . . . Chompsky, who caught the case for the police department," Dearborne said. "Cleary overstepped her bounds. To me, this is a local homicide investigation."

Shara nodded. What could she say?

"With Flowers front page news, I can wait a day or two before dumping it back in their laps so you can be there for Renee without any distractions."

"It's appreciated," Shara said, then walked to a car where Briggs, Alexis, and Nina Rios waited for her.

Shara had spent most of the night making phone calls to prove her theory about Cheyenne while Renee slept. Alexis slept in fits and starts in a chair in Renee's room.

Renee's ordeal had clearly taken a toll. She needed rest. Lots of rest. For starters, Renee would remain in the hospital for the day for observation, then be released at 6 p.m., if there were no complications. It had been agreed upon that McCandless alone would take a statement from Renee regarding what she recalled of the shooting. He had proven himself more than capable to LeBrea and Dearborne. The doctor had helped by insisting that it wasn't in Renee's best interest to have to retell her story three separate times. And there would be no questions about the kidnapping for at least another day. Doctor's orders. LeBrea would take Renee's statement when she was ready and provide copies to Dearborne. For a change, it seemed all the clashing agencies were cooperating with one another.

Alexis slept the entire ninety-minute drive to Philly. She looked better than the night before, Shara thought, better yet when they arrived at her home in Philly, but she still seemed a bit lethargic. Shara herself dozed and was surprised when Briggs tapped her on the shoulder. They were at his home.

"Tell me the two of you didn't stay up all night keeping vigil over Renee," Briggs said, looking at his daughter and then Shara.

"We didn't want to leave Renee's side," Shara said for both of them. She intentionally omitted the phone calls she had made.

"Leaving me to soothe some ruffled feathers," Briggs said.

"LeBrea?" Shara asked.

"I think he's more disappointed than angry," Briggs said. "Maybe it goes with the territory . . . working a kidnapping, but he's more than a little fond of you."

"No shit," Shara said, only mildly surprised. She realized she hadn't been imagining the mutual attraction between her and LeBrea.

"So you going off on your own, well . . . it's like you didn't trust him. It stings," Briggs said.

"Alexis told you about my dream," Shara said, looking from Alexis to Briggs.

"Which is why I covered for you," Briggs said. "I don't know what to make of that dream of yours, but I wasn't about to put Renee as risk. I remember that psychic link you had with Mica Swann in that one case. I scoffed. It went against everything I'd believed in. But you made me a believer. And with Alexis having powers of her own . . . . Whether I believe in your dream or not wasn't the issue. That it could have become reality was enough for me. Still, it's not something I could tell LeBrea."

"He'll get over it," Shara said. "He's no child."

"Speak with him," Briggs said. "Say whatever the hell you want, but he kept us all going. You owe it to him. You know, massage his ego a bit."

Shara nodded. "When he's cooled down." She paused. "Look, can Alexis come with me? I've got some loose ends to tie up, and she could really help."

"Brash?" Briggs asked.

Shara nodded.

"Sure," he said. "Not too late, though. She looks like she could sleep all day."

Chapter Forty-Two

After they'd both showered and changed clothes, Alexis and Shara left in Shara's car.

"You're looking better," Shara said.

"I'm feeling decent," Alexis said. "So where are we going?"

"To Cheyenne's home. Tying up one last loose end. *Then* I'll tell you everything and we decide what to do."

The ride was short. Shara knew Alexis was curious and wanted to pepper her with questions. Instead, Shara asked about Alexis's new power. It was a short ride and Alexis wouldn't have a chance to pry before they got to Cheyenne's house.

"It happened at school," Alexis said. "There was this girl in my class, Kimberly. She was a real sweet kid. She had always been shy, like me, but there was no trauma I knew of that would make her so withdrawn. We were sorta friends.

"Sorta friends?" Shara asked.

"Birds of a feather, I guess," Alexis said. "Since I returned to school, I've been looked upon as a freak. High school is like that. Seems everyone is looking for your weakness. With my speech impediment and limp, not to mention the stories about my rape and beating, there was a lot of whispering behind my back. And there are the cliques. I didn't seem to fit into any particular niche. Kim, like I said, she was shy by nature."

"You didn't probe into her mind to try to find out why?" Shara asked.

"I stopped doing that once I learned how to tune others out. It was none of my business why Kim was shy."

"But it became your business," Shara said.

"Only when she became more withdrawn than usual. She was a good student. We sat next to one another in several classes we shared. I noticed she became inattentive over a period of about a week, which wasn't like her. And she began biting her nails. Right down to the quick. She had had these beautiful nails. That was about the only thing about her others envied. She'd polish them twice a week. She would paint these beautiful symbols and designs on her nails. Once or twice she even painted the nails of some other kids. It could have been her entry into one of the many cliques in school, but Kim wasn't interested. Anyway, all of a sudden she's biting her nails and she stopped polishing them. A couple of times in the lunchroom I'd see her wiping tears from her eyes. We'd eat together at times. Other times she just wanted to be alone. Now she wanted to be alone all the time."

"So you pried," Shara said.

"Something was wrong," Alexis said, as if that explained it all.

"Alexis, you have this gift, which you can put to use for good. There's nothing wrong with using it."

"I feel like I'm invading someone's privacy. I *know* how you felt before I could control myself."

"I'm not going to argue with you about it," Shara said. "You've got to come to terms with your abilities. You will. So you took a trip into her mind. What did you see?"

"She had been . . . pleasuring herself in her room—"

"Masturbating?" Shara asked.

"Yes, masturbating," Alexis said. "It sounds so gross—"

"Okay, pleasuring herself," Shara said with a smile. "And . . . ."

"And her brother walked in. He was a year older than she was—a senior. He threatened to spread it all over school if she didn't give him a hand job."

"She fell for that?" Shara asked.

"I'm just telling you what happened," Alexis said. "She was scared . . . and embarrassed. It's pretty hard to think straight when you're . . . caught in the act. And don't forget, we're teens. We blow everything all out of proportion."

"I take it she relented. Gave him what he wanted," Shara said.

"Yes, that once. She knew he would want more. God, Shara, her mind was so full of what would unfold. A blow-job. Then he'd want to play with her breasts. Then finger her . . . privates."

"And finally have sex with him," Shara said.

"No finally about it," Alexis said. "She envisioned him inviting friends over and each taking their turn with her."

"A seriously disturbed young woman," Shara said. "So what did you do?"

"I put it straight," Alexis said.

"It's like pulling teeth, Alexis," Shara said. "How did you put it straight?"

"I altered both their memories. Like I said at the hospital, I wasn't aware I could do it, but something within me told me I could."

"What alterations did you make?"

"I had Kim walking into *his* room finding him, you know—"

"Masturbating," Shara finished for her. "Jacking off. Pleasuring himself."

Alexis signed a laugh. "Saying a guy was pleasuring himself just doesn't sound right," she said.

"You got that right," Shara said. "So did she avenge herself?"

"You don't understand," Alexis said. "She had *no* memory of his ever having seen her . . . playing with herself," Alexis said.

"So many phrases for masturbation," Shara said. "Isn't our language incredible," she said and laughed.

"If things were reversed, I knew Kim would never use it against her brother," Alexis said, ignoring Shara's comment. "And she didn't."

"So how's she doing?"

"As shy as ever," Alexis said. "But she's let her nails grow and is painting them again. She's paying attention in school. She's less secretive than she'd been that week after he caught her."

"So you used this new power of yours for good," Shara said. "And if you hadn't intruded into her mind, you would never have known just what was bothering her. I'd say you did good."

"I only use it as a last resort, like with Kim and Renee," Alexis said. "Not only is it draining physically, but I feel guilty afterwards. Who gives me the right to alter someone's memory without their consent?"

"Isn't that what being traumatized is all about?" Shara asked. "Not being able to cope. Your friend was tearing herself up. Maybe her brother wouldn't have gone any further. Then again, maybe it would have unfolded just as she imagined. She wasn't about to seek help. You have nothing to feel guilty about. And with Renee, well, who knows how long she would have remained catatonic if you hadn't altered her memory of the shooting."

"It's no easy balancing act," Alexis said. "You know, deciding when to intervene and when to let nature run its course."

"It's something you'll come to grips with," Shara said. "Seems so far you've done pretty well." As she finished the sentence, she pulled up to Cheyenne's house and parked by the curb.

At Cheyenne's door, Shara took out her lock pick after knocking and receiving no answer. Shara also called Cheyenne on her cell phone. It was no longer in service. Before Shara could attack the door, Alexis tried the door knob. The door wasn't locked. Alexis looked at Shara and they both laughed—Alexis signing her laugh. There was no more laughing, though, after they entered.

"I guess she got it unfurnished," Alexis said. The living room was devoid of furniture. A quick check of the rest of the house confirmed the place was bare. In every room, though, there were plants. Dozens of every variety. All dead. In the kitchen, still more withering vines, but no table, no dishes, no utensils, and no food. In the refrigerator were a dozen vases and jars filled with water.

"I knew she was fond of trees and plants—" Alexis started.

"More than just fond," Shara cut in. "She was created by the forest. Or *is* the forest," Shara added.

Alexis looked at Shara as if not wanting to believe Shara's words.

"It was staring me in the face," Shara said. "Cheyenne even challenged me at Flowers's cabin to learn the truth. While you slept, I followed a hunch. I checked with authorities in Colorado. No Cheyenne Woods was ever employed in law enforcement. The DMV in Colorado hadn't issued a license to a Cheyenne Woods. That led me to Lysette and something else that had been bothering me. We never saw Cheyenne at night. Lysette confirmed it. They were lovers. I'd assumed Cheyenne stayed with Lysette overnight when Cheyenne first told me. Not so. Cheyenne would come over to the club during the day. They never spent a night together. I think Cheyenne had to return to the forest for nourishment or to recharge her batteries, so to speak."

"And from that you deduced Cheyenne is a . . . creature of the forest," Alexis said, skeptically.

"There's more, Grasshopper," Shara said, teasing Alexis. "Cheyenne knew of your powers to alter memories, which even I didn't know. How do you explain that? She was at Flowers's cabin to comfort Renee. You even told me she was there *several* times. Why wouldn't she free Renee or let us know where Renee was? And, there was no way Cheyenne could have located the cabin before I did. Flowers wasn't a suspect until just a few hours before we found him. Yet Cheyenne had already been there. All which defies explanation. And the clue that Renee's abductor might not have been a convicted felon, that, too, came from Cheyenne. She already knew who he was. You still doubt me?" Shara asked.

"No, but from the looks of you, there's more," Alexis said.

"Oh yes," Shara said with a smile. "Cheyenne freed herself from her bonds at the cabin, yet she didn't try to stop Flowers herself. Hell, how did she get captured in the first place? She freed Renee to see if Renee could go against her true nature and kill. That's something we've both experienced firsthand in the forest. Observing and experimenting. Fucking with our minds. And, let's not forget my fever dreams. The husk I inhabited showed me the cabin and Renee tied up in the cabinet. But that body was detached. Devoid of all emotion. The fucking forest. And then there's this place. Cheyenne's gone. She won't be returning, just like she told me at the cabin. I know where she is."

"In the forest," Alexis said. "You want to go there," Alexis added. It wasn't a question.

"No, I don't want to, but we must, and I'll tell you why," Shara said. "I'm certain Cheyenne killed Brash. He was strangled with a vine. Come on, clue after clue I ignored. How could I have been so naïve? My mind was so focused on Renee, I didn't tie all of this together until Cheyenne appeared at the cabin."

"Why would Cheyenne kill Brash and frame you?" Alexis said.

"To see how I'd react to another distraction," Shara said. "I know I'm right. Let's go and find out."

Alexis nodded without enthusiasm.

"I know how you feel," Shara said. "I want nothing to do with the forest, yet we seem drawn to it despite our best intentions. And now it's manifested itself into a human form to observe us outside the forest itself. And to fuck with our lives. We *have* to confront it."

Chapter Forty-Three

The forest shed its cloak as Shara and Alexis approached. The forest appeared to be a typical South Jersey wooded area except for the chosen few it let enter.

"It's expecting us," Shara said.

As always, the forest appeared lifeless. The trees were bone white, stripped of their bark, and leafless. There was no grass, no bushes, no wildlife, no insects. While the temperature was fifty degrees outside, it was comfortable within. There was no breeze, no humidity, and no sounds.

On the ground was the lifeless form of Cheyenne, though Shara only recognized her from her clothes and hair. Her face resembled a dried prune. There were just sockets where eyes had been. Hazel eyes, Shara recalled. Her red-tinged brown hair was no longer vibrant, but it was Cheyenne's. Dried skin clung to Cheyenne's arms and legs. It was as if her entire body had been sucked dry. A cat walked by, nudged the body, mewed, and then went to one of the trees and sat down.

"Show yourself," Shara called. "You had no right to play god with Renee." She had no idea what to expect. The forest had never manifested itself in any form until it created Cheyenne. Alexis had been opposed to this confrontational approach Shara had decided upon. They had argued during the seventy-five minute ride to the forest.

"Alexis, for too long the forest has called the shots,"

Shara had told her. "First it cured you slowly . . . and you were healed *only* when you were in the forest. It whetted your appetite for more. Then it offered you an impossible proposition you had to accept—confront and defeat your demons if you wanted to be truly cured. Oh, and I had to confront my demons as well if you were to be cured. And on and on it's gone. Once, just *once* we stood up to the forest, and the fucker blinked. After you defeated the albino for the second time, it wanted you to go through the forest. I refused to allow it. You weren't harmed, were you?"

"But it *could* have harmed me," Alexis countered. "It might harm you now if you're belligerent."

"I'll take the risk. It's not done with me. The fever dreams prove that. But I'm not going to be cowered."

Alexis had grudgingly agreed to allow Shara to take the lead. Now she stood tightlipped beside Shara as Shara demanded the forest to show itself.

The forest responded with silence.

"Stop fucking with us," Shara yelled, kicking the lifeless body that had been Cheyenne. The body began to crumble within itself and was swallowed up by the earthen ground they stood upon.

"Then stop coming to us when you need our help." Behind them stood Cheyenne as she had appeared outside the forest. Just as quickly the apparition disappeared.

"I never asked anything of you," Shara answered.

Alexis tumbled to the ground, mute and in the vegetative state she had been in until healed by the forest.

"Do you want Alexis like this . . . forever?"

Shara looked up. Cheyenne was sitting on a branch of a nearby tree. Before Shara could reply, she again disappeared. Alexis recovered and stood up next to Shara, her eyes filled with fear.

Suddenly Shara heard what must have been hundreds of voices, and Alexis was covering her ears. Another version of Cheyenne emerged from the ground. "If not for us, Alexis would hear the thoughts of all around her. She can't control her psychic abilities without us," Cheyenne said. "Would she want that?" Just as abruptly, the voices ceased, and this Cheyenne evaporated before their eyes. Shara saw Alexis trembling. Shara was about the shout "Enough" to the forest when something caught her eye.

The figure of Denise emerged from a path and took two steps toward Shara. Her eyes were crazed, not unlike those of Norman Flowers when Shara had looked into them. The forest had had its way with Denise, Shara saw.

"Do you want her back in your life?" Cheyenne said, appearing by Denise's side. Denise then backed up and was gone. Cheyenne vanished without moving.

Shara next saw Renee tied in a cabinet that suddenly appeared. It was the one Shara had seen in the cellar of Norman Flowers's cabin. Renee was sobbing uncontrollably.

"Did you want Renee alone with no one to share her fears and anguish?" It was Cheyenne, this time appearing next to Renee and wiping a tear from the youth's cheek. Renee disappeared but Cheyenne remained and walked toward Shara until they were face to face. "Did you want her to die in that cellar? Did you want Renee to perish with her whole life before her? You have a convenient memory. Yes, there has been a price for what we have done for you, Alexis and Renee, but Alexis is whole and you and Renee are alive today because of us. It's *you* who have sought us out. *You* who returned here again and again. *You* come here with your self-righteous indignation, but without us, you and Renee would be lying side by side in a cemetery. And don't forget we gave you the clue to locate Flowers. Without it, Renee's time would have run out. Should we have remained silent?"

"I suppose you helped me by framing me for Sam Brash's murder," Shara said sarcastically. "Or is that part of my payment for helping Renee?"

Cheyenne moved a step closer to Shara. "That has been taken care of," Cheyenne said.

"I'm to believe that?" Shara asked. "How do I explain my fingerprints? Pretty damning evidence."

"There are no longer any fingerprints," Cheyenne said. She opened her hand and specks of dust dropped from her palm. "There's no evidence against you at all."

"Why the charade?" Shara asked. She could muster up no further anger. Cheyenne . . . the forest was right. Shara and Alexis had returned countless times of their own accord. "Why send Cheyenne among us?" She knew she was talking to the forest. The figure before her *was* the forest in human form.

"Curiosity. Growth. Observing you and your kind in *your* surroundings," Cheyenne said. "Now leave," she added before Shara could speak. "We tire of your pettiness."

"One last question. Why spare the cat?" Shara asked.

"Because we can," Cheyenne said. "It was an innocent in all of this. It can live and thrive here in the forest, though it can never leave. Now go."

Shara saw the black vortex approaching from behind Cheyenne. She and Alexis had seen it several times before. If trapped within, they would join the other tortured souls like Denise who had tasted the wrath of the forest.

Shara and Alexis ran. Cheyenne's voice echoed as they outran the fingers of blackness that would ensnare them. "You'll be back."

Outside the forest, which had transformed itself back into non-threatening woods, Shara shook her head. "*Never!*" she said, looking at the forest with loathing. Deep down she knew she was fooling no one.

Epilogue

(1)

Shara and Alexis were back in Philly by 2 p.m. Shara dropped Alexis off at her home and was driving back to her apartment to shower before leaving to pick Renee up at the hospital. Shara had driven just a few blocks when her cell phone rang. It was J'aime. Shara was tempted to let the call go to voicemail. She really wasn't in the mood to speak to J'aime. But J'aime hadn't called her since their last lunch two weeks ago. Instinctively, she decided to take the call.

"Shara, it's J'aime," the girl said, her voice trembling. "Brett's out. He called. He's coming over. I'm scared."

Shara knew now wasn't the time to ask questions, like how the hell had Brett gotten out. Last Shara knew, he was in a juvenile facility awaiting disposition of his case.

"Where's your aunt?" Shara asked.

"At work."

"Call the police," Shara said.

"No, please, Shara. You promised to protect me from him. I need you . . . *now*."

Before Shara could answer, J'aime disconnected. Cursing to herself, Shara was in Center City in twenty minutes.

When Shara got to J'aime's aunt's apartment, the front door was slightly ajar. Shara drew her gun and entered cautiously. She heard sobbing coming from a room down the hall to the right. At the open door to the room, Brett

Maynard lay on his back, shot twice in the chest. Shara saw a gun in his waistband. J'aime sat on the bed cross-legged wearing only a bra and panties. Shara checked the boy for a pulse. Found none.

"Are you all right?" Shara asked. She walked to a phone and picked up the receiver.

"Don't call," she said. "Not yet." She paused. "I'm not injured."

Shara walked over and picked up a gun that lay on the bed between J'aime's legs.

"How did he get out?" Shara asked.

"He escaped," J'aime said. "Hell, he could have escaped from that juvenile facility a week ago, once he was healed from the gunshot wound, if he wanted to."

"Why did he want to now?" Shara said.

"He heard our mother had been arrested," J'aime said.

"He blamed you?" Shara said.

J'aime nodded.

"Where did you get the gun?" Shara asked.

"My aunt had it for self-protection. Awhile back there had been a rash of burglaries, home invasions. She showed me where it was."

"And you knew how to use it?" Shara asked.

J'aime again nodded. "Brett taught me."

Shara again picked up the receiver. There seemed nothing more to discuss.

"Why did you have to stick your nose in where it didn't belong?" J'aime asked. "You fucked up everything."

"Pardon?" Shara asked, putting the receiver down. "Your brother was raping you in broad daylight—"

"No, he wasn't," J'aime said. Shara saw she wasn't chewing on her lip. She was pretty damn calm for having just killed her brother. "We were lovers," J'aime said.

"That's not what I saw," Shara said.

"You saw wrong. I just didn't want to screw in public," J'aime said. "Brett would fuck me anywhere. We were in the store to boost an iPod. Some supermarkets carry them now. He didn't like the look you were giving us, so we left. When Brett gets frustrated he . . . well, he likes to fuck. I told him to wait until we got home. Our mother was working. But he wanted to do it right then and there. We were arguing, but I really didn't care if I lost. Then you got involved. And, fool that Brett is, he goes all stupid and tries to shoot you."

"But if he wasn't raping you—" Shara began.

"I'm—*we're* almost sixteen," J'aime interrupted. "He *wasn't* fucking me, and I wouldn't have given him up, but he didn't know that. He *thought* he knew what statutory rape was, so he reacted like an asshole. He didn't know that since we were both minors, both the same age, and I'd consented that he couldn't be tried for statutory rape."

"So why did you lie to me?" Shara asked. "Were you embarrassed?"

"You provided me an opportunity," J'aime said. "It just all went horribly wrong."

"What are you talking about? What opportunity?" Shara asked.

"Brett and I were in love. I've never met anyone more gentle," J'aime said. "But my mother loved him, too."

"Loved him ?" Shara asked

"When we were seven, our mother took Brett to bed. *They* became lovers. Or at least fuck buddies."

"Is that why your father left?" Shara asked.

"That, and, although I didn't know it at the time, he was convinced my mother wasn't going to harm me. When he left he said, 'You're seven. You'll be okay now.' I had no idea what he meant until later."

"You said Brett raped you when you were twelve," Shara said. "Another lie?"

"We became *lovers* when we were twelve. He never

raped me. I seduced him . . . when my mother wasn't around. I'd walk around like this," she said, spreading her arms so Shara could see her bra and panties. "I'd leave the door to the bathroom ajar. After a shower, I'd wear only a towel covering my bottom. I'd take it off in my room with the door wide open. I knew he was looking at me. We became lovers. Secret lovers. But our mother came home early one day and found us in bed together. She was fit to be tied. Brett had tired of her, but she wouldn't let him go. One day she sent him to the store and came into my room. She told me she wished I was dead like my sisters. She told me she should have done to me what she did to them when they were infants. It was only then that I knew she'd killed my sisters. Only then I understood what my father had told me. He'd hung around until he was certain I'd be safe."

"So I was your puppet," Shara said. "You fed me just enough information so your mother was arrested for killing your sisters. Then you wanted me to go to bat for your brother. What I don't get is why did you kill him?"

"The schmuck still loved my mother . . . still *fucked* my mother, though I didn't know until just a few weeks before you caught us in the car," J'aime said. "When I confronted him, he said he loved us *both*. Wanted us *both*, selfish bastard that he was. He was pampered, you know. He always got what he wanted, and now he wanted both my mother and me. I was going out of my mind trying to figure out how to get him for myself."

She paused, looked at her brother's body, and shook her head. "He knew I was responsible for our mother's arrest. He knew it was because I wanted her out of our lives so it would be just the two of us. He was livid. You saw how he got when you accused him of raping me. Like I said, he goes all stupid. He came to kill me. Check him. He has a gun. He must have been seething all the way over knowing my other two sisters' bodies would be exhumed, which would prove our mother's guilt. Like one murder wasn't enough." She shrugged. "Maybe he thought she could use a postpartum defense for one, but it wouldn't wash with three kids. Anyway, he would have killed me without a second thought, even though I'm sure he still loved me. I just beat him to the punch."

"Self defense," Shara said and shrugged. "I don't know if I buy it, but I guess the police will." Shara had to admit J'aime was good, but there were holes in her story. Holes she knew because of what J'aime had told her. Why, for instance, had J'aime greeted her brother wearing only a bra and panties. She saw jeans and a top on the floor next to the bed. Had J'aime wanted to keep her brother off guard when he arrived? Was she offering herself to him? Then, while anger gave way to lust, she shot him, knowing his rage would eventually return. And, why hadn't J'aime called the police *before* her brother arrived, knowing he was on the way? The police would have responded in far less than the twenty minutes it had taken Shara to arrive. The answer, Shara thought, was staring at her in the face. J'aime had already killed her brother when she called Shara. She wanted Shara to handle the police as she had when Brett had tried to shoot her. Shara had no proof, though, and, truth be told, she really didn't give a damn. A fucked up family, they all should be behind bars. But Shara was determined not to get involved any further. Two out of three ain't bad, she thought to herself. "What now? Kill yourself now that you've got nothing to live for?"

J'aime laughed. "This isn't Romeo and Juliet. I've lost the love of my life, but there will be others. I see how boys look at me at school. When I was with Brett, I ignored their stares. Now I invite them," she said with a smile. "And I'll see my mother rot in jail where she belongs. Better yet, she'll feel Brett's death far more than I will. She'll suffer a fate worse than death. Her bitch of a daughter killed her only son. I'll relish each and every one of those days." She stopped talking and suddenly looked sapped. "Will you call the police now for me?" she asked, sounding like the sixteen-year-old she was.

Shara went over to Brett's body and took the gun from his waistband and put it in her jacket pocket. Explain *that* to the police, she thought. "Clean up your own mess, J'aime," Shara said and left.

(2)

Shara arrived home with Renee at seven-thirty that evening. She wanted to put J'aime out of her mind, just where she belonged, but on her ride up to the hospital, J'aime kept intruding. J'aime was a master manipulator, much like Denise. If she didn't get therapy—a hell of a lot of therapy—she would become one twisted adult, a danger to herself and others. But that was none of Shara's concern. She had interceded once, and look where it had gotten her. Thoughts of J'aime brought her back to the forest. Denise, Norman Flowers, and J'aime had all become malevolent. They took and gave nothing in return. The forest, on the other hand, was most definitely selfish, but not totally self-absorbed. The price for what it offered was steep, but the forest had never taken anything without giving someone of equal or greater value in return. Strange, Shara thought, that the forest was more humane than many humans Shara had recently come into contact with.

Once at the hospital, Shara exorcized J'aime and the forest from her consciousness. All she cared about now was Renee and what she could do to speed her recovery. Renee had been discharged from the hospital, as promised. Physically she was fine. Emotionally Shara wondered if she'd ever be whole.

Renee napped on and off on the way home. Shara

wasn't about to pepper her with questions. Renee had given a statement to McCandless about her ordeal. It wasn't a story she'd want to rehash again for Shara right now. When Renee felt the need, she would open up and Shara would be there for her. Shara would also follow the recommendation of the doctors at the hospital. Renee would need some professional help to conquer her demons. But that would come later. For now, Shara wanted to build a comfort zone around Renee. Slowly reestablish a routine.

On the Schuylkill Expressway, Renee woke up and stretched.

"Hungry?" Shara asked.

"Starving," Renee said. "Anything but peanut butter and jelly."

Shara looked at Renee, but the youth didn't elaborate. *Patience*, Shara decided. "What about Nick's?" Shara asked.

"Really?" Renee said. Shara could hear her excitement. Other than Pat's or Geno's cheesesteaks, Nick's was Renee's favorite restaurant. Shara's too. Located in South Philly, Nick's had the most delicious hot roast beef sandwiches Shara had ever tasted. Each sandwich was piled high with hot, fresh cut roast beef or ham and slathered with natural gravy that dribbled down your fingers. The bread was fresh and soft. Just thinking about it made her mouth water. Crisp fries on the side made for a perfect meal. Crisp *gravy* fries, to be exact. The same gravy that topped the sandwiches made the fries equally delectable. Shara had once asked if she could get some extra gravy to take out and had been turned down. Nick's would give you mustard, peppers, and horseradish, but the gravy stayed on the premises. Both Shara and Renee had unsuccessfully tried to replicate the gravy at home. They never got close.

At Nick's they found a table, ordered, and were served in less than five minutes. It was another of Nick's charms. No long waits for your meal. As usual, it was crowded, noisy, and boisterous. Political correctness hadn't made its way to Nick's. Regulars parked themselves at the bar. Smoking was allowed. One was never asked if a non-smoking table was desired. It wouldn't have done any good. Smoke wafted from the bar throughout the restaurant.

Renee attacked her sandwich with a vengeance. Shara smiled. They ordered a second helping of gravy fries, which they shared.

"I'm stuffed," Renee said as they walked to Shara's car. "You know what's so neat about Nick's?" she asked.

"Yeah, but tell me again," Shara said.

Renee laughed. "The aftertaste. Good as that sandwich was, it'll be with me for hours. It's like eating it all over again."

"Not to mention licking your fingers," Shara said.

Renee nodded, then licked her fingers and smiled.

Two hours later, Renee was asleep in her own bed. A restless sleep, Shara could tell from the tossing and turning, but asleep nevertheless.

Shara went to sleep and was awakened by Renee's sobbing. She went into Renee's room. Renee was sitting up in her bed, fully awake. Tears cascaded down her cheeks. Shara sat down next to the youth, and Renee hugged her and refused to let go. Shara thought Renee was ready to tell Shara about her ordeal.

"I . . . I killed him, Shara, not you," Renee said. "I wanted him out of my life . . . forever. It's something I have to live with. Something I . . . I need to live with. Something—"

"Something we'll both come to grips with together," Shara said.

Author's Afterword

Why end the "Eyes" series with the next book? If you've followed the series, you might be aware that I only decided to extend *Hungry Eyes* into a series because I had far more of Shara's character to explore than I initially anticipated, which would keep the series fresh. Shara was haunted by her half-brother from the time she was eleven until she was in her early-twenties. She basically lost a decade of her life that could never be recaptured. She had to first come to grips with her half-brother, then begin to start living a life of her own. She found love in *Judas Eyes*. She found family—not a biological family—in *Blindsided*. And in that book the darkness within her emerged for the first time since *Hungry Eyes*. It was something else she had to come to terms with. In *Blind Vengeance,* she learned how to cope with losing control; control being essential to her nature.

Meanwhile, something more was developing. Alexis, while mentioned in *Hungry Eyes* doesn't become flesh and blood until *Eyes of Prey*. And Renee didn't enter the picture at all until *Judas Eyes*. As a bit of a teaser, I'll let you know right now that the final book of the series revolves more around Alexis *or* Renee than Shara. And, it might not be whom you think. It certainly surprised me as I plotted out the final book in the series. Alexis has her psychic powers, physical limitations and demons of her own she may not have conquered. Most definitely fodder for a series lead.

Renee has gone through a traumatic experience in *Blind Vengeance* that could have further ramifications. The impact of her abduction opens many doors into her character's development. While the "Eyes" series, per se, ends with the sixth book there's always the possibility of a new series where Shara plays a secondary role with either Alexis or Renee becoming the focus of the series. So, reader, who would you like to see become the main character of a new series (if the choice was between Alexis and Renee)? And, of course, why? Feel free to email me at gauntlet66@aol.com with your suggestion/comments.

With just one book remaining, the ride is almost over, but I have to wonder, will one of the characters plague my dreams, demanding another story or two be told? That's what happened with Shara and it's quite possible you haven't seen the end of those characters I created for the "Eyes" series.

Barry Hoffman
August 2013

Further Epilogue To Blind Vengeance

[Author's note: I have a problem with epilogues. I have too many loose ends I want to tie up. In ***Judas Eyes*** *I wrote a chapter dealing with Shara's convincing Renee (and herself) to let her be Renee's legal guardian. In* ***Blindsided****, Shara didn't just leave to be alone with herself at the end. There was a long chapter in which she comes to grips with Alexis and Renee's attempt to "domesticate" her as if she were an animal who had spent her entire life in the wild. And here in* ***Blind Vengeance****, I felt the need for Shara to explain herself to Paul LeBrea.* ***All*** *of these epilogues felt right in my first handwritten draft. Some even made it onto my computer. All were eventually discarded. All detracted from the natural ending of the respective book. Some things are best left to the imagination. But . . . I didn't toss these chapters into the trash. They were extraneous and never made their way into the next book in the series. Yet, they gave a further glimpse into Shara's discovering herself—Shara getting a life, and the bumps in the road she encountered in doing so, is what the first four books centered upon. In this book she shares center stage with Renee, foreshadowing a pivotal change in the final book in the* ***Eyes*** *series. So, consider this a bonus chapter. It's not crucial to the book, but I enjoy it just the same. Note, that in this version Renee was unaware it was she who had killed Norman Flowers. She wouldn't discover the truth until the final book in the series.]*

Three days after Renee returned to Philly, Shara took Briggs's advice and went to see Paul LeBrea. There were fences to be mended. Maybe more. Winding down from the forty-eight hour adrenaline rush from Renee's abduction to her release, Shara found her mind returning to the detective she had betrayed. Used and abused—something she was very good at. Yes, it had been necessary to keep LeBrea in the dark *after* Shara had found the location of Norman Flowers's cabin. Shara wasn't one to second guess her actions. But she had repaid LeBrea's goodwill and trust with betrayal, just as she'd done with Deidre Caffrey on numerous occasions. Shara wasn't proud of her manipulation of Deidre, but she seldom dwelled on it for long.

So, why was she so bothered by her deceit with LeBrea, she wondered? Why was he constantly within the grasp of her consciousness? Initially Shara deluded herself into believing her guilt was fueled by the role LeBrea played in Renee's safe return. There was no doubt in Shara's mind that LeBrea was the fuel that kept the engine of the investigation running. With everyone feeling frustrated by setback after setback, LeBrea had stepped in and rallied them from the outset. He commanded—rather than demanded—their allegiance with his take charge attitude, attention to detail and perseverance. He encouraged and accepted the input of others. LeBrea was no one-man show, but most definitely the conductor of the orchestra. He had taken on the weight without complaint. Only when Shara stabbed him in the back at the end had he appeared deflated. He had been professional but distant when he had questioned Shara at the hospital where Renee had been brought after she had been freed. He hadn't spoken of his disappointment. They had simply parted ways. There had been no closure.

Briggs's advice resonated within Shara. Meet with LeBrea, Briggs had suggested if only for closure. But it was all so much bullshit. Loathe as Shara was to admit it to herself she was attracted to the guy. She thought the feeling mutual. LeBrea embodied everything Shara wanted in a man. He was her equal in every sense of the word. Shara didn't want closure. She wanted LeBrea.

Renee seemed to have read her mind just that morning. Renee was still coping with the trauma of her abduction. She had told Shara every grisly detail, but even though both had cried at Renee's debasement, Shara had the feeling Renee was reciting a book report. She hadn't yet told Shara her fears, sense of humiliation or the emotional toll the war of wills with Flowers had taken on her.

And Renee still puzzled over the haze that engulfed her when it came to Flowers's death. She sensed something amiss. Shara feared she might regain her memory; recall she and not Shara had killed Flowers. Shara cringed at the implications of the return of Renee's memory. And, while Renee said nothing, Shara was aware Renee's dreams were plagued by reliving her ordeal. She would need some professional counseling. Shara and Alexis could help her just so much.

Still, Renee wasn't totally self-absorbed. She'd been genuinely interested in every aspect of the investigation. She was intrigued with Shara's fever dreams. Like Shara, she wondered through whose eyes Shara had lived the dream. Shara hadn't yet told her it was Cheyenne . . . or more aptly, a manifestation of the forest. It could trigger Renee's memories. And Shara had spoken about LeBrea. *A lot.*

That morning Shara had been staring into space, watching something on television but taking in nothing at all.

"Thinking about LeBrea again," Renee said. It wasn't a question.

"Was not," Shara said, blushing. "Fuck, who am I kidding," she admitted. "Yeah, I treated him shabbily."

"That's *not* what you're thinking about," Renee had countered. "You've fallen for him hook, line and sinker."

"I've got Clay," Shara had said lamely.

"You can't have feelings for two men?" Renee had shot back. "Gimme a break. You know how fond I am of Clay. He's got this aura of mystery about him. I sometimes think he can read my mind. I *know* he can read yours," she said, and laughed. "He's way cool, but he's in Virginia. You two have one fucked up relationship."

"Which means what?" Shara asked, wanting Renee to put into words what she had been thinking.

"Meaning you and LeBrea connected and not just on a professional level. And you're afraid," Renee said, but didn't elaborate.

Shara threw a Nerf ball at Renee who laughed. Damn, Shara thought, it was good to see Renee laugh again. Good to see that wonderful smile of hers, if only for a fleeting moment. "You are so bad," Shara said. "Afraid of what? Don't leave me hanging."

"Afraid of commitment," Renee said. "Seems to me Clay and LeBrea are very much alike. But Clay's safe. He's in Virginia. He's not moving here to Philly and you're not relocating to the sticks to be close to him. You don't have to consider taking your relationship to another level. With LeBrea you'd be jumping out of an airplane without a parachute if the two of you hit it off. You'd have no excuses. That terrifies you."

"Says you," Shara said, then broke into laughter. "I sound like a teenager. You're right. I like him. Like him a lot. And I can't argue with you about Clay being safe."

"Then do something about it," Renee said.

"I already fucked LeBrea over once," Shara said. "I wouldn't give *me* a second chance of I were him."

"Level with him," Renee said. "Tell him about your fever dreams—your premonition. At least give him a chance to blow you off. Then again, he might understand. Then you'd be in deep shit," Renee said, with another smile.

So a day later here she was, standing behind Paul LeBrea at the Southwest Detectives office. LeBrea seemed totally focused on a file he was reading.

"Hey stranger," Shara said. LeBrea seemed startled. Shara saw LeBrea look at her and saw the hurt in his eyes. "Hey," he said, without emotion.

"We gotta talk," Shara said.

"I'm kinda busy—"

"I owe you an explanation," Shara said. "Let me speak my piece and then you can blow me off if you want." Before he could answer Shara went on. "Not now. Not here. Over dinner. My treat."

LeBrea was stroking his beard as if contemplating Shara's offer.

"C'mon. Give a girl a break," Shara said.

LeBrea finally shrugged. "I *do* want to hear how Renee's doing," he said. "My treat, though. Call me old-fashioned.

They agreed to meet at the Roosevelt Pub on Walnut Street.

That evening Shara and LeBrea ordered drinks and dinner. Sipping a beer, LeBrea maintained his silence and refused to make eye contact with Shara.

"Not going to cut me any slack, are you," Shara said.

LeBrea raised his head briefly, but said nothing, then averted his glance again.

"Fuck it," Shara said, getting up. "I thought you were a stand up guy, LeBrea, but I see I was wrong. You want to be an asshole, do it by yourself." Shara turned to leave.

"How's Renee?" LeBrea asked, scarcely above a whisper.

"Excuse me," Shara said.

LeBrea sighed. "Sit down and tell me how Renee's doing," he said a bit louder.

Shara remained standing.

"Please," LeBrea said.

Shara sat down. "Look, you're angry at me for good reason. Let me just have my say. You can tell me to go fuck myself or you can accept my explanation. Your call."

LeBrea nodded. "First tell me about Renee."

"She's coping," Shara said. "We talk. Well, I let her do most of the talking. Venting. There's a disturbing lack of emotion as she tells me what that bastard Flowers did to her."

"Shock," LeBrea said. "She needs professional help."

"I'm fully aware," Shara said, abruptly. "I'm sorry," Shara said, knowing she'd been curt. "I'm wound a bit tight," she added and shrugged. "Right now, she doesn't want to speak to a stranger. My instinct is to give her both time and space. Only then will she accept the thought of counseling." Shara paused. "Should I go now?"

LeBrea betrayed the hint of a smile for the first time. "You know how to play people, don't you," he said. It wasn't a question.

Now it was Shara's turn to avoid eye contact.

"You betrayed me," LeBrea said. "It cost Norman Flowers his life. Worse, you and Renee could have been killed. I can't come to grips with your lack of concern for your actions."

"If I'd confided in you, Flowers would have killed Renee and then committed suicide," Shara said.

"Conjecture on your part," LeBrea said.

"No, Paul. *Fact.*" Shara told LeBrea about the forest and her fever dreams. Told LeBrea that if the police and FBI surrounded Norman Flowers's cabin, Flowers would have killed Renee and then himself. "These dreams I have, they're not mere premonitions. I *saw* what would have gone down, as if I were in the cabin."

"Assuming your . . . fever dreams were accurate, you could have told me," LeBrea said.

"And you would have believed me?" Shara asked. "Let me go to the cabin alone?" she added and waved a hand dismissively before LeBrea could answer. "If I didn't experience the dreams I wouldn't have believed me. Time was paramount. I couldn't gamble that you would have accepted my . . . vision, I guess you could call it. I couldn't chance you would have brushed me off. You'd have thought that maybe I'd cracked under the pressure. My dreams would have sounded like the ravings of a hysterical woman who'd gone over the edge. You would have ignored me. Renee would have died. Ironically, the only person to ever see me having one of my fever dreams and their after effects was Renee. But she couldn't vouch for me, could she?"

LeBrea stared at Shara. "You're right. I'd have never let you go in alone."

"Because you have feelings for me," Shara said.

"Because it would have been suicidal," LeBrea said. "You're not a cop trained to infiltrate a secured cabin. If I believed you I would have gone in alone. No Feds."

"Because you have feelings for me," Shara repeated.

LeBrea laughed. "You think pretty highly of yourself."

"You wouldn't have been so pissed, so disappointed if it wasn't personal," Shara said. "You like me. Maybe want to jump my bones. You took my betrayal as a personal slap in the face. Dammit, Paul, you saved Renee. You pushed and prodded. You refused to give into the despair and rallied us when we faltered. And you know it. And what did I do? I refused to let you in. I lied to you, went behind your back and went after Flowers myself. I let you down. And it was personal. Deny you have feelings for me, but I like you Paul. I admit it. You've been on my mind. I want to get to know you better. I did what I had to do and I'd do it again. But I don't want to lose you. Lose your friendship . . . and maybe something beyond friendship. So, believe me or tell me to get the hell out of your life."

"Eat your burger," LeBrea said, after a pause. He took a bite of his. After a few moments he glanced at Shara. "More than friends?" he asked.

Shara shrugged. She didn't know if LeBrea was serious or simply toying with her.

"I don't go after women who are taken," LeBrea said. "You *are* in a serious relationship, aren't you?"

"You've been asking?" Shara asked, not able to resist a smile.

"It . . . it came up in conversation with Briggs during the kidnapping," LeBrea said.

"I bet it did," Shara said. "Like the two of you had time for small talk while trying to find Renee's abductor." She held up her hand before LeBrea could respond. "Look, I've been in a serious relationship, as you say. But we're at an impasse." She explained to LeBrea how Clay was loathe to move to Philly and she was equally opposed to living in a small town where everyone knew your business. "Neither one of us is going to budge and we're treading water right now, but we both know there's no resolution in sight. We're not exclusive." Shara paused a moment. "Pissed as you were at me you were still thinking about me, weren't you?"

LeBrea took another bite of his burger. "You intrigue me, that's all,"

"Am I forgiven?" Shara asked. "I didn't mean—"

"I know," LeBrea said. "Guess I knew all along there were mitigating circumstances I wasn't privy to, unless I had totally misjudged you. And, in all fairness, you're probably right as to what my reaction would have been if you told me your plans and the fever dreams they were based upon. If you had come clean at the time I may have dismissed your vision due to the pressure you were under. We would have gone at it tooth and nail with Renee's life hanging in the balance. So, forgive you? That may take some time, but I understand your reticence in confiding in me."

"Does that mean a second dinner—a date if you will—isn't out of the question?" Shara asked.

"You intrigue me," LeBrea said. "I wasn't lying. And, yes, I do want to get to know you better."

After dinner LeBrea invited Shara over to his apartment for a nightcap. They'd spent what was left of dinner talking shop. LeBrea told Shara about some of his more interesting cases. Shara was a bit more guarded but told LeBrea some war stories of her own. Told LeBrea how she'd become Renee's legal guardian and had helped keep Renee's father from serving a life sentence for killing his wife.

Shara didn't play coy with LeBrea at his apartment. Life was too short to drag out physical intimacy until the third or fourth date. Inviting Shara to his apartment had its own implication. In accepting Shara had agreed to more than just a drink. Within fifteen minutes of arriving at LeBrea's apartment the two were in his bed. Only time would tell if their mutual attraction was merely physical or the beginning of a relationship she felt they both craved.

www.ingramcontent.com/pod-product-compliance
Lightning Source LLC
Chambersburg PA
CBHW060850250626
47159CB00008B/2678
9781948929424